ANGEL DOOM

PROF CROFT 12

BRAD MAGNARELLA

THE PROF CROFT SERIES

PREQUELS
Book of Souls
Siren Call

MAIN SERIES
Demon Moon
Blood Deal
Purge City
Death Mage
Black Luck
Power Game
Druid Bond
Night Rune
Shadow Duel
Shadow Deep
Godly Wars
Angel Doom

SPIN-OFFS
Croft & Tabby
Croft & Wesson

1

"It's about time!" the blue-haired woman cried as she opened her door. "Heavens to Betsy, I was wondering if you were *ever* going to show!"

"Yeah, sorry," I said. "Busy morning. I fell a little behind."

"I had an *appointment* with you people," she said, eyes smoldering from their wrinkled beds. "Nine fifteen, it was to be. Not nine *thirty*. Not nine *forty-five*. And sure as Sherlock not *ten o'clock*. Nine *fifteen!*"

The eccentric old woman produced her phone and accessed *Average Joe*, an app that matched people in need of home-maintenance services to those with a knack for particular skills, but at nonprofessional rates. In this case, boiler repair.

Unfortunately, Miss Widows had been using *Average Joe* for more... culinary purposes.

"See?" She tapped her finger against the appointment confirmation on her phone hard enough to shed bright bits of nail polish onto the glass. I shifted my tool bag prop to my other hand and angled my head for a better view.

"You did, indeed," I agreed. "And all I can say is I'm sorry."

The truth was it had taken longer than expected to get everyone in place.

"Well, poo on your *sorry* and poo on *you!*" She stuck the phone back in her pocket. "I have half a mind to call another company. One that understands what stress and worry does to an old woman's insides. In fact, consider it done!"

"Hey, I don't blame you," I said quickly, trying not to sound too desperate. "But I'm here now—and listen, I'm willing to take fifteen percent off your order for the inconvenience. I'll even upgrade your status to Preferred."

She'd started to swing the door to her East Village home closed, but she paused. Slowly, her halo of blue-frosted hair reemerged from the gloom until her hungry eyes were peering up at mine.

"Preferred?" she repeated.

I'd thought that might strike her fancy.

"It's a new feature that *Average Joe* reserves for its most valued clients—and I happen to have an in with the developer. From now on, your orders will be sent to the front of the queue and broadcast as priorities. No more waiting around for slugs like me." I winked, sharing a joke at my front's expense.

Miss Widows licked her lips, then broke into an unnatural giggle, her powdered brow and rouged cheeks crinkling into an unsightly mask. When a warm draft of bloating and decay broke against my face, I forced myself to nod and chuckle along with her.

Catching herself, she pinched her lips suddenly. "Oh, do forgive my earlier crabbiness, ah—what was your name again?"

"Craft," I said, using the alias we'd created. "Evan Craft."

"Yes, Evan, I'm a worrier by nature, and it just does awful, awful things to my digestion. But I appreciate your willingness to make things right, and I'll accept your generous offer. Please, do come in."

She backed into the house, one of the few in the neighborhood to have survived its infamous descent into blight. Indeed, the new developments rising around hers made the historic brick building with its marble-arched doorway and windows an anomaly—much like the woman herself. There was a good reason both had survived the city's recent past, but she'd concealed her doings well.

"Oh, do I *worry*," she said, snapping the bolt closed behind me for emphasis. The hair on my nape stiffened as a skein of magic spread over the old wooden door. "But can you blame me after everything this neighborhood has been through? Even now, people are disappearing right off the sidewalk. Why, just last month it was a young man from your company. Poof—gone like the wind!"

"I heard about that," I said, perhaps a little too thinly.

She tsked and shuffled ahead of me. "Like I've always said, you can never be too careful in this city."

"No, you can't," I agreed, sneaking a look around.

The corridor passed a sitting room stuffed with antique furniture and creepy porcelain dolls. Cats were perched high and low, their glowing eyes tracking us. The few times the police had come to her house, they'd left insisting that Miss Widows was just a harmless old cat lady—but there was nothing harmless about her or her "cats." They began plopping down and converging ominously in our wake.

From a pocket, I produced a handful of potion pellets and tossed them onto the faded rug. The pellets were already misting as the creatures veered over to inspect them.

Oblivious, Miss Widows pushed open a swinging door onto an antiquated but colorful kitchen.

"The basement is that way," she said, gesturing to a door at the kitchen's far end. "But first can I offer you a treat? I'm rather famous around here for my cinnamon cocoa and snickerdoodles." A dainty kettle just happened to be steaming on the stove, while warm air seeped from her oven. Both carried irresistible smells, but of course they would. The food and drink were enchanted, designed to incapacitate.

"Oh, no, ma'am," I demurred. "I don't want to put you out more than I already have."

"Oh, pish-posh, Evan. You'd be doing me a favor. I can't eat these all by myself!"

"Well... you twisted my arm," I said with a chuckle. "How about a few cookies, then?"

Though she grinned, I noticed her dimples fell well short of her shrewd eyes. "Oh, we are in for a treat," she whispered, donning a frilly cloth mitten and turning toward the oven.

I edged closer, drawing a set of iron cuffs from the back of my pants. She reached for the oven door. In a maneuver I'd practiced at least a hundred times leading up to this moment, I brought the right bracelet down. It was a little off center, but it snapped around her wrist, locking into place with a satisfying rush of clicks.

Hell, yeah!

I cinched it tight, then wrenched her other arm behind her. With the iron neutralizing her casting abilities, the fae being was powerless as I snapped the left bracelet closed, too.

"Well, gracious *me!*" she exclaimed.

"Got her," I said into the magic-enhanced wire taped to my shoulder.

The front door yielded to the splintering blow of the Sup

Squad's iron battering ram. Footsteps raced through the foyer and into the kitchen. I turned to find my lovely wife, Detective Ricki Vega, staring down the sights of a service pistol loaded with cold iron rounds.

The old woman looked from her to me, aghast. "Evan? How dare you deceive me!"

I snorted at the irony.

"Miss Widows, if that is your real name," Ricki snapped, "you're under arrest for abduction and false imprisonment. We have a warrant to search your home."

"I can't have *this*," she exclaimed indignantly. "Oh, no, no, *no!*"

"You should have thought of that before you started treating *Average Joe* like a food delivery service," I said.

Her irritation when I'd arrived late hadn't been for show. She'd been hunger-raging.

As Ricki read Miss Widows her rights, the room began to change. The walls darkened, mold spread across the tile grout, appliances dulled, and dust and cobwebs accumulated on every surface. The air turned thick and musty, making my nose twitch. Ricki glanced around but kept her cool, even as Miss Widows started changing, too. No longer able to cast glamours, she lost her vibrant colors and began contorting into something haggish and arachnid, angular joints jabbing through her clothes.

I cinched the bracelets further as her wrists thinned inside a gray exoskeleton.

"C'mon," I said, pulling the drow hag through the swinging doors while Ricki covered her.

The hag's pets were scattered across the sitting room floor, their hairy legs sticking up. Only they weren't cats anymore—they were spiders. Cat-*sized*, granted, but now that the glamours were gone, there was no mistaking them for anything else. I looked at Miss Widows for a reaction, but the two lines of yellow eyes that perforated her face beside her shrinking, wrinkling nose stared straight ahead.

"Her fingers!" Ricki called.

Black spines had replaced her glittery nails, and one was jiggling inside the keyhole. *Crap!*

Before I could react, the bracelet snapped open. Her free arm came around, a spine aiming for my face. I flexed backward into a limbo-like pose, somehow managing to keep my feet. The spine missed, but the cuffs in my hand were empty now. As the hag pulled away, I straightened into Ricki's line of fire.

Checking her weapon, she called, "She's coming your way!"

The hag was halfway down a back corridor when a stocky figure stepped into her path. Detective Hoffman had breached a rear entrance, but he hadn't expected to find the suspect bearing down on him. He shuffled back a step in surprise before driving his shoulder into her gut and grasping her around the waist.

"Got her!" he grunted as they crashed to the floor.

"Careful," I called, rushing forward with the cuffs.

In the next moment, black spiders burst over Hoffman's face. He released the hag with a cry and began spluttering and slapping at the arachnids. Though they looked—and I'm sure felt—real enough, they were a harmless glamour. The hag disappeared through a door. Drawing a wand from my tool bag, I gave chase, hitting Hoffman with a neutralizing blast in passing to clear away the creepy-crawlies.

The door led back into the kitchen from the other side. Though the drow hag was nowhere in sight, the door to the basement was ajar, and I could hear her sharp feet racing down a set of wooden steps.

"Sorry about that," I panted as Ricki joined me. "I didn't expect her to pull a Houdini."

"At least she can't leave the house," she said, referring to the wards I'd planted. She nodded at the basement door. "She in there?"

"Yeah, and it's probably where we'll find the victims. I'll check it out."

"Not without me. I've been busting ass on this case for the last two months."

She wasn't exaggerating. Since returning to full-time duty she'd been intent on making up for lost time, starting with a cluster of mysterious disappearances and deaths in the neighborhood. Though I hated to put her in harm's way, I had to remind myself we were working as professionals now, not a husband-wife team.

"All right. Stay close, Detective."

"Roger that, Croft," she replied with a sarcastic look.

I set my tool bag on the counter, drew out a second wand, and started down the steps. Though the hag had glamoured the basement when the police came calling, she didn't bother now. It was a damp space that smelled of old running shoes. I ducked beneath strands of webbing. When we reached the bottom, I grew my light out.

In a room off to our left, silk-wrapped bodies dangled from exposed wooden beams, the older ones shrunken and gray. After incapacitating her victims, the hag strung them up and kept them alive as a food supply. Based on the frequency of disappearances, the victims lasted for about a month. Something skittered over the pipes in the far wall, where I caught a row of V-shaped eyeshine.

I signaled to Ricki to check on the victims, leaving me to advance solo.

Though the hag's eyes had dimmed again, I could feel them watching me. The air tingled suddenly, but infused with neutralizing potion, both Ricki and I were immune to the creature's enchantments.

"There are only two ways you're getting out of here," I called. "In cuffs or a body bag, your choice."

With a shriek of frustration, the hag leapt out and raced toward me on spindly legs, her multiple eyes blazing. Two shots rang out. She stumbled, a smoking stump where her head had been. I danced back as her body erupted against the floor, hundreds of spiders pouring from her deflating clothes. They skittered in every direction before melting into a gray sludge, no magic to sustain them.

"That works, too," I said, lowering my wands.

Ricki stepped forward and panned the mess with her sidearm. It was good to see her back in detective blacks, the jacket and blouse matching her pulled-back hair. The look suited her role in the city, just as my trench coat and cane suited mine. In my *Average Joe* disguise, I felt a little naked.

"Any survivors?" I asked, angling my head toward the hanging room.

She shook her head grimly. "But at least there won't be any more victims."

Hoffman hustled down the steps with his weapon and stared at the pile of clothes. "Is that her?"

"Yeah," Ricki replied, holstering her sidearm. "Case closed. Just a matter of notifying the victims' families."

Hoffman looked from the suspended bodies back to the drow hag's remains. "Go on," he grunted. "I'll handle the scene. Hey, I'm not trying to horn in on your work—you'll get the credit. I just know you've been missing out on family time."

Ricki's face softened. "I'm strangely touched, Hoffman."

"Yeah, man." I clapped his shoulder. "Super appreciated."

"Well, it doesn't mean she's off the hook with the paperwork," he said.

"Like I'd entrust that to someone who can barely spell," Ricki shot back, falling right back into their old partnership.

Hoffman smirked. "Go on, you two. Enjoy your girl."

"There she is!" Ricki sang.

From Mae's grandmotherly arms, Abigail squealed and batted her hands at the air. Ricki's fatigue seemed to evaporate as she rushed up and nuzzled our daughter's delighted face. When Abi looked past her to me, I waved and grinned stupidly. Even after three months, she still had that effect on me.

"How's she been?" Ricki asked.

"Other than a little angel?" Mae chuckled as she handed her over. "She's fed, burped, changed, and should be about ready for her nap."

"You're a saint," Ricki said.

Though we were both chronically underslept, we'd lucked out in so many ways. Not only in having a good-natured little girl, but also friends like Mae Johnson who offered (demanded, actually) to care for her while we were at work. We'd set up the guest bedroom for when she and Bree-yark wanted to stay over, which was most nights. As I dropped my bag beside the coat rack, Bree-yark appeared from the kitchen.

"How'd the job go?" the goblin asked, wiping away his milk mustache with a forearm.

"Damned near perfectly." I was still kicking myself for the cuff-picking incident. "One less drow hag on the city census."

"Good," he grunted. "Nasty things, as I'm sure you saw for yourselves."

"Unfortunately. Thanks again for the intel. Sorry we couldn't use you in the sting."

He waved a hand. "Aw, no worries. We had plenty to keep us busy here. Right, Abi?"

He hunkered in front of our daughter and covered his eyes. She watched expectantly. When he opened his hands and cried, "Peek-a-yark!" she gurgled appreciatively. But it was when he wriggled his goblin ears that her eyes really lit up and a squeal erupted through her spittle. Ricki smiled as she wiped Abi's chin with her bib.

"Don't over-excite her," Mae cautioned. "She's got sleepy time coming up."

Tabitha sighed heavily from her divan. "Have you given any more thought to my *gag* idea?"

Though my cat acted put out by all the infantile noises—as much from Abi as the adults—it seemed a small part of her succubus heart had softened since our daughter's arrival. Not entirely a shock. I'd long suspected she had a weakness for kids, going back to an early case involving a boy named Oliver.

Bree-yark performed a final "Peek-a-yark," to more delight from Abi, another warning from Mae, and an exaggerated groan from Tabitha.

"Can I fix anyone coffee?" I asked.

We settled in the living room, where Abigail ended up slumped against my belly, a pacifier locked between her gums. This was my favorite part of parenting—the low-key hanging out. The only ones missing were Tony, who'd recently started fourth grade, and Alec, the teenaged son of my shadow. He was back in his alternate version of the city, and it would be months before I could make the jump over to visit him.

"So will you get some time off after this?" Mae asked.

Ricki and I exchanged looks. "I'd love to," my wife sighed, setting her coffee down, "but Homicide is completely backlogged."

"And my dimension of the city isn't sleeping, either," I added, thinking of the recent spate of nether-creature banishments. Getting to help Ricki on her East Village case had been a luxury, especially with my ongoing responsibilities at Midtown College. I was teaching one less class, granted, but I was behind on my research. Wizard or not, I was still expected to keep up with my faculty obligations.

"You two just look so doggone *tired* all the time," Mae said.

"Yeah," Bree-yark added. "We get that you want to make New York safe for little Abi and her friends, but you can't baby-proof the entire city."

Mae nodded sagely. "Look, it's not our place to tell you your business, but we know the way you are about your responsibilities. And you're not gonna be any good to anyone, including your sweet baby, if you're dragging yourselves around, half-dead."

When Buster climbed onto her shoulder, she opened a packet of peanut-butter crackers from her purse and held one up. The lobster-like creature took the cracker in his lip tentacles, broke it apart, and began pushing the pieces into his mouth with eager chirps.

"We're just encouraging you to set some boundaries," she finished.

"Plus, it's been kinda lonesome down in the man cave," Bree-yark said, referring to the room he'd renovated off my basement lab.

Ricki tilted her head at me in a way that said, *They're right, you know.*

I nodded in assent. Even Hoffman had told us as much in so many words.

"We'll see what we can do," I said. "Maybe we can shift some resources around."

Mae's eyebrows drew down sternly. "I hope you're not just saying that to placate an old woman."

"No, no," I chuckled. "I've been meaning to contact the Order about sending temporary help. Grimstone County was quiet last I heard from Wesson."

"You mean the *cowboy*?" Ricki asked.

"Yeah, but he's done a lot of growing up. Well, you know... relatively speaking."

Ricki shared her confidence in my assessment with a flat look. "I can also put in a request for more detectives," she said. "Missing Persons is slammed, but I know Robbery has been slow lately."

Mae's face brightened. "There now, you see?"

"Oh, and there's a *Big Machines* marathon on this weekend," Bree-yark said, not ready to give up on recruiting me to the man cave. "Those things look even more amazing on the wide screen. I'm just sayin'."

"Maybe I can sneak down for an episode," I allowed. "But right now, someone else needs to go down." Abigail had been alternately drifting off and wriggling back to life, but now she was completely sacked out. I stood, turning her against my shoulder, and crept into our room, a finger to my lips.

"Good riddance," Tabitha muttered as I closed the door behind us.

I took a final breath of Abigail's warm head before lowering her into her crib. Her arms and legs kicked and her pacifier pistoned several times as she settled into place. I drew her blanket to her chest and tucked in the edges. Then I watched our daughter, our future magic-user. We wouldn't know for sure until she was at least thirteen, but I felt it—the same magic that moved through me would one day move through her.

As conversation resumed outside, I considered what Mae and Bree-yark had said.

They were right, of course, but how could I rest when I knew the kinds of things that were out there. The same concerns drove Ricki, even if we rarely spoke of them. We tended to manage by doing. But there was the promise I'd made to always be there for Abigail, and I couldn't fulfill both duties. Not well, anyway.

From the dresser, my mother's emo ball caught my eye. I'd set it there while preparing my disguise that morning. As I took the orb in hand, it glowed to life, its deep-seated compassion warming my heart. She'd prepared the enchantment when I was still an infant. In the event something happened to her, she hadn't wanted me to grow up without a mother's love. Smiling sadly, I returned the ball and looked down at Abigail.

My commitment had to be to my daughter—not doing *for* her, but being *with* her.

"Of course the Order could blow that right out of the

water," I murmured, leaning my arms against the crib's cherrywood railing.

It had been months since my meeting with Arianna when she'd revealed I had angel blood. She suggested my role could change within the Order, but I'd heard nothing since. No new mentor, either, which she'd also floated. What I did have was an angel-powered whip in my basement. Though instructed to safeguard it—and though a similar whip had enabled me to destroy a major Greek being—I was still uncomfortable with the thing in our building, even inside my warded safe.

I wondered how much the Order's recent silence was them wanting to give me time with my new girl and how much was them still consulting the collective. I'd gotten that the existence of an Avenging Angel had thrown them a major curveball. They were probably still deciding how best to proceed.

But I was getting ahead of myself—right now, I just needed extra personnel.

I was about to leave the room to call Claudius when my watch started to flash. Dammit, another nether creature in the city. With my mind and body revving into banishment mode, I made myself stop long enough to say goodbye to Abigail. As I patted her belly, a knot of guilt tightened inside my own.

"I'll try not to be long," I whispered.

3

The address was an industrial gray apartment building in a working-class neighborhood. An elderly man was exiting as I approached, and I compelled him with my wizard's voice to hold the front door. Two flights later, I was standing in front of my target's apartment.

I texted the number to Detective Hoffman, ending with **I?** —short for "info on occupant requested." As I put the phone away and knocked, I imagined him grunting out some choice words. A Code I sometimes led to a Code B, and Ricki wasn't exaggerating. Homicide had more than enough bodies these days.

I knocked again, this time hard enough to rattle the door. Twenty-four minutes had elapsed from alarm to arrival, an eternity when it came to amateur conjurings. When no one answered, I tried the knob, then stood back, my drawn sword aimed at the lock.

"*Vigore*," I hissed.

In a detonation of wood, the door blew open. I hurried

inside, a shield of hardened air already spreading into place around me.

"Hello?" I called. "Anyone home?"

The living area appeared mundane at a glance, but that wasn't unusual with amateurs. Though I was moving too quickly to make out the titles on the bookcase, I imagined that at least a few covered the sacred and/or occult. I was already picking up an ozone-like scent issuing from a back room.

"Anyone home?" I tried again.

I arrived in a small kitchen and pulled up, the back of my sword hand to my mouth.

I averted my eyes from the victim, blood swishing hard in my ears, and scanned the surroundings: stovetop of spell ingredients, crude symbol on the floor, toppled pile of ash and animal entrails. Though no longer smoking, the last gave off a warm, wet odor, like dog hair, that competed with the casting's greasy aftermath. I steeled myself before returning my gaze to the victim.

She was barely in her twenties, possibly a student at the neighborhood technical college. Her dark blond hair was banded into a ponytail, and she'd pulled on a denim work shirt over a plain T, as though preparing for a day of cleaning or DIY.

I had a hard time meeting her eyes, which seemed to stare into mine. Her arms were at her sides, hands angled inward as though presenting the evidence: *Look what it did to me.*

Her torso was completely hollowed out, all the way to the hull of her rib cage in back. The summoned creature had fed quickly and thoroughly, suggesting it had arrived from a deeper plane than your average nether bug.

I scanned the windows—all closed and intact, thank God

—before examining the floor. Even against the brown linoleum, the trail of blood from the victim wasn't hard to track. It led to a bathroom off the kitchen.

Rising, I followed it, my grip damp around my sword and staff. Though I'd battled bigger and badder, these moments never failed to unnerve me. Just-summoned nether creatures had a penchant for unpredictability.

With a foot, I eased the bathroom door wider.

The trail climbed the shallow end of the tub, where I could make out something's vein-mapped back glistening above the rim.

I edged a little closer, then released my breath.

The nether slug was familiar to me. Featuring a complex arrangement of tubes and enzymes, it dissolved its victims' insides and imbibed them like gruel through thick straws. Revolting, but not from as deep down as I'd feared. And there would be no fight. Engorged, and exhausted from its climb, the slug was struggling to shimmy toward the puddle of water around the tub's rusty drain.

I plunged my sword into its back and summoned an enclosure around its sudden wriggling and slaps. In the light of the surging banishment rune, I shouted, "*Disfare!*"

The creature exploded into blood and a black phlegm that oozed down the enclosure's sides. I dispersed the invocation and turned on the shower, sending the mess sluicing down the drain. I swallowed back the burn of illness, knowing some of the mess belonged to the young woman in the kitchen.

Finally, I cut off the water and texted Hoffman a follow-up: **B** for body.

"Kristin Shanks," Hoffman grunted. "Twenty-two. Moved here from Albany last year to go to school. Wanted to get into building management, apparently. So why'd she go getting mixed up in this crap?"

He squinted from her covered body to the casting evidence.

"Could be all kinds of reasons," I said. "But oftentimes it just comes down to plain old curiosity. You see that more with the... the younger ones." I still hadn't gotten over the image of her hollowed-out torso, or what was left of it circling the drain.

I'd been right about her bookcase. Though most of the books were for school, the bottom shelf spoke to someone who'd been seeking and spell-dabbling. A familiar pattern in my work. I'd already removed the dangerous titles, placing them in my interplanar cubby hole for later incineration.

"Well, she's lucky she only got *herself* killed," Hoffman decided. Though he accepted the supernatural, he still regarded it with suspicion, if not open hostility. Especially when it resulted in bodies. "Seems there's been a lot of these lately."

"Hmm?" I replied, still thinking about the victim. "Oh, yeah, they come in waves. A popular book or streaming series featuring witchcraft and wizardry can set off a sudden interest, and I'm told urban fantasy is hot right now."

I also had a theory that surges in the city's already powerful ley lines could drive energy-sensitive types to experiment, much like the moon's influence on the tides. But I still squirmed every time a blockbuster show came out.

"So I can write this up as an accident?" Hoffman asked to be sure.

"Yeah, I'll add my part later. In the meantime, I'll have

Ricki track down the vic's friends, see if there are any other amateurs in her circle." It was much easier to stop a conjurer before they conjured than after, as our present scene underscored. I was about to say as much when my watch started flashing.

Hoffman's puckered gaze dropped to my wrist. "You're freaking kidding me. Another one?"

"Yeah, gotta run," I said, rushing from the room. "I'll text you when I get there."

"Better not be another body!" he called after me.

4

"You sure this is the place?" the cabbie asked.

As he idled in front of a fence topped with loops of razor wire, I consulted my cane and the crumbling asphalt drive beyond the padlocked gate. We were on a service road behind the housing projects in the Lower East Side, close enough to the water to smell its briny tang. The conjurer had to be near.

"Yeah." I passed a couple twenties over the seat. "Thanks for getting me here so fast."

Two conjurings in one day was rare, two within a one-hour window even rarer, but it happened. And, lucky me, this one was clear across Manhattan from the last. Even with the cabbie's commendable driving, twenty-one minutes had elapsed between alarm and arrival. Another eternity.

"I'd offer to wait, but..." The cabbie angled his head toward the looming housing projects.

"Understood and no worries," I said quickly as I stepped out into an October drizzle. "Thanks again."

Bree-yark had offered to drive me to the first conjuring—and he would have driven me here, too—but I didn't want to abuse our friendship. He was already doing plenty by helping look after Abigail.

Plus, something in my magic suggested I needed to be doing this alone.

I raised my trench coat collar against the rain and inserted the end of my cane between the padlock's shafts. Manifesting a small sphere of hardened air, I expanded it until the lock snapped and fell to the ground. A basic invocation for a basic task. I gripped the gate, pushing and pulling until the chain loosened enough for me to duck through the opening. Basic physics worked a lot of the time, too.

Leading with my cane, I hurried down the curving drive, not entirely surprised when a large drainage culvert rounded into view.

I've been here before, I thought, *when Ricki and I were after a werewolf-vampire hybrid that turned out to be the mayor's stepdaughter.* That had been three years earlier, but it felt like three decades. So much had happened since, not least that my one-time adversary and I were now a family.

Straddling a stream of slimy water, I advanced down the culvert. Graffiti-covered walls shook with the passage of motor traffic high overhead. Beyond an intersection of north-south cylinders, a pair of white tennis shoes glowed into view. They hovered above the floor, specter-like, until I saw they were attached to someone in a space off the tunnel.

The shoes' splayed angle didn't bode well for the wearer.

I grew the light from my separated staff, revealing a small service room where the rest of the victim lay. A man this time, fifty-something with a flat cap that had remained on his head against all reason. Like the young woman, he was thoroughly disemboweled, as if someone had taken a giant ice-cream scoop to his center.

And where did the scoop scramble off to?

I peered past the expected casting circle, this one appearing to have been made from metal shavings. An open spell book lay beside a rudimentary camp stove. Candles stood at five points, but only one continued to burn. Its light reflected from a glistening trail that led from the victim's body and up the near wall.

I tracked it with my eyes and—*damn!*—nearly fell as I splashed back into the tunnel.

The summoned creature had pressed itself into a nook right above where I'd been standing. From my new angle, I made out a transparent wing pulled taut around a swollen body. A single milky eye peered out.

Not a slug this time, some kind of flyer. I considered its awkward placement, high and recessed, before deciding on fire.

With a Word, I activated my blade's second rune and sent a narrow stream of flames into the damp nook. A piercing whine went up. The creature wriggled from its steaming lair and batted into clumsy flight. But swaddled in fire, it could only slap from wall to wall, its reverberating cry losing strength.

As the winged horror plummeted, I caught it with a staff thrust and invocation, enclosing it in a sphere of hardened air. Then I squeezed it like a fist, the pressure quickly overcoming the final bonds holding the creature together. It exploded into smoke and black ichor.

A clean banishment, but it didn't make up for the fact I'd arrived too late. Again.

I was preparing to disperse the creature's remains into the creeklet running down the tunnel, but I drew a glass tube from a coat pocket instead. Opening a hole in the sphere's bottom, I filled the tube with the creature's residue and capped it before sending the rest floating off toward the East River.

I'd been struck by a sense of off-ness. Maybe nothing more than two conjurings happening within an hour of each other, but I'd learned to heed such intuitions. And this one felt like my magic talking.

Pocketing the tube, I took a longer look around the service room. The spell book was different than what I'd found in the girl's apartment, as was the style of casting. Seemed to rule out a connection between them. Just another unlucky conjurer. Lacking actual magic, he'd reached into a shallow nether realm and grasped a nasty grub. I'd seen more than a hundred similar cases in my time.

So why was this one throwing flags?

I looked at his open pack, a battered Jansport he'd used to haul his spell implements and ingredients down here. He'd probably come from one of the nearby projects, seen magic as his way out...

But I couldn't shake the feeling I was *supposed* to think that. Just like I was supposed to think the last woman had gotten into magic out of youthful curiosity.

Years before, I might have felt nothing and gone on my grim way. Not now.

I took a deep breath and exhaled through my nose, clearing my mind of all logic and reason. Like a diver, I sank into the raw depths of my magic. Mysterious currents swirled around me, pushing and pulling. If the currents were the source of my nagging feeling, they might also reveal its cause.

But they thinned suddenly.

My hearing had picked up something. I opened my eyes, snapping the room back into focus.

There it was again—a soft splash and drip. Someone from farther down the tunnel coming stealthily toward the conjurer. I pressed my back to the wall and whispered, drawing the candle's shadows around me.

The steps drew nearer.

Maybe this is my answer, I thought, pulse quickening.

The edge of a shadow appeared on the far wall of the tunnel. I waited for it to advance, for the figure to step into full view, but it went still. As I adjusted my sword and staff, the shadow withdrew along with the steps, more quickly than they'd arrived. I jumped into the tunnel with a splash.

Ahead, the figure broke into a run.

"Hey!" I shouted.

5

The figure was too fast for my light, which swelled white and beacon-like from my staff. All I could make out was the back of a hooded cloak, its fabric thrashing with each splashing stride.

"I just want to talk to you!" I shouted.

Whether or not he'd been involved in the conjuring, he might have seen something. Or maybe he knew the conjurer. But despite my appeal, the runner didn't slow. If anything, he was pulling away.

"*Vigore!*" I called, thrusting my sword toward his legs.

The force blast was meant to trip him up, but the runner cut left, leaving my invocation to push up a small wall of water. As I arrived at the intersection, the water returned in a surge, soaking through my socks.

Panting for breath, I peered down the intersecting tunnel. A foot off the floor of the main tunnel, the sight of its narrowness cinched my chest. But besides a steady trickle of water, I couldn't see or hear anything down the cylinder's length.

He didn't have that *much of a lead.*

When I picked up a whiff of burnt ash, I rotated and uttered a Word that threw a shield into place—and not a moment too soon. It caught the violent roar of a fire blast that pushed me back a step.

I grunted and planted my feet, incanting to reinforce my protection. Water boiled into steam around me. As the flames relented, fierce turquoise eyes flashed from the opposite tunnel. A magic-user? He must have cast an illusion to send me in the wrong direction, because the hood framing his face told me this was the same person I'd been chasing.

"*Respingere!*" I shouted, fear and anger powering my invocation.

A spell-caster lurking around a deadly conjuring wasn't an accident, and this one had just tried to flame-broil me.

The pent-up power left my shield in a bright flash. The magic-user threw an arm up, revealing a wooden wand, its tip a burning ember. With defensive magic sizzling through the air, he skidded to a stop after a couple feet, his combat boots furrowing the water.

"Who are you?" I demanded.

His extended wand rippled the space between us, not with heat this time, but force. I cleaved the invocation with my drawn sword, sending it to either side, and countered with my staff, circling it smartly. The space around him glinted into a fist of hardened air, pinning his arms to his sides.

He struggled like a caught fish.

"Who are you?" I pressed, stalking forward. "What are you doing in here?"

He wasn't wearing a cloak, I saw, but a rain poncho. In his struggle, the hood fell away, his exposed head bald and shiny with moisture. The ebony skin was tattooed with fine white lines that seemed to shift as they glinted in the light of my staff. Energy-channeling patterns I recognized as druidic.

How in the hell is a druid mixed up in this?

When his scowl revealed teeth filed to points, I stopped suddenly.

First, we burn out its eyes, came a seething, recollected voice. *That it may no more curse us with its evil sight.*

For a moment, the steam rising around us took on the form of smoke. My right eye throbbed as sweat coursed around it. Gripped by an overpowering sense of déjà vu, my mind and mouth stammered.

"Y-you," I said, reflexively tightening the fist of hardened air around her.

Because this wasn't a man, but a woman—one I had battled before.

In a sudden twist of light, she disappeared.

"So tell us more about this druid," Detective Hoffman said, dragging a hand around his wreath of brown curls.

It was late in the day, and at my urging, he and Ricki had gotten the conjuring cases assigned to a special task force. Mayor "Budge" Lowder promised to rubber stamp any future task force requests after he'd undermined our last one—we had only to send it to one of his deputies. It was partly a concession to his screwup, but he also trusted our instincts when it came to supernatural cases in the city.

"You remember the St. Martin's case from a few years ago?" I said to Hoffman. "It started with a message in blood on the rector's back?"

He grunted from his seat opposite me at the conference room table. "Yeah? So?"

Ricki gave me a knowing look. The "Demon Moon" case had been our first official collaboration.

"Well, while trying to interpret the message, I discovered a druid group living in the North Woods section of Central Park," I said. "'Black Earth,' they called themselves. That was before the mayor's eradication campaign, of course."

"You mean the one where he torched the whole goddamned show?" Hoffman asked.

I nodded, recalling how Ricki and I had gotten pinned in the park's southern end during the first round of napalming. I still had a little skin discoloration on my neck from the close call.

"In any case, this Black Earth cult was obsessed with star readings. Their charts pointed to the present age for the return of a major demon lord, Sathanas. They'd actually gotten that part right—he was what I battled under the church—but they mistakenly believed I was in his employ. Their high priestess was ready to turn my eye sockets into smoking craters. She was who I encountered in the tunnels today."

"And you're sure it was her?" Ricki asked.

"It's not the kind of face you forget. Especially when you're thinking it's the last one you'll ever see."

First, we burn out its eyes, I heard her saying, her lunatic stare bright in the smoldering tip of her wand. *That it may no more curse us with its evil sight.*

With the aid of the seared-in memory, I completed a sketch of her tattoos.

"Here," I said, turning the pad around for them to see. "The bald head, turquoise eyes, and filed teeth are distinctive

enough, but these are for channeling energy from her god."
As they studied the tattoo patterns, I touched the socks I'd
draped over the back of an adjacent chair, still damp from the
storm tunnels. I willed my blade's fire rune to ember hotness
and passed it under them a couple times.

"We'll run her description through the database,"
Hoffman grumbled at last. "Assuming the damned thing's
been updated in the last decade."

He'd been resistant to the idea of the task force, mainly
because it meant he couldn't close the files on that day's
conjurer deaths as accidents. Worse, it meant reopening
some recent cases where I hadn't reached amateurs in time.
But I needed to see if any patterns jumped out. When Ricki
told him they could use the task force to justify more help for
their mundane cases, Hoffman grudgingly agreed.

"But what connects the bodies to this druid chick?" he
asked. "It's gotta be more than her just being down in the
storm tunnels."

"Well, it makes her a person of interest at the very least,
right?" I said. "She might have seen something, heard something. She could also have been why the conjuring happened
in the first place."

I didn't share my nagging feeling that the day's conjurings
had been staged, partly because it would only draw a deeper
scowl from Hoffman, but mostly because I had nothing
concrete to back it up. And why would someone stage them
in the first place?

"Great, so we don't even know what side she's on," he
muttered.

"If her cult is dedicated to stopping the return of a demon
lord," Ricki asked over him, "why would she be involved in
dangerous conjurings?"

"To say this druid was crazy when I met her four years ago is like saying gangrene gives off an unpleasant odor. And both tend to get worse with time. I put in a few calls, one to Jordan Derrow—a druid friend of mine," I added for Hoffman's benefit. "I'm waiting to hear back, but he should know where Black Earth ended up after they were smoked out of Central Park. Might also have some info on their doings."

"Lot of *should*s and *might*s," Hoffman grumbled. "Like I said, we'll stick her description in the database, see what pops up. We'll put out an APB, too."

Ricki patted the small stack of files between them. "We can also knock on doors for these old cases. Neighbors, building managers. See if they remember anyone fitting the druid's description."

Hoffman leveled his exhausted eyes at mine. "Anything else, Croft?"

"Oh, I have something for forensics," I said, producing the tube with the creature's remains from a coat pocket. "It's what's left of the thing I banished in the tunnel, but can we check it against the victim's DNA? See if it matches?"

"Why wouldn't it?" he asked. "You said it hollowed him out."

"Just following up on a hunch," I admitted.

Lips compressed, he took the tube and slung his crinkled jacket over a shoulder. "I'll run it down before they decide to bail for the night."

"Thanks, Hoff."

He returned a dismissive wave, but I'd worked with him enough to know he was on board.

When the door closed behind him, Ricki turned to me. "Ready to share what you weren't telling him?"

"That obvious?" I grinned as I tested my socks again.

Deciding they were dry enough, I began pulling them on. "It's my magic. With the latest conjuring, it started prodding me, suggesting something was off. And then the druid showed up, seeming to confirm the off-ness. But it's more than that. They say history doesn't repeat itself, but often rhymes... and that's what this feels like. A rhyme."

She raised an eyebrow. "With the Demon Moon case?"

I nodded. "That started with a cluster of random conjurings, only they weren't so random. They were calling up shriekers."

"I spent an evening with a couple of them," she reminded me.

That was the night I'd encased her in a protective circle against her will. "Hey, desperate times, desperate measures. The shriekers were supposed to be the lead soldiers in Sathanas's army, something the Black Earth druids sensed back then. Now we have another cluster of seemingly random conjurings. They're calling up random creatures this time, true, but Black Earth is back in the picture."

Ricki's eyebrows nearly touched. "Suggesting another demon lord?"

As I finished lacing my shoes, I considered her question —the very one I'd been asking myself all afternoon. "Doubtful," I decided. "The last time, the Order was still in exile, in no position to sense Sathanas, much less head him off. Today, our most powerful members are watching the layers around our world. If something that big-time were making a move, it would be making equally big-time waves."

Her brow let out slightly. "That is reassuring."

"Anyway, I put in a call to Claudius to get the Order's thoughts. Still waiting to hear back."

"I made some calls, too. Talked to a few of Kristin

Shanks's friends in the city and back home." Ricki consulted her tablet computer. "No one claimed to know about her having an interest in magic. If anything, they acted surprised by the question, like it was really out of character for her. She was a jock, apparently."

That deepened my suspicion about the scenes being staged, but it was too soon to jump to that conclusion. A lot of amateurs kept the conjuring dimension of their life hidden until it was too late.

"Anything on the tunnel vic?" I asked.

"Hasn't been ID'd yet. Once we have a name, I'll start interviewing his associates."

Though I was trying to see my wife through professional eyes, I couldn't *not* notice the paleness of her face. That was her fatigue tell. "Hey, I know I'm asking a lot of the department's resources right now," I said gently. "Including yours."

She came around, sat on my lap, and kissed me firmly. "You don't have to explain yourself. I'm not Hoffman."

"Good, because that would be really awkward right now." I patted her hip.

She squeezed my jaw in mock exasperation. "You know what I mean. If your magic's talking, we should all be listening."

I nodded, knowing she was right.

And that scared the hell out of me.

6

Despite my earlier promise to my daughter, I remained in the conference room long after Ricki had gone home for the day.

I paced slowly around a city map onto which I'd plotted all of the amateur conjurings in the last six months. Blue stickies indicated the cases I'd reached in time, while the yellow ones marked the ones where I'd arrived too late to spare the conjurer. Including that day's cases, I was looking at thirteen yellows, but with no apparent pattern. Not until I considered the dates I'd written on the dry erase board.

The ones with the yellow stickies showed an accelerating pattern.

Just the way the dice tumbled? I wondered. *Or does it actually mean something?*

I'd already pulled a book on star and moon patterns from my interplanar cubbyhole, but there didn't seem to be any upcoming celestial events. None that were obvious to my amateur eye, anyway.

I wondered if it was time for a scrying spell. With strands of the last victim's hairs, I could attempt to tap into his final moments. I would experience them, up to and quite possibly through the creature noshing his insides. Pretty freaking unpleasant, but that wasn't what made me shrink from the idea. Acting as the scrying object would mean opening myself up to an attack, and if powerful druids were involved...

Might want to shelve that for now, Chief.

I paused to recall Arianna's counsel from our last meeting. I had been telling her that while my faith in my magic seemed to be growing, I felt compelled to do the busy work and I was always questioning whether I'd done enough.

The work remains important, she'd replied, *but finding the balance will come.*

A check of my watch told me I'd put in a solid day. It was time now for some balance.

I cut the lights, spread a polyethylene sheet with a premade casting circle over the floor, and sat in its center cross-legged. As I'd done inside the tunnel earlier, I exhaled through my nose, allowing my thoughts to flow out with the air. The sinking sensation followed. Strange but familiar currents, strengthened by the casting circle, pushed and pulled against me. But with them came the uneasiness I'd felt earlier while talking to Ricki. Whatever my magic wanted to tell me felt big. Maybe too big.

"Find the child."

I jerked, the suddenness and clarity of the voice catching me off guard.

"Ch-child?" I stammered, not sure if I was speaking out loud or in my head. "What child?"

"The child," the voice repeated, farther away. "Find the child."

The voice sounded strangely like... my father's.

"Wait!" I called, but it was gone now.

Something heavy landed on top of me. I returned to the
conference room to a chaotic jousting of arms and legs. A
sharp blow caught me in the side as I slapped for my cane,
but it wasn't within reach. Disentangling myself from the
grunting mass, I scrambled toward the door and flipped on
the lights.

I wasn't sure what I would find, but I hadn't been
expecting an elderly man with a mess of dyed-black hair.

"Claudius?" I panted, lowering the hand I was aiming at
the senior member of my Order.

"Is that Everson?" He leaned toward me as he gained his
feet, parting his hair to squint from his blue-tinted glasses.
"Yes, good, good, I'm in the right place. My apologies for the
dramatic entrance. I, ah, thought I'd adjusted for your
position."

He moved a finger around his palm as though rechecking
his math.

"What are you even doing here?" I asked, rubbing the
soreness from my side.

"Well, I got your message earlier, and the Order has some
news to share. I could have called, but it being the evening
time, I was hoping we could meet over pizza. It's been a long
time since my last New York slice."

My growling stomach reminded me I'd skipped dinner.

"Sure," I said. "There's a place right up the street. My
treat."

"Great!" he cried, rubbing his hands together. But he
paused, his face dimming suddenly as though recalling his
errand. "But I should tell you, Everson, it's not going to be all,
ah, good news."

"Mmm, that was tasty," he said, pushing the final length of wood-fired crust into his mouth. He looked down at my paper plate. "You haven't eaten much."

Though the pepperoni slice *was* tasty, I'd only managed a couple bites.

"Yeah, my digestion doesn't play well with the portent of bad news," I said.

Claudius's brow furrowed as he sucked his Diet Coke through a straw. Following the earlier rain, the evening was clear and mild, and we were sitting at an outdoor table with a view of Park Avenue, the unofficial boundary between Civic Center and Chinatown. I caught myself scanning the far side of the street, alert for Bashi's White Hand enforcers.

"Ah, yes, the news," Claudius said, wiping his mouth. "We'll get to everything in a moment, but first, let me share some good tidings. Your request for backup has been approved and will be dispatched shortly."

"Wesson?" I asked hopefully. Despite a few bumps—and, yeah, egg on our faces—James Wesson and I had racked up some solid wins out West. Plus, I preferred working with a familiar face.

"I wasn't told," Claudius said. "But the Order only had to take one look at your cases to see you needed reinforcements. I volunteered to deliver them myself, but my route-finding hasn't been so hot of late. I'm afraid I lost a magic-user somewhere on the second plane... Or was it the third? Anyway, until I recover her, I'm only to transport myself."

That sort of mishap had always felt inevitable, but though I was morbidly curious to hear the story, I needed to keep him on topic.

"Did the Order say if they found the cases unusual? Connected to something bigger?"

Claudius affected a thinking face. "Hmm, I don't *believe* so. In what way, exactly?"

With a sigh, I reviewed the message I'd left for him, about my magic prodding me and the run-in with the druid.

"Ah, yes, yes. No, Arianna didn't say one way or the other. She only asked that you continue to heed your magic. She stressed this, in fact. She has a lot of faith when it comes to your listening abilities."

That always surprised me. At the conclusion of my cases, I may have appeared to have conducted my magic like a pro, but during them, I always felt as if I were running in a dozen different directions at once.

Seeing my doubt, Claudius said, "Well, what is it telling you now?"

"It wants me to 'find the child.'"

His face brightened. "See there?"

"Does that mean anything to you?" I didn't mention that the voice had sounded like my father's. I wasn't even sure anymore.

Claudius's bristly eyebrows drew down. "'Find the child,'" he repeated. "Is one missing?"

This was pointless. "All right, I'm ready." I knocked on the table. "Let's get to the bad news."

"Ah, yes." He pushed his grease-soaked plate to one side.

My heart beat sickly. A part of me was still traumatized by the old "Order," which had kept me in line with threats, even hinting at death spells. Though that was history and Arianna and the true Order were the closest I knew to benevolence incarnate, my nerves didn't care. They shook every time an official so much as frowned.

"This has to do with your angelic nature," Claudius began.

I wiped my damp palms on the thighs of my slacks and swallowed. "Okay."

"But first a little history." He pulled a crumpled piece of paper from a pocket with some handwritten notes and cleared his throat. "The Avenging Angels were sent here to face the nine original demons. But they were zealots, Everson. Not as nasty as the demons, no, but nasty in their own rights. They inflicted a good deal of damage and death on the humans they were meant to protect. Seeing this, the Creator quickly swapped them out for the First Saints. You know the rest, of course."

I'd known the first part, too, but I nodded anyway.

He skimmed the next section of his notes. "Let's see, the two-thousand-year war between saints and demons, the agreement, the betrayal... um... Saint Michael banishing the final three demon lords—Belphegor, Beelzebub, and Sathanas—and starting what would become our Order, yes? But in light of your angelic blood, it has become clear that one of the Angels was on Earth long enough to start a line, too. And the senior members believe they've traced your lineage back to an angel named Faziel."

"Faziel," I repeated.

"Oh, don't say it out loud!" He thrust his waving hands toward me. "I shouldn't have said it myself."

I glanced around, my heartrate kicking up again. "That's bad, I assume."

Claudius patted his hands toward the table as if to calm himself before steepling his fingers in front of his lips. "Yes. Well, the Order believes so. You see, the angels didn't take the fact of their banishment very well. Fortunately, they were recalled before they could rebel. But Faziel—" He caught himself. "We'll call him Faz from now on. By starting a line, *Faz* lived on in the blood of his progeny."

I remembered the looming figure I'd seen when I'd opened myself to the angel-powered whip. No face, no distinct features, just an outline and a giant pair of wings that seemed to merge with the surrounding mist.

"And under the right conditions, he can take form?" I asked.

Claudius nodded. "We're starting to believe so, yes."

"Is that what happened in the shadow realm?"

"Again, we believe so."

He was resorting to Order-speak, but that would have explained why no magic-users existed over there. Faziel must have trained his anger on the descendants of his replacement —Saint Michael's line.

"Do we know *how* he took form?" I asked carefully.

Claudius frowned as he studied his notes. "No, ah, not yet. But until we do, we'll need to err on the side of caution. Not saying his name, for example. Also, we're trying to come up with a plan for the whip. Is it...?"

"Still in my safe? Yes."

"Okay, good," he breathed. "It's not just the angel that concerns us."

My thoughts immediately went to the Street Keepers in the shadow realm, or what remained of them. The Greek gods had decimated their leadership. "There aren't any motorcycle-riding cults to him here, are there?"

"Oh, no, no, nothing like that, but you're not the only one who carries his blood."

I'd wondered about that. "Has the Order located others?" An angelic line could break any number of ways, several bad, but I felt a crackling shot of anticipation of getting to meet others like me.

"Well, only in theory. They're out there—they'd have to be —but the question of purity comes up. If the line has been sufficiently diluted, they would have no power to speak of. No idea of their lineage, even. They might be ardent churchgoers or especially committed to ideas of justice, but perhaps nothing more."

I suffered a twinge of disappointment. "Was there anything else?"

He consulted his notes with a frown. "No... I believe that was all."

I knew I was only getting what Claudius recalled or had thought to write down, but I trusted Arianna was working behind the scenes and would tell me if something urgent came up.

"So I should keep his name out of my mouth and the whip in my safe," I said in summation. Basically what I'd already been doing.

"Exactly!" Claudius stuffed the note away. "Well, I should get back to my search for that lost magic-user." He said it as though he were referring to a television remote. "It's just a matter of retracing my steps... If I can remember them."

We hugged farewell, and then I watched him slide from his chair and into a portal under the table. A green appendage groped out, prompting me to jerk my feet up. It retreated back inside before the portal snapped closed.

I chuckled in disbelief as I lowered my feet again, but our angel talk had left a ganglion of foreboding in my gut. Maybe because it meant one more thing to worry about on top of the recent amateur conjurings. But I'd done everything I could for the day. It was time to get home to my family.

"Mr. Croft?" someone said from behind me.

I turned to see a man of Asian descent with sheared blond hair. The fact that he knew my name put me on edge. His mercenary stare didn't help. I noticed a white SUV had pulled up to the curb while Claudius and I were saying our goodbyes. The silhouette of a driver watched from behind the tinted glass.

"Who's asking?" I said.

"Mr. Gang would like to speak with you."

Great, this was one of Bashi's henchmen. "Tell him I'm not interested."

A gun appeared at his hip. "It wasn't a question."

7

As I looked from the bore of the man's weapon back to his mercenary eyes. I was a little surprised it had taken his boss, Wang "Bashi" Gang, this long to come after me.

A couple years earlier, I helped my friend, the Blue Wolf, eliminate a powerful dragon shifter with whom Bashi had been negotiating a major opium deal. The Blue Wolf gunned down several of his White Hand enforcers in the process and trashed one of his homes. More recently, I liberated a shaman from Bashi's Chinatown opium den, which couldn't have improved my standing with the mob boss.

But I wasn't overly concerned. The second I'd heard the henchman's voice, I'd invoked a form-fitting shield. I casually lifted my coat from the chair back and draped it over an arm encased in protective energy.

"Mr. Gang has my number," I said. "He's welcome to call me."

"That is *not* what he wants." The man adjusted his stance, showing more of his weapon.

"Nice toy, but isn't your playground across the street?"

"Chinatown is *growing*," he said viciously. When he raised his eyes, I glanced over and saw that, indeed, Pilky's Pizza was bracketed by a pair of new businesses, their signs in Chinese script. "You are on our turf."

"My apologies. I'll fix that now."

It had been years since I'd been forced into a car at gunpoint, and I wasn't going to fall off the wagon now. Bashi may have had contacts inside the NYPD, but so did I, and mine outranked his. I would make sure he got the message to back off until my task force completed its work. Then I'd figure out how to placate him.

As I cane-tapped toward One Police Plaza, the henchman looked over at his driver in exasperation before hustling to catch up to me. He clearly wasn't used to being brushed off after invoking his boss's name.

"Mr. Croft, these are not mundane bullets I carry."

"No?' I was about to add something dismissive, but hesitated.

He wasn't bullshitting. I picked up an aura around his weapon, its subtlety speaking to fae magic. Powerful enough to fracture *my* magic? Bashi may have been a lot of things, but he hadn't lorded over Chinatown and the vice trades going on four years now by being stupid. He'd studied his potential enemies.

I slowed to a stop. Thinking he was in control again, the henchman's face relaxed and his voice regained its haughty texture. "That's better, Mr. Croft." He opened his arm toward the car. "Right this way."

I nodded in acceptance while signing with my far hand, pulling more energy into my shielding. Decision time: release enough power to disarm him, blast him over the low-rises across the street, or aim for something in between? I didn't want to draw Bashi's ire more than I already had—there was my family to think about—but I wasn't getting into that car.

I'd all but decided on a midrange blast, when a distinct rumbling from One Police Plaza presented another solution. The man looked between me and the approaching vehicle as I raised a hand.

"What are you doing?" he hissed.

A large, armored personnel carrier with the NYPD Shield pulled over, dwarfing the white SUV. The passenger door opened, and a tall man in Sup Squad gear emerged, rifle in hand. Three more members of the team followed, taking up covering positions around the carrier.

"Everything all right, Croft?" Trevor asked, striding toward me.

"I was just chatting with one of Mr. Gang's underlings." I clapped the henchman's shoulder, noticing he'd slipped the gun into a concealed holster behind his hip. "I'm sorry, what did you say your name was?"

Outnumbered and outgunned, he glared at me and reached into a pocket. The Sup Squad raised their weapons.

"Relax," he seethed. "It's just my *card*."

He produced a black rectangle and pressed it into my hand. "This isn't going away. Call me when you're ready to meet. *Soon*."

As the man got into the SUV, Trevor asked, "What was that about?"

"Oh, Bashi has a bone to pick with me," I said, glancing at the card—no name, just a number and an impression of a white hand—and pocketing it. "Thanks for pulling over. Things were about to get untidy."

"Hey, we've always got your back."

"Ditto for you guys. Where are you headed?"

"A call on a possible ghoul sighting on Roosevelt Island. Nine times out of ten they're tweakers, but there's always that tenth. Speaking of which, I saw the memo on your task force. Anything we can be doing?"

As the adrenaline of the encounter with Bashi's man thinned along with my shielding, I considered where things stood. Amateur conjurings that didn't feel so random, a fire druid's presence, and most recently a call to "find the child." The pieces were gathering, rotating into an orbit around me, but nothing had cohered yet.

"At the moment, no," I said. "But that could change."

"Let us know. We'll be ready."

We slapped fives and bumped fists. As he and his teammates climbed back into the carrier, I flagged down a cab.

I had just given the driver my address when my phone buzzed. The display showed an unknown number. Possibly Bashi—he'd called me directly in the past. I almost sent the call to voicemail before choosing to end the suspense.

"Hello?" I answered.

"Yes, I'm looking for Mr. Croft?"

But it wasn't Bashi. The voice belonged to an older woman.

"Who's calling?" I asked.

"I'm sorry, this is Bishop Sheridan."

Disturbing images flashed through my mind: the subbasement of St. Martin's Cathedral; a gray-haired woman convulsing in a casting circle; a black-robed figure gargling demonic words and wielding a dagger. I was seeing the climax of the Demon Moon case. The robed figure was Father Vick, possessed by the demon lord Sathanas. The woman was the caller, Bishop Sheridan of the New York Episcopal diocese.

ought hadn’t

"Oh, ah, hi, Bishop," I said clumsily. "How are you?"

Soon after Sathanas nearly escaped into a city bathed in the demon moon's red glow, Bishop Sheridan visited my apartment to thank me. We hadn't spoken since, but I had received a few invitations to her masses. I always seemed to have a scheduling conflict, which couldn't have looked good.

"I'm fine, thank you," she replied. "How about you?"

"Oh, trying to juggle family life with teaching and my side work."

Though I hadn't the slightest idea why she was calling, it was another verse in the rhyme: a cluster of conjurings, the Black Earth cult, and now the return of the bishop? Even Bashi had played a role back then, I realized, demanding I track down the conjurer who'd killed one of his couriers.

"Well, your side work is actually why I'm calling," she said. "I have a favor to ask of you."

"Oh, yeah?" I shimmied myself straighter in the cab's backseat. "What's going on?"

"It involves a parishioner at St. Martin's. She needs help of a kind that only you may be able to provide."

I thought of all my commitments, not least to my family and Abigail. Just that afternoon I'd pledged to tamp down my work, but in the last few hours it only seemed to have piled to greater heights.

"How urgent are we talking?" I hedged.

"It's her son. He's... well, he's missing."

My heart jolted as the voice from earlier returned like a crack of thunder: *Find the child.*

"When can we meet?" I asked.

8

Sited on a massive fount of ley energy in downtown Manhattan, St. Martin's Cathedral was among the oldest and most powerful buildings of worship in the city. I had attended as a boy, and as my gaze climbed the bronze doors of the narrow facade to the Gothic spire, I felt time collapse around me.

I remembered hopping up the steps on Sunday mornings, clinging to Nana's hand. I remembered studying the saints and angels on the stained-glass window inside, utterly transfixed. Many years later, I would battle a demon lord beneath the same cathedral. Three years after that, I would marry my wife here.

To say I had mixed memories of the place was an understatement.

A cold wind flapped my trench coat, returning me to the present. I glanced at the waxing moon. Though I'd already consulted the lunar cycles, I was relieved to find its bone-white glow unmarred by red. Not another demon moon.

Bishop Sheridan met me at the door and invited me

inside, as arranged. The powerful threshold relented, but I still lost a good portion of my magic as I stepped through the doorway. That was the way holy protections worked, even for allies. My incubus spirit, Thelonious, shuddered weakly.

The bishop received me with a warm hug before grasping my elbows at arm's length.

"It is so good to see you again, Everson," she said, moisture standing in her eyes. Into her seventies now, the deepening lines of her face reinforced her authority rather than weakened it. Even so, I picked up some psychic scarring. Precious few had looked upon a manifested demon lord and lived to tell the tale. We had that in common.

"You too," I replied. "I'm anxious to help out in any way I can."

Ever since her call, my heart had been drilling my sternum. Could this be the child my magic was urging me to find?

"She's this way," she said. "We're housing her here for her protection."

I was about to ask what she needed protection from, but I would hear everything shortly.

The bishop led me through several doors and across a courtyard to a covered walkway lined with closed rooms. One had housed the late Father Victor. We stopped two doors down, where a chair had been parked outside along with a coffee mug holding a pack's worth of cigarette butts. The bishop knocked gently. A shadow passed beyond the curtained window, and the door cracked open onto a red-rimmed eye.

"He's here," the bishop said.

"Um, okay." The door opened onto the rest of the woman.

Mary Swal was in her young twenties, but the worry that

pinched her eyes and hollowed out her cheeks added another fifteen years. Even her brunette hair, fastened with plastic barrettes, looked thin and worn-out. She retreated into the studio apartment, where she'd set up a trio of chairs near the foot of the bed.

"Thank you for coming," she said in a quiet smoker's voice. "Can I get you something to drink? A soda?"

"Oh, no, thank you," I replied.

As the three of us settled into the chairs, I realized this was Malachi Wickstrom's old room when he was an acolyte in residence. He'd gone on to become a prophet and assembled the Upholders, a group with whom I'd journeyed into the time catches. He ultimately succumbed to a demon. Though we'd stopped some major infernal beings in the last few years, they'd still inflicted some gutting losses.

Mary cleared her throat. "I don't know how much you've been told, so I guess I'll just start at the beginning."

I drew my notepad from a coat pocket. "Take your time."

She nodded and dropped her eyes. "I had my son, Edgar, three years ago. It was a difficult birth, and he had a lot of medical problems. He was diagnosed with a genetic condition that made him age prematurely. I wasn't well off, so the Church helped. A lot. I don't know what I would have done without them." She glanced over at the bishop before dropping her eyes again, her fingers picking at a tuft of gray thread on her sweater.

"I know I could have been a better mom, but I didn't always understand Edgar's needs. He was my first child, my only child, and he was sick so much. When he was two, a therapist came over to work with him. During the session, Edgar got hold of a kitchen knife—I don't know how, I kept stuff like that away from him—and he cut her across the eyes."

When she began plucking at the thread more fervently, the bishop rubbed her back. I didn't realize Mary was crying until a tear spackled the lap of her faded jeans.

"Do you need a minute?" I asked.

She shook her head and blotted her nose with her sleeve. "No, I want to keep going. I saw something in Edgar's face that day. Anger, but not the kind that belongs to a two-year old, not even one with his condition. The only way I can explain it is that it made him look a lot older than he already did."

Possession? I wondered, jotting it down.

"After that, I restrained him. Not with handcuffs or anything—these were soft restraints, from a medical store. Because if I didn't, I knew he'd hurt someone again. What he'd done to the therapist left her blind in one eye. But I wasn't just scared for them or... or myself. I was scared for Edgar." She looked up with pleading eyes. "I was still his mother. I didn't want him put in an institution."

I'd wondered why she was going into so much of his back-story, but that explained it. She needed to justify her treatment of him.

"I couldn't be with him all the time—I still had to work and run errands. But I made sure he was fed and cleaned before I left. I also got him a tranquilizer in a child's dose. That probably sounds awful," she added quietly. "But without it, he'd scream and try to hurt himself. That went on for almost a year. Then last night I came back from a shopping run and he... he wasn't in his bed."

Though I was still struggling with her neglect of Edgar, the new parent in me felt the spearing dread of losing a child.

"The restraints were cut," she continued. "I—I looked everywhere, but instead of finding him, I found that." She gestured toward her window-facing desk. On top was a piece of paper in a plastic bag. "It was on my bed."

"May I?" I asked, reaching toward it. When she nodded, I brought it onto my lap. The handwritten note read:

Mary Swal,

You are a disgrace to motherhood. Cruel, selfish, unfit to care for a dog, much less your son.

Edgar is with us now. If you tell the police, we will release the photos and you will be arrested. Even if they were to find him, you would never see him again. The smartest thing you can do is leave him in our care. He will be better off. So will you. Search for him at your peril.

We are watching.

There was no signature or claim of responsibility, and the writing looked intentionally blocky.

I turned the bag around to where the photos were. I squinted at a frail old man with liver spots and a hooked nose before realizing it was Edgar. His wrists and ankles were bound to the rails of a hospital bed, and a broad strap fastened his waist to the mattress. The photos were instants. Edgar's large, unfocused eyes stared up at whomever was taking his picture.

"Are the police involved?" I asked.

"No," Mary replied hoarsely. She had been staring at the floor while I studied the damning letter and photos, her drawn-in shoulders making it look as if she were trying to hide inside herself. "I believe the threat."

"Do you suspect anyone?" I asked. "The father, maybe?"

She remained silent for an uncomfortable length of time. "Edgar's father was never part of his life," she replied at last.

"Ever notice anyone watching your place?"

"Not watching, but the week before Edgar disappeared, a woman came to the door in a business skirt and jacket. She asked questions about him. I thought she worked for one of the state services, but she never asked to see Edgar. I didn't think much about her visit at the time—I was just glad when she left."

"What kinds of questions?"

"About his well-being, mostly. Hard to remember—I was so afraid she'd come to take him away. But I remember one question that seemed weird. She wanted to know if he'd undergone any sudden changes."

I jotted that down. "Did she leave a card or anything?"

"No, she didn't even tell me her name. She just said she'd come back."

"What did she look like?"

"Tall, with straight blond hair to here." She touched the side of her neck near her shoulder. "It was almost white, but it didn't look bleached. And she was very pale, like part albino or something." Her fingers circled her face and brushed her lips. "Except for her eyes. They were this weird green, like melted glass."

Fae? "Any other defining features?" I asked. "Marks or tattoos?"

When Mary shook her head, I looked over my notes, then at the plastic bag, still on my lap. What could someone have wanted with a sick child?

Though the threat note was a start, I wanted to examine the energies in her apartment. I could also select something of Edgar's for hunting. According to Bishop Sheridan, she had spirited Mary here following that morning's service with only her purse and the clothes on her back, nothing of Edgar's.

"Would you mind if I went by your place?" I asked Mary. "I'll be discreet."

Mary's next head-shake was urgent. "Please don't. They can't know I talked to anyone."

Her eyes appealed to the bishop, who leaned toward me. "It's taken a lot of courage for Mary to speak to the two of us. If someone is watching her apartment and you show up to look around, they could put two and two together."

I had my stealth magic, of course, but I sensed there was something the bishop didn't want to say in front of Mary.

"All right, Mary." I placed the bag with the letter and photos inside my satchel. "I'm going to do everything I can to find your son."

When she looked up, a spectrum of emotions filled her eyes: guilt, fear, anguish, hope. Though I still had my own very conflicted feelings about how she'd treated her son, I reached forward. Her hand was as thin and cold as a piece of bony meat, but she squeezed back fervently with both of hers.

"God bless you, Mr. Croft," she whispered tearfully.

The bishop and I returned to the front of the cathedral in silence. At the bronze doors, I turned to her.

"I felt called to help Mary," the bishop said, as though anticipating my question. "Just as I felt called to bring you in. Regardless of how I feel about her as a mother, Mary and her son are at the crux of something involving forces greater than both of them. Dangerous forces. I'm convinced of this." Though she was peering up at me, her squinting eyes seemed to be surveying a stormy horizon.

"I was called, too," I said, recalling the voice. "Do you have any idea who the father is?"

That suddenly felt important. As the bishop's gaze cleared and returned to mine, she shook her head.

"Mary may not even know. She came to St. Martin's through one of our parochial schools—an education and training program for troubled teens. She was pregnant by the time we found housing for her."

Nodding, I patted my battered satchel. "I'll start on the note tonight. See what I can pick up."

"Please keep me apprised."

"I will." At the open door, I hesitated. "Hey, I hate to ask this, but do you have any reason to doubt Mary's story? With the hardship of raising Edgar, could she have... disappeared him herself?"

"I don't believe I would have been called if that were the case."

"No," I agreed after a moment. "Me, neither."

9

It was after ten by the time I got home. I looked in on Ricki and Abigail, both asleep, before fixing myself a large travel mug of Colombian dark to carry down to my basement lab.

The light was on when I got there, the television murmuring beyond the wall to the man cave Bree-yark had built out. He often came down after Mae had gone to bed to "watch a couple shows." He almost always ended up sacking out.

I sipped from the travel mug as I pulled several spell items from my shelves and cupboards and arranged them on my iron-topped island.

After my talk with Claudius, I was more wary than usual of my warded safe. If what he'd said was true—that the angel-powered whip could call up a being who had wiped out Saint Michael's entire line—then they were basically entrusting me with the keys to Armageddon.

No pressure or anything, I thought, giving the safe a wider berth on my next pass.

But right now, I needed to focus on the missing child.

That was where my magic was urging me to go, and Arianna had counseled me to listen. By the time I finished the prep work and coffee, I had a sigil-enhanced casting circle and a wire stand that held a horizontal slice of a distilling stone.

I was also slightly more awake.

I produced the threat note and brought it to my nose. A little mothy. I cut off the top quarter with a pair of scissors. The rest would serve as a backup. I placed the strip in the circle's center, beneath the wire stand, and stepped back into my own circle inset in the floor. I was all set to cast when scratching sounded on the wall beside the bathroom.

Sighing, I strode over, depressed a false light switch and opened the hidden door to the man cave. Bree-yark was sawing logs on one of the two recliners, his goblin feet splayed toward the television, but it was Tabitha who'd done the scratching. She sauntered past me with a sour face as though I'd kept her waiting an unreasonably long time.

"What are you doing down here?" I asked, closing the wall behind her.

"Not that it's any of your business, but Bree-yark invited me. Your baby's smell was making me nauseous."

"She smells like milk. Something you drink in very large and expensive quantities, I should remind you."

"Yes, *drink,* darling. Not *inhale.*"

"Hey, not up—"

She leapt onto the island.

"—there," I finished as she plopped onto her side. I quickly closed the casting circle before any of her shed hairs could gust inside and contaminate the space. She peered blandly at the arrangement.

"What's this?" she asked.

"A boy was taken from his mother, and I'm trying to locate him."

"Oh," she said, lowering her head back down. Had I caught her brow crease in concern? I was tempted to poke at her softness for kids, but it would only make her fight harder against one of her few redeeming qualities.

"Well, you know the rule, you can—"

"Stay only if I remain quiet and out of the way," she finished for me. "Yes, I know all of your petty tyrannies from memory by now. I've only suffered under them for eight years," she added in a mutter.

"It's for—"

"Your safety as much as mine," she said, completing my sentence yet again. "I know all of your inane rationalizations, too."

We really had been together a long time.

"Not that they saved me from your sadistic angel friend," she grumbled.

She was referring to my attempt to open the whip's protection before I'd understood its angelic nature. The whip's energy had yanked her succubus spirit into the angel's realm and nearly ended her. Something she still held against me. In fact, I was surprised she was willing to lounge so close to another one of my castings, but now that she was settled, convincing her to move wasn't going to happen.

"Okay, the silence begins now," I said.

"Then why are you still talking?"

"I'm serious."

She sighed. "There you go again, darling."

I side-eyed her before raising my cane to the strip of paper. "*Rivelare.*"

Energy coursed down the length of wood, setting its opal

aglow. A moment later, the paper at the circle's center fluttered. A faint mist lifted from the ink, wafting through the wire mesh and into the slice of distilling stone.

A medium I'd been practicing on, the distilling stone was safer than casting a direct reveal spell and more accurate. It would take time—that was the only drawback—but there *was* energy in the ink. The crystals in the stone's glassy face illuminated and began to slowly cycle through a progression of colors in search of a match.

While the stone worked its magic, I emptied the photos of Edgar onto the edge of my casting island and spread them out. They showed the boy from different angles with a few closeups of his restraints. A bad look, especially with Mary leaving him solo for long spells. But my personal feelings about his care didn't change the fact he was missing and that my magic had given me an order.

Find the child.

And still that ambiguous sense that the voice might have been my father's...

I dug into one of my storage boxes until I came up with an antique magnifying glass. A gift from Gretchen, my former mentor, who'd claimed it was enchanted. I cleaned the smudged lens with my shirttail and tapped into it. Not surprisingly what magic remained was thin, practically mummified.

"*Attivare,*" I whispered anyway.

The brass handle managed the faintest glow before dulling again. I snorted. Gretchen's *gift* had been an excuse to unload her junk. The glass still worked as a magnifier, though, and I held it over the boy's drawn face.

"Who's that?" Tabitha asked.

"The boy I mentioned."

"Ick," she remarked.

I focused on his eyes—parts of Mary's story, such as Edgar cutting his therapist, had me thinking possession—but all I could pick up was an empty stare, probably an effect of the tranquilizer.

"He looks like he's a hundred and three," Tabitha pressed.

"Yeah, well, there's a reason for that."

"Whatever. He's *not* a boy."

Ignoring her, I looked over the other photos. When I reached the close-up of his wrist restraint, I leaned over the magnifying glass, then jerked back as something leapt out.

"What in the hell?" I gasped.

With a pleased snort, Tabitha lowered her head again.

As I caught my breath, I realized the brass handle was glowing. The enchantment had come to life, the glass picking up a reflection in the bedrail, rendering it into something sensible, and projecting it.

A corrective enchantment—something Tabitha had already figured out.

I scowled at her before bringing the magnifying glass back to the same spot. The object returned: the kidnapper's camera. It was a Polaroid, a gloved finger depressing the button to take the photo.

I frowned as I worked the glass around, determined to pull the figure into focus. But the corrective enchantment was struggling. A shadowy face leapt in and out a couple times, enough that I could make out some sort of head covering, before the enchantment gave up and the brass handle dulled again.

The druid? I wondered. *Or someone connected to the pale woman? Maybe even the pale woman herself?*

My phone buzzed, making me jump. I checked the display. *Speaking of druids...*

"Hey, man, thanks for getting back to me," I said to Jordan Derrow.

"Can you meet?" he asked. "I've got some info on Black Earth."

10

A cab dropped me at Central Park North. Shoulders hunched to the chill wind, I searched the midnight sky, then dropped my gaze to what had once been a forbidding thicket, home to the druid cult I'd nearly lost my eyes and life to those years ago.

I considered how inexperienced I'd been back then—and solitary.

With a croaking caw and a flurry of feathers, Jordan's raven form landed on the stone wall. He tilted his head at me, the moon reflecting in his burnished eyes. Then he flapped down to the sidewalk and, in a rush of magic, sprouted up as a druid, complete with a cloak and long quarterstaff.

"Thanks for coming," he said, grasping my offered hand.

"I should be the one doing the thanking. You had the longer commute."

His druid circle was based in Harriman State Park, forty miles north as the crow flies. Or raven, in his case. Though I hadn't seen him since my wedding, he and his wife had sent a small wreath following Abigail's birth. The sacred object was meant to protect the young and hung on the wall above her crib.

Not one for chit chat, Jordan angled his head toward the park. "You ready?"

A thin beard traced his jawline, while sigils at his temples glowed pale in the moonlight. A hint of the raven remained as he regarded me with his serious eyes. I nodded, and he took lead down a set of stone steps illuminated by moonlight. Following its replanting, North Woods remained mostly saplings, and I could see our destination ahead. Even so, I separated my cane into sword and staff, ready for anything.

"The Black Earth cult lacked the grounding and balance of nature druids," Jordan began without preamble. "And their god, Brigit, is about as temperamental as they come. Our two circles had some run-ins a number of years back. One of our young had gone missing, and everything pointed to Black Earth."

"To what purpose?"

"Sacrifice, probably. One of several perversions found in god-powered cults."

Years before, I'd traced Black Earth's roots to ancient Britain. Worshippers of the fire goddess Brigit, the cult survived the Roman occupation by going underground and cloaking themselves in the new religion. What emerged was a fusion of beliefs, including an obsession with Sathanas, who'd replaced one of their major fiends. I thought they'd phased out human sacrifice, too, but apparently not.

"Jesus," I muttered, praying the covered head in the photo hadn't belonged to one of theirs.

"The incident culminated in a battle that ended in our casting out the unnaturals and warding them from our woods," Jordan continued. "We lobbied other druid circles to

No.

follow suit, effectively isolating Black Earth. That was when they established themselves here." He nodded toward the rocky ravine we were coming upon.

"We kept tabs on them, but they seemed content to stay put. Petra was leading them by this point, a venomous priestess. It's rumored she sacrificed the cult's male druids, establishing Black Earth as a pure matriarchy." He peered at me darkly over a shoulder. "Knowing what I know of her, I believe it. By locating here, she and her circle were free to practice all manner of depravities in the city's shadows."

"Right," I said, recalling that period all too well.

"But then your mayor burned down the park—including some centuries-old trees," he added sternly. "Black Earth fled."

"To where?"

He paused as we rock-climbed down the ravine and crossed a small stream.

"That's the big question," he said. "We stayed vigilant following the park's burning, thinking Black Earth might try to infiltrate our woods again, but they never showed up. Every indication suggested they'd dispersed. But when I received your message about the encounter, I took a closer look."

I pictured Jordan peering into a blood-filled raven's skull, one of his circle's methods for scrying.

"Their energy remains in the city," he said. "It's a faint layer, the kind you can miss if you're not looking for it, but it's not left over from their time here. Too many years have elapsed. Leads me to believe they're still practicing, just not openly. They could be using any number of spells for concealment."

Jordan stopped and began stirring the ground with the

end of his quarterstaff. I recognized the clearing, even with the boulders charred. It was where I had blundered into the Black Earth's midst that first time four years earlier.

And he will appear unto mortal eyes as saintly, Petra had said of me. *And earnest and righteous will seem his pleas, but do not be ye deceived, for he ariseth from the darkest pits and bringeth death and ruin.*

I blinked away the memory of her burning wand nearing my eye, and found Jordan kneeling, sifting the stirred-up earth through his fingers. With a frown, he cast it aside and rose.

"They would not have returned here. The ground is tainted."

"Yeah, a few thousand gallons of napalm will do that," I remarked.

He walked over to one of the smaller boulders and rested a hand against it, as though offering it comfort. He nodded to himself, stepped back, and without warning, drove the end of his quarterstaff against it. Energy flashed from the contact, and in a series of deep snaps, the boulder cracked in two.

The exterior of the boulder may have been just as tainted as the ground, but the mineral-rich core, which had spent years absorbing the druid's energy, remained pristine. Before the energy could disperse, he thrust his staff into the breach. Speaking druidic words, he drew the essence into the wood and shaped it.

"Your staff," he said.

I handed it over, and he performed a transference.

"Given their present concealment, there isn't enough energy here to track them," he said, returning my staff to my hand. "Not from a distance, but it should tell you if they're close."

"Much appreciated," I said, feeling the tension of fresh magic. "Any idea where they could be based?"

"A group like theirs requires two things. First, contact with the earth. They may be god-powered, but they still require a grounding element. And two, a vantage point from which to monitor the stars."

I mentally tagged a few areas that might fit the bill.

"How about why they'd be hanging around amateur conjurings?" I followed up.

"Not yet, no. But I sense their purpose is dark and goes against nature. I have more work to do," he said abruptly, eyeing his staff, which held the other half of the siphoned essence. "I should head back to my circle."

We exited the park the way we'd come in.

"Thanks again for coming," I said, clasping his hand.

"And thank you for notifying me. This is serious business."

I nodded, having reached out to him as much to alert his community as for his aid.

"But I must warn you again," he said. "Black Earth is very dangerous. The fact they believe they're doing divine work makes them even more so. You're fortunate you caught Petra by surprise—and alone. They numbered more than twelve at last count. And if they're presently involved in sacrifices, they may be commanding power beyond even yours, Everson."

"I'll be careful."

He hesitated before taking flight. "Take special care of your family."

He didn't need to remind me that Black Earth had a history of targeting the young. With a grim nod, he broke skyward, the sight of his raven form merging with the night seeming to deepen his ominous warning.

11

"You have four readings for next week," I reminded my Thursday morning class. "They deal with the afterlife across myths. Be ready to *discuss*. Participation is fifteen percent of your grade, and this class is way too small to hide in." I aimed two fingers at my eyes and then at them, drawing some nervous chuckles as the students filed out.

I was hardly one to flex. With just three hours' sleep, and a ton on my mind, my own participation that morning had been suspect. Why couldn't the cases have waited until the weekend? Fortunately, after ten years of teaching and wizarding, I'd developed a decent ability to split my attention. That, plus coffee spiked with invigoration potion, had gotten me through the two-hour lecture.

I was polishing off the final, cold swallow from my travel mug when my phone buzzed. It was Ricki.

"Hey, is everything all right?" I asked, my thoughts immediately going to our kids.

After my meeting with Jordan last night, I'd stayed up until the wee hours, reinforcing our apartment's wards and preparing a protection for Tony—a small amulet he was wearing under his shirt at Greenwich Elementary. I also asked Mae not to take Abigail out in the stroller for the next few days.

"I've got some info on the cases," she said.

I relaxed slightly, taking a seat on the corner of my desk. "Great, let's hear it."

"Well, we ID'd the tunnel vic. His name's Chester Miles, a resident of Ferguson Towers. Lived alone in an efficiency. I pulled a couple books of his you might want to look at, but the neighbors didn't know anything about him dabbling in magic. Like with Kristin Shanks, they acted surprised someone was even asking."

"What are the book titles?"

As she consulted her notes, I picked up a collision of voices and ringing phones in her busy unit. When she read them off, I nodded to myself. Common gateway books to casting. But had someone known to plant them?

"Anything on the druid?" I asked.

"Nothing in the database. We're going to start talking to neighbors and apartment managers on the cases you had us pull, see if anyone remembers seeing her. We have another detective looking into security footage. Oh, and we're expecting the lab results on the creature's remains a little later today."

"That was quick."

"Task forces take priority. What are you going to be doing?"

"I'm about to head back to my own lab." I checked my watch. "The distilling stone should have something for me by now."

Though the druid's connection to the amateur conjurings

remained important, my magic had assigned me an explicit task—*find the child*. I'd given Ricki the CliffsNotes version of the missing boy that morning with her promise that she wouldn't alert the NYPD unless and until I gave the green light.

"Any word on your wizard backup?" she asked.

"Not yet, but I expect I'll hear something today. Claudius said help was en route."

In the silence that followed, I couldn't tell whether she was skeptical of Claudius's assurance or just didn't like the idea of me pursuing the case alone. But with the NYPD off limits, I couldn't very well call on the Sup Squad for backup.

"I'll be careful," I promised her.

"Yeah, you say that a lot."

Back at the apartment I found Mae feeding Abigail from a bottle. When I offered to take over, she parked me in front of a roast beef sandwich that was as thick as one of my spell books and ordered me to eat. I had a bad habit of skipping meals when I was deep in my work, something Mae knew all too well. I avoided the usual lecture only because she was so smitten with my daughter, who was suckling and sighing contentedly in her arms.

"Is Bree-yark here?" I asked, peering around.

Tabitha was dozing in a shaft of sunlight on her divan, while Buster was curled up in the shade underneath. I would have given anything for an hour's rest myself, but whatever fatigue I felt paled in comparison to the hell Mary was going through. Forty-eight hours with no idea who had taken her son or why.

"He's out running some errands," Mae replied, pausing to dab Abi's cheek. "Listen, do me a favor and tell him if you need him. He's getting fidgety, and as much as I love the fellow, I can only take so many of his army stories and songs in one day."

I smiled. "Will do. If you'll excuse me, I'm going to take the rest of this to-go."

I kissed Mae on the cheek, Abigail on the crown, and carried the plate down to my basement lab, anxious to see the results of the reading and whether it had parsed out something I could hunt.

The casting circle was still intact and glowing faintly when I arrived, but the distilling stone was dim, indicating it was done. I set the plate with the rest of the sandwich aside and stepped quickly forward.

"*Attivare*," I whispered.

Like a computer screen waking up, the stone glowed back to life. I had been anticipating what color it would show. Red for fire magic? Indigo, suggesting fae magic? Or would it be a sulfuric yellow, indicating something demonic? With all the parallels to the Demon Moon case, a part of me was bracing for the last. But the color the stone revealed was none of them. It glowed a pale gray.

That's not right.

I dispersed the casting circle and examined the space. The ink on the strip of paper was so faint now I could barely read it, but there was no stray matter in the circle that could have acted as a contaminant. Bad stone? No, I'd used it before. And if the magic caught in the ink had carried protections, they should have been filtered out. That left one explanation: the magic was unknown to the distilling stone.

"Bummer," I muttered.

But the bigger question now was whether I could track it. I tapped into a special sigil I'd built into one side of the circle and immediately felt the pull of the hunting spell. I wasted no time bringing my cane around and coaxing the spell into the opal until the cane tensed in my grip, then jerked north.

Yes!

I was collecting potions and spell implements when the door opened. Bree-yark backed inside carrying a box of bottles and paraphernalia intended for the minibar. "Everson!" he barked as he closed the door with a foot. "Thought you'd still be at the college." His eyes fell to my jiggling cane. "Whoa, looks like you hooked a big one."

Remembering Mae's request, I said, "Wanna help me reel it in?"

12

"Okay, whoa," I said as we crossed One Hundred and Tenth Street.

The hunting spell had pulled us up to Morningside Heights, and now my cane was beginning to pivot east. But could that be right? It was indicating the campus of Grace Cathedral, one of its council buildings already showing above the trees. When car horns sounded behind us, I realized Bree-yark had slowed to a crawl.

"Should I pull over?" he asked.

"Sorry, keep going, then take the next right."

He picked up speed, using hand gestures to inform the passing drivers what they could do with their horns. The campus—or *close*, as it was called—was large, taking up three city blocks. Near the north end, the cathedral itself grew into view, a towering neo-gothic structure big enough to hold two or three St. Martin's. The last time I'd been inside had been to "borrow" a robe of invisibility to infiltrate what had turned out to be the Refuge, where my father and the Order were exiled.

This was also among the last places I'd expected the spell to lead me.

As Bree-yark wheeled onto a street that ran past a hospital, my cane pivoted south, confirming that my target was in the cathedral's close. I had Bree-yark turn again and park near a stone staircase that dropped into Morningside Park.

"So this is the place, huh?" he asked, regarding the leafy close. "Pretty nice."

"Yeah," I said, thinking, *too nice.* But it was where my spell was pointing. "Let me check with someone." I pulled out my very outdated flip phone, still about all I could manage around magic, and accessed Bishop Sheridan's number.

"Hello, Everson," she answered.

"Listen, I just got a strong hit on the note left at Mary's. Can you think of any reason why it would have led me to Grace Cathedral?"

"Grace Cathedral? Are you sure?"

The doubt in her voice made me question my spell work. Had the ink picked up another energy, maybe the protective field around the cathedral? That could have explained why the distilling stone failed to ID the source. Still, it had led me to this location, meaning the letter had been here at some point.

"Should I call their rector?" the bishop asked when I didn't respond to her right away. "He sits on the Interfaith Council."

"No, no," I said quickly. Not knowing who was involved in the abduction or why, I didn't want to tip anyone off. "Let's keep this between us for now, at least until I know what we're dealing with."

"I understand. Grace Cathedral had to suspend some renovation projects, and a couple of their buildings have been sitting empty for months. Perhaps someone is using one of them?"

"That could explain it," I agreed. "How's Mary doing?"

"Holding up as well as can be expected under the circumstances."

"All right, let's not tell her anything until I have something more concrete." I didn't want to get her hopes up only to have to shatter them like glass ornaments. I was on the trail of the note-writer, not her son. There was no guarantee I would find him here. I ended the call and patted the steering wheel.

"Mind keeping the engine running?" I asked Bree-yark.

He returned a dejected look that said, *Aw, I thought we were going in as a team.*

"If I need backup, you'll be my first call," I promised.

"Good, 'cause I restocked the arsenal in my trunk this summer, and it's just been sitting there. Some people need to dance, Everson. It's in their blood. Me? I need to battle. That's what's in mine."

As a goblin, he wasn't wrong. "I'll see what I can do, but the getaway takes priority."

We bumped fists, and I climbed out. Accessing the sidewalk along the close, I began walking south, lining up buildings with the pull of my cane. To lessen any suspicion, I paused to take the occasional photo with my phone. Just a shoulder-season tourist awed by the beauty and majesty of Grace Cathedral.

I'd gone about a block and a half when the spell locked onto a stone building in the center of the close. Holy energy from the nearby cathedral joined with the building, coursing over and around its two stories. As I approached through a garden, I saw that the building's back half was covered in scaffolding.

Maybe the bishop is right.

"Hey!" someone shouted.

I turned to find a bulky security guard hustling toward me. He intercepted me in front of a thick chain blocking the walkway.

"This is a restricted area," he panted. "You can't be back here."

"No, I wasn't planning on going any further. What is this building?"

Instead of following my nod, he continued to stare me down. "You can't be back here," he repeated.

"Right, I got that part. I was just—"

He seized my arm. "All right, c'mon."

"Hey! What the hell?"

"You want to be a smartass, you can do it somewhere else."

I protested some more as he marched me back toward the street, but I was using his proximity and contact to check him out. Coincidence that he'd just happened to be hanging around that building when I walked up, or something more? And why the fanatical bouncer treatment? Nothing magical moved through the hot grip that wrapped my upper arm, but his aura had an edgy, single-minded feel to it.

He's under someone's explicit orders.

As we neared the sidewalk, I glanced back. Three more guards were watching from around the building. Yeah, that wasn't normal.

The guard released me with a shove. "Don't let me catch you loitering here again."

I staggered to a stop, grateful to be out of Bree-yark's view. We would have had a major brawl on our hands, otherwise.

"Hey, quick question," I said.

The guard, who'd already begun to turn, squared his thick shoulders toward me. He had a wide head to go with his body, and from under the span of his sweaty brow, eyes that were equal parts dumb and penetrating glared into mine. The distant guards stepped over for better views. There were four of them now.

"You're testing your luck, dipshit," he growled.

"When the many are reduced to one," I asked in my wizard's voice, "to what is the one reduced?"

It was a special koan that shorted out simple possessions. The guard opened his mouth, but his brow furrowed suddenly. I could all but see his mental cogs grinding in different directions. By the time he shook his head, though, the cogs resumed their former action. He blinked his eyes back into focus.

"The hell did you just say to me?" he grumbled.

I couldn't attempt anything more aggressive, not with half the force watching us.

When the muscles around his jaw bunched up, I thought he was going to draw his holstered sidearm or test my chin with his fist, but he thrust a thick finger down the street. "Beat it."

"Much appreciated," I said, as though he'd answered me. In a way, he had.

He waited for me to begin cane-tapping away before lumbering back to his post near my target. The brief encounter had exposed the building's outer defenses. Now it was a matter of forming a breaching plan.

13

"Nothing?" Bree-yark asked when I returned to the Hummer.

"More like too much." I closed the door and filled him in on my meeting with the guard.

Following the encounter, I'd continued to Cathedral Parkway. Assuming I was being watched, I dropped into Morningside Park, where I dawdled and took some more photos before climbing the stone staircase back to the Hummer. I didn't sense any eyes on me now, but I hunkered low anyway. Bree-yark straightened in anticipation.

"So, we gonna storm the place?" he asked.

"Not *exactly* what I had in mind..."

"Even after that meathead manhandled you?"

"Listen, I think the security guards are legit, just under someone's orders. Fortunately, I have an easy way past them." I'd already pulled a stealth potion from my pocket, and now I activated it with a Word. Tiny gems sparked and flashed inside the tube, turning the gray sludge into a steaming green liquid.

"But you don't know what's inside the building," Bree-yark pressed.

"Not yet." I paused to down the bitter potion. "But if I need to, I'll pull back and reassess." What I wasn't saying was that I didn't want bullets flying willy-nilly during a potential child rescue.

I produced another potion from my pocket—this one with a dark brown suspension—and handed it to him. "I may need a distraction to get back here. If so, I'll call and tell you what to do with this."

He accepted the potion reluctantly and stood it inside one of the cup holders in the center console. "All right, but if I don't hear from you in twenty, I'm going in. And there's not gonna be anything *stealth* about it."

"Only if you armor up."

"Deal," he agreed, smiling with all his teeth.

With my wizard help yet to arrive, and unable to call on the Sup Squad or NYPD, I could use the backup. With the stealth potion taking hold in my system, I consulted my watch, clapped Bree-yark's shoulder, and slipped from the vehicle.

I retraced my earlier route at a fast trot. At the chain barrier separating the garden from the stone building, I paused, watchful for any response. Two guards, including the one who'd escorted me from the property, were in a conference near the side of the building, while another patrolled close by.

That I was invisible to them confirmed they lacked preternatural senses. No wards or magical tripwires showed in my wizard's vision, either.

As another guard patrolled into view, I ducked under the chain and took the least crowded route to the building's far side. I edged along the scaffolding to where yet another guard stood near a rear entrance covered in plastic sheeting. His aura carried the same single-mindedness as the guard I'd met earlier.

Aiming my cane at a cluster of bushes opposite him, I whispered, "*Vigore.*"

The invocation thrashed the leaves. As he moved forward to investigate, a hand on the grip of his duty weapon, I slipped behind him and past the plastic. Something slammed into my diaphragm, and I fell to my knees, gasping for air.

Holy hell...

The rear was doorless, and I had just crossed the building's threshold without realizing it. Despite being an ally of the Church, and this being a lesser building, I had entered without a formal invite. Electric-like energy coursed through me, driving an already weak Thelonious deeper into my soul. With an aching breath, I managed to push myself upright. The initial shock was leaving me, but the threshold had stripped away a considerable swath of my magic, including much of the stealth potion.

Dammit.

In the dimness, I peered around the construction site and consulted my cane. Enough of the hunting spell remained, but it was no longer giving me a direction. Of course the building itself could have been the source. Drawing a thin veil of shadows around me, I listened intently but heard only a cloistered silence.

I advanced down the main corridor. The building wasn't large—two stories with a wooden staircase at either end. I peered into empty rooms as I went, each one the size of an office or small classroom.

Were we dealing with a church official? One who'd

learned about Mary's neglect and decided to take matters into their own hands?

I peered into a final room near the far stairs and stopped. This one hadn't been cleared out. I looked over a sitting area, past a settee long enough to double as a bed, to a stout wooden desk that faced away from a covered window. A small sheaf of paper sat to one side, the sheets blank. I lifted the top one and brought it to my nose. It carried the same mothy scent as the threat note.

It was written here.

I searched the desk drawers—all empty—and scoured the rest of the room for anything that might have ID'd the kidnapper, but there were no personal items. Back at the settee, I cut the pale cover off of a small cushion. If the kidnapper had handled the cushion at any point, or better, used it as a pillow, the cover would carry all kinds of bio matter for tracking.

As I folded the cover and slipped it into an evidence bag, I felt another energy in the space. I scanned the room in my wizard's vision. No, not another energy, I realized—a current coming from the far wall.

Veiling spell?

That had me thinking fae again, but I'd known church officials to possess preternatural powers, too. Father Vick, for instance, had performed shadow exorcisms before succumbing to the demon lord Sathanas.

As I advanced on the wall, my pulse picking up, I noticed a feature that had escaped me earlier—a depressed handle. I wasn't looking at a veiling, but a sliding door. Finding it locked, I dropped a granule of dragon sand into a keyhole hidden by a brass guard and whispered an invocation. Smoke hissed out, and the melting catch released.

I pulled the door, fully expecting a closet. I was surprised to find a second, smaller room. The space was mostly barren, save for a wooden rack canted up at a steep angle and facing away from the door.

I circled it and found Mary's son strapped to the planks.

14

I tried to say his name, but couldn't find my voice. The surprise discovery had jammed my heart into my throat.

Edgar looked exactly as he had in the photos. His head was bald, save for a few game strands. His frail body was bent and shriveled like an old man's. Leather straps held him in place, from his forehead to his ankles. What I had mistaken for a rack in the dim space was actually a wooden pallet propped up by a second on its side, their mattresses leaning against the wall.

I jerked into action, bringing my fingers to his knobby neck, terrified it would feel cold and stiff. But his skin yielded to the pressure, and I picked up a faint pulse.

Swallowing hard, I found my voice. "Edgar?" I whispered.

When I unbuckled his forehead strap, his large head slumped forward. I caught it and called his name again. It might have been my imagination, but his eyelids seemed to flutter over his bulbous eyes. I didn't imagine the mark in the center of his brow, though—a small oval of blackened flesh.

What in the hell did they do to you?

As my shock thawed, anger moved in. I shoved out the supporting pallet and lowered his to the floor. I worked quickly to remove the rest of the straps. The one across his chest hid another char mark, this one in the shape of a hand.

All the looks of torture, I thought, which induced another hot rush.

I removed a fitted sheet from one of the mattresses and wrapped Edgar in a tidy parcel, safe for carrying. As I worked, a steely fear began to permeate my anger. I had caught a break by locating Edgar while his kidnapper was out, but I sensed that my window of opportunity was narrow and closing.

I sensed, too, that I didn't want to be here when the kidnapper returned.

I finished wrapping him up and checked my phone. The combination of the building's energy and stone construction was only allowing in one bar of signal. I used it to call Bree-yark.

"Everson!" he barked. "I was just kitting up."

We must have been coming up on the twenty minutes. "Stay there, I need a distraction. That potion? Throw it as far as you can into the garden while keeping out of sight of the guards."

The potion contained a likeness of myself, one magically adept at evading pursuers. And when the guard who'd ordered me off the property saw it, he'd *definitely* pursue—along with the other guards, I hoped.

"You found him?" Bree-yark whispered.

I glanced down at Edgar's swaddled body, only his sallow, chinless face peering out. The sight further stoked my parental instincts. "Yeah, but we're going to need to make tracks."

"Okay, I'm moving out."

I lifted the wrapped boy in one arm, keeping my cane arm free. Fortunately, Edgar was as light as a sack of mail.

"All right, buddy," I whispered, hitching him up. "We're getting you out of here."

From the main room, I peered into the corridor. Empty and quiet. I advanced quickly until I was hidden in the shadows near the plastic sheet I'd entered through. Beyond its translucence, I spied the guard's figure. Now it was up to Bree-yark. Fortunately, I didn't have long to wait. Shouts sounded in the distance, and the guard hurried away. I pushed through the plastic sheet and went the other direction.

Clear of the threshold, my powers returned in a heady rush. What remained of the stealth potion took hold again, encompassing Edgar and me in a haze. Not full strength anymore, but strong enough.

I hustled from the building and along the garden's north path. By their shouts, the guards were chasing my likeness south. I hit the street, the Hummer soon coming into view. I expected the kidnapper to appear in front of us or blast me from behind. Neither happened, and I was soon rapping on the back door.

The lock released, and I climbed inside, setting Edgar across the seat. Bree-yark was already pulling away as I yanked the door closed behind us.

"Anyone see you?" he asked.

"No, I don't think so."

As we passed the garden in front of the stone building, I glimpsed the guards chasing a shadowy figure. "Told you not to come back here, asshole!" the guard from earlier bellowed. A pair of shots cracked.

But I was too preoccupied with Edgar's condition to appreciate my potion's effectiveness. I uttered words of healing, illuminating the opal inset in my cane.

Bree-yark slowed toward a stop light at Cathedral Parkway. "Where to?"

"St. Martin's." We needed to get him to his mother and the protective power of the holy sanctuary. But I had to wonder how much protection that really offered. After all, his kidnapper had been holding him inside a similar sanctuary. The kidnapper might even have been a church official. But where else was there to go?

"I'll jump on the West Side Highway," Bree-yark decided, turning right.

By the time I finished my work, a gauzy layer of healing magic enveloped Edgar's swaddled body. With the boy stable, I leaned over to inspect the mark on his forehead. Clearly a burn, one that had been inflicted by someone's thumb. I thought about the one on his chest in the shape of a hand.

I couldn't help but connect it to the White Hand in Chinatown. Bashi's enforcers often left their handprint insignia on hits to inspire fear. And then there was the pale woman who'd been asking about the boy. Her description sounded suspiciously fae-like, and Bashi's henchman had been carrying fae-enhanced rounds last night. But why would he or the fae be interested in the boy?

Of course, I could have been seeing a connection where none existed.

My cane rattled beside me and my watch began to flash. Crap, another breach. I removed my mystical map from my satchel and unrolled it. The fresh point of light was well behind us, in the South Bronx.

"Got something?" Bree-yark asked.

"Another conjuring, but keep going." I pulled out my phone and called Trevor of the Sup Squad.

"Croft," he answered. "What's up?"

"There's an alarm I can't get to right now. It's in the Bronx and looks like another amateur conjuring."

"We're not too far from there. What's the address?"

I zoomed in on the map until I pinpointed the epicenter. "East One Hundred Fifty Eighth. Third townhouse on the north side. You'll want composite rounds. Oh, and check the APB Detective Hoffman put out. If you encounter a woman fitting her description, stay back. She's a powerful fire druid."

"Okay, we're on it."

As I ended the call, Bree-yark swore. "Accident ahead."

Before we could join the line of taillights, he swerved onto an exit and worked his way to Ninth Avenue. It would give us a straight shot to St. Martin's, but with all the stop lights, we were looking at a longer commute. I nearly called Ricki to arrange a police escort, but I wanted to honor Mary's request to avoid the NYPD.

I called anyway to give her an update.

"We found him alive, and we're on our way to St. Martin's," I said after she'd answered.

"Thank God," Ricki breathed, as relieved for me, I suspected, as for the boy. "Can you talk?"

"Yeah, for a few minutes."

"All right, a couple of task force related things," she said. "First, we picked up footage of your druid at the site of a conjuring from two weeks ago. She disappeared when you showed up."

"No kidding?" So her presence in the tunnels hadn't been a fluke.

"Yeah, she's clearly connected to the conjurings. Also, the

results came back on your creature gunk. No DNA from the victim."

"None?"

"Not according to the lab."

I thought back to the man's hollowed-out torso and the winged creature engorged with blood and organs. But if not the victim's, then whose?

"I'm still making calls on the other cases," she said. "Anything else we can be doing?"

"No, keep it up. You guys are doing great. After I drop the boy off, I may have to head to the Bronx for another conjuring. Trevor and the Sup Squad are en route now."

I was about to say more when my watch and cane alerted again. My map was still across my lap, and I consulted it, hoping the wards were just reminding me of the breach in the Bronx. But this was a new one, in Chelsea. I scanned the passing street numbers out the window. We were only a few blocks away.

"Hey, Ricki, I've gotta go."

"Something up?" Bree-yark asked as I ended the call.

During the Demon Moon case, a pair of conjurings had happened nearly simultaneously, but at opposite ends of the city, ensuring I couldn't reach both in time. Was that the idea now? And had foregoing the one in the Bronx just handed me an unexpected gift?

As I looked from the boy, whom I urgently wanted to get to safety, back to the map, my magic nodded. It was telling me to go to the conjuring.

"Another rhyme," I replied. "Left at the next light."

15

As the Hummer rolled into a space along West Twenty-Second, I propped Edgar's head on a folded throw blanket. Bree-yark craned his neck around. "Don't worry, Everson. I'll stay with the boy."

"Thanks. I'll shield the car just in case."

"Do what you've gotta do. And if you need help..." He cut his eyes toward the trunk to indicate his arsenal.

I climbed out, pausing to whisper an invocation. The air around the Hummer made a warping sound as it hardened. I pushed additional power into the protection before turning and hustling toward the alleyway my map had indicated.

Only two minutes since the alarm sounded. Should reach this one in time.

I consulted the spell Jordan had transferred to my staff, but it gave no indication the Black Earth druids were near, which surprised me.

The alley was a residential dead end, plastic trash receptacles spaced along its length. I accessed the hunting spell for the conjuring. It was pulling me straight, no angling, which ruled out the buildings. The conjuring should have been taking place in the alley itself, but I couldn't see a damned thing.

I grew a shield around myself anyway and switched to my wizard's senses. About three-quarters of the way down the span of concrete and garbage cans, the currents of ley lines suddenly ended. Beyond it, vague energies stirred. An actual veiling this time.

Thrusting my staff, I bellowed, "*Rivelare!*"

My invocation met the concealing magic, causing it to waver. As my vision returned to the physical plane, the veiling failed entirely, revealing a cluster of gray-robed figures, some wearing packs. Two of them spun toward me, the light from their burning wands illuminating familiar patterns in the shadows of their hoods.

Black Earth druids!

The remaining druids crouched and moved in ways suggesting they were rushing to finish something. Before I could see what, fire jetted from the two druids' wands, bathing my shield in red hot flames.

I met the blistering force with an inclined body, activating the fire rune in my blade to absorb the excess heat. As the attack flagged, I released the power stored in my shield. It caught the druids high, knocking one to the ground. The other staggered into a haphazard retreat, a forearm to her face.

"A little different than four years ago, huh?" I said.

I remembered Jordan's warning about the danger they posed, but I couldn't relinquish my advantage of surprise.

With a sweep of my sword, I released a large force invocation. It plowed into the remaining druids, clearing them from a figure down on the concrete. He lay in the same sprawled-out manner as yesterday's victims, the stomach of his shirt a blood-matted concavity. I'd caught the druids in the act.

Of what I wasn't sure yet.

The first druid to gain her feet hurried toward a descending flight of steps at the back of a building, cradling what looked like a draped box against her chest. It felt important, vital, that I stop her.

Swinging my sword over, I shouted, "*Vigore!*"

But another druid acted first, screening my target with a swirling mass of fire. My invocation was sucked into the convection and smothered. The effect stole my breath and opened a burning ache in my chest.

As I gasped for air, the remaining druids reassembled, backing down the steps behind the druid with the box. The fiery invocations from their wands were defensive now, flaming funnels to keep me back and to protect their retreat. Recovering my breath, I dug into my pocket, grasped a tube of ice crystals, and took aim.

"*Ghioccio!*" I rasped.

The cone of frost that shot from the tube met their flames in a hissing plume. I ran behind the spewing invocation and past the victim's extended legs, noting the crude casting circle beyond him.

With condensation raining down, I plunged into the stairwell and splashed down the steps. The druids had already disappeared beyond a door at the bottom. Before throwing it open, I pulled up.

They set a damned incendiary trap.

By the time I dispersed the ward that glowed ember-like in my wizard's vision, they had a one-minute lead. In their haste, though, they'd left an astral trail, bright as a comet's tail. I followed it through a basement area sectioned off into storage cages for the tenants who lived above.

The trail led up a flight of stairs and through another door—this one unmined. It opened onto a corridor featuring a row of apartment doors. I followed the trail to one at the far end. No traps, but locked.

I aimed my sword at the bolt guard and shouted, "*Vigore!*"

In a spill of metal fragments, the door banged open. I rushed through—and came to a sudden halt. From a living room table, a set of elderly faces rotated toward me. For a moment, I could only stare back.

"The hell do you think you're doing?" a woman at the head of the table asked.

"Oh, I thought, ah—" I stammered before starting over. "Did a group of robed people just run through here?"

"A group of robed *whats*?" she asked, holding a fan of playing cards.

As the other women began to murmur, I understood what had happened. The astral trail had been an illusion, meant to lead me astray—much as Petra had done the day before in the tunnels. I had just crashed these ladies' afternoon bridge club.

I checked to ensure *they* weren't illusions before drawing out my wallet and setting several twenties on a bookcase. "That should cover the damage to your door," I said, retreating. "Carry on."

Back in the corridor, I turned and eyed the remaining doors. The druids had left through another unit—the victim's, most likely—but there was no telling which that was, and Jordan's tracking spell wasn't talking.

Swearing, I retraced my route through the basement, up

into the alleyway, and back to the street. I looked along the span of rowhouses in both directions, but there was no sign of the druids. They may have translocated, like Petra had done the day before. I wondered now if she'd been the one carrying the box.

Need to know what was inside that damned thing.

Shoving my sword back into my cane in frustration, I returned to the alleyway and hunkered beside the victim, a young man with box-braided hair. His disembowelment wasn't as clean as the others, but he was officially a body. With a harsh sigh, I texted the info to Hoffman and returned the phone to my pocket.

I glanced over at the casting circle, then stopped and looked again.

The circle and its associated symbols were messy, but not because the druids had wanted to make it appear amateurish. I walked around the circle, snapping photos with my phone. The druids had been in the middle of altering it. They hadn't finished, though, and I could see where they'd attempted to clear it away altogether.

That would have been when I hit them with the force blast.

I walked a wider loop, peering behind garbage containers and along caged window ledges, but there was no sign of a nether creature. I thought of the lab results on the last creature's remains: no DNA match to the victim.

And that was when it all clicked.

Two conjurings were taking place here. The first consumed the victims' insides. The second conjuring, the one the druids had been adapting the circle for, called up shallow nether creatures. Stuffed with animal blood and entrails, the shallow creatures were meant to explain the victims' disemboweled states. Meanwhile, the actual disemboweler was placed in a container and spirited away.

That was what the first druid had been carrying.

I flipped through a mental file of summoned beings that would require human remains. Several creatures from deeper down fit the bill, but demonic creatures, with their need for soul material, topped the list. My magic nodded some more. I'd lost the druids, but I'd learned why my magic had directed me here.

So they're calling up demons. But why? And where are they stashing them?

I circled the site one more time, blood pumping hard in my temples, before heading back to where we'd parked. Though I'd only been away ten minutes, it was starting to feel like too long.

As the Hummer came into view, I checked its shield. Pins and needles rushed through me, and I broke into a run. Had I pulled energy from the shielding during my melee with the druids? Couldn't remember. Either way, it was down.

I arrived at the backdoor and yanked it open. Save for a small depression in the folded blanket, the space was empty.

"Bree-yark!" I shouted at the back of his head. "What happened to Edgar?"

He didn't answer. I opened his door to find his hands locked around the wheel, eyes fixed straight ahead. I seized his forearm, relieved to feel heat, but his muscles were as taught as steel cables.

"Can you hear me, buddy? Where did Edgar go?"

The shock of losing the boy and seeing Bree-yark incapacitated cast my head into an ill spin. So much so that I nearly missed the tensing of my cane, the resonant tone of an alarm between my ears.

"They took him," someone said from behind me.

I turned and met a pair of turquoise eyes set back in a hood. I realized then that Jordan's tracking spell had been trying to alert me. Light flashed from Petra's wand, then darkness.

16

"Wake up."

Petra's seething voice. My eyes came open.

It felt like only a moment had passed since she'd struck me with a mind bolt, but I was no longer standing beside Bree-yark's Hummer. I was sitting in a faux leather chair in a dim hotel room. Ahead of me was a bed with a faded brown coverlet and a crooked headboard. On a desk that hugged the wall to my left, I spotted my cane. My trench coat and satchel were draped over a chair back.

I went to launch myself upright, but I couldn't move. I couldn't even speak an invocation.

A holding charm.

"I want you to notice a couple of things."

Her voice was coming from my right, but I couldn't so much as turn my head. I could only strain my eyes over until she took peripheral form. In the gloom, I picked up flashes of her irises, sending panic through my powerlessness.

"For starters, you're alive. Had I wanted to end you, I could have done so two dozen times by now."

There were all kinds of reasons to keep a wizard breathing, and I could think of few that were encouraging. I replayed the conjuring I had interrupted. If her druid cult was calling up demonic beings, maybe she saw my powers as an asset. Or maybe she just wanted me awake when she burned out my eyes.

"You needn't fear me," she said. "I'm not the same druid of years ago."

Sure, lady. One doesn't simply stop being a psychopath with the wave of a wand.

When she stepped into view, I flinched back—or tried to. I'd expected her to be in robed attire befitting her priestess status, but she was wearing jeans and a black T-shirt beneath an army-green jacket. Regardless, our original encounter remained seared in my memory, reinforced by Jordan's warning from last night.

"Do you need proof of my mercy?" she asked.

She produced her wand, its tip already smoldering red. As she brought it forward, I clenched my eyes closed. Sweat sprang from my brow and ran—steaming, no doubt—down my temples. But it was the glow beyond my lids, hot and growing, that resurrected my terror from four years earlier.

"There it is," she said. "I have no wish to harm you."

Feeling that the heat had withdrawn from my face, I chanced a peek. She was standing back, the dimming wand in her folded arms. I blinked away the afterimage of the scorching tip and released my breath.

"I know about your lineage, Everson. I know you banished the demon lord Sathanas. I believe we're pursuing the same thing and can perhaps help one another. My former group has descended into deviltry."

My suspicions spiked at her claim of *former*, but I hadn't

actually seen her with the others in the alleyway. Jordan's spell had alerted me to her presence only after they'd cleared out.

I stopped to consider the rest of what she'd said. That confrontation four years earlier had stemmed from her conviction that I was a demonic agent. She seemed to have straightened that much out in her mind, but what explained her presence at the recent conjurings?

With the wave of her wand, she released the holding charm. My muscles relaxed from its paralytic grip. I cut my eyes to the desk and my casting implements. With a Word, I could recall the cane to my hand and the fight would be on. But though Petra followed my gaze, she made no move to block me.

Instead, she said, "You must have questions."

I cleared my throat. "Where's Bree-yark? The one who was in the car?"

"Your friend is fine. I had him drive us here. He's sitting in his vehicle a block away, awaiting your return."

"And the boy?" The sickness I'd felt when I discovered him missing returned like a heavy deposit of gravel in my stomach.

"The druids took him."

"Where?" I demanded. "And why?"

"That's part of the puzzle. I'm prepared to share what I know." She gestured toward the desk, where she'd arranged two chairs. A star chart had been taped to the wall above. "Do you pledge your help?"

I eyed the hand she extended toward me. The power of a binding agreement crackled around it. If she was telling the truth, her information on her former group could prove invaluable to tracking the druids—especially now that they had Edgar.

"Nonbinding," I said. "I don't know you well enough."

She considered my amendment before nodding. "I can do that."

I waited for the power to thin around her hand before accepting her firm grip.

She moved back, giving me space to stand. She said nothing as I walked over on very stiff legs and retrieved my cane. I sent a small quantum of energy through it as a test, then released the sword partway from the staff. No signs of tampering or foreign magic. When I turned back to Petra, her wand remained in her crossed arms. Not in the casting position, but easy enough to put there if I gave her a reason.

I lowered my cane to my side, deciding to trust her. For now.

"Let's start with what you know," I said.

Five minutes later, Petra and I were sitting at opposite ends of the hotel room desk. Surreal didn't begin to describe the fact of our meeting.

To be safe, I'd texted Ricki an update with my location. It turned out we were in one of the budget hotels off Times Square—the same one I'd visited during a case that had resulted in me binding a succubus spirit to a certain ginger kitten. Though the hotel had cleaned up its act, the weekly rate was still cheap. That plus its central location made it a good base of operations for Petra. I supposed the criminal element in the neighborhood was of little concern to a druid who'd once called Central Park home.

"I should start with the events around our encounter," she said as I adjusted my chair.

"I'm all ears."

"The stars had foretold the return of Sathanas. Our circle awaited his arrival, we braced ourselves, but nothing happened. I consulted the charts. I held seances with Brigit. Meanwhile, doubts were taking hold around me. I saw it on the faces of my Black Earth sisters. I heard it in their voices. The passing months only grew those doubts, and when the city incinerated our sanctuary, my fate was sealed. I had a relocation plan, another park, but none of the sisters came. They had been conspiring with my second in command, and I was ousted, the power of Brigit wrested from me."

Though Petra's voice continued to seethe, it wasn't from anger, I realized, but the way air moved past her filed teeth. It sounded like the pain of old wounds reopening.

"Cast out, I left the city. My home became a shelter across the river, in Jersey. With no connection to Brigit, no sign of Sathanas's return, I questioned the prophesies. I questioned *everything*. And because of these"—she gestured to her facial tattoos—"I was attracting attention of an unwanted kind." I noticed a crook in her nose that hadn't been there the last time, evidence of recent breaking and healing. "But I had no power to call on anymore. That was the hardest year of my life. Through the kindness of a social worker, I was moved to a halfway house and employed as a dishwasher in one of the city's kitchens. I attended night classes at the local college. I also went into counseling for recovering cultists."

I was having a hard time picturing this bogeywoman who had haunted my dreams on and off for the last four years suddenly powerless. Not only that, but scrubbing dishes, sitting for exams, and participating in therapy circles.

"Wow," was all I could think to say.

"I was determined to complete my *deprogramming*, as my therapist called it, to end that phase of my life. I was promoted from dishwasher to kitchen manager. I soon ended up in the main office, in their finance department. Everything was going to plan. And then Brigit returned to me in a dream."

Though I had been conscious of keeping a healthy distance from Petra, I caught myself leaning forward now.

"I hadn't heard from my former group in years, but they had been led astray. Brigit wanted to restore power to me. I ignored the dream, tried to push it back down into darkness, but night after night it persisted. The therapist prescribed an alpha-blocker so I wouldn't dream, but the ones with Brigit always seemed to break through. Finally, I went to the place where I'd buried my wand. I hadn't the will to destroy it back then, but I was determined to now. I wanted the dreams to end. I wanted to get back to my recovery and my new life. I dug up the wand, seized it at either end, like this. But before I could snap it, Brigit's power came storming back. I'd forgotten what that felt like."

When she looked up, dangerous flames moved behind her turquoise irises and shone from the crook in her nose.

"It was nighttime, and the burst of light from the wand attracted two foul men. One of them pulled a knife. I called on the fire of Brigit. It was weeks before the police were able to identify their remains. But while they were thrashing inside Brigit's flames, I knew the life I had been living since my expulsion was the lie, not my servitude to the goddess. I recommitted myself to her then and there."

She suddenly appeared larger, more powerful.

"What happened to the other druids?" I asked, anxious to know what we were up against.

"Another entity had entered Brigit's realm. Something dark and vile. Brigit managed to expel him, but not before he claimed a portion of her power and seduced her devotees. They went with him."

That must have explained why Jordan's spell had alerted me to Petra's presence but not to the druids'. Hers was the only power that remained true to Brigit. The others' were tainted with infernal energy. Indeed, the druids' fire in the alleyway had felt different than Petra's. More hellish.

"Did he have a name?" I asked.

"If so, it was never spoken in Brigit's presence."

I wondered if this demon's infiltration into Brigit's realm had happened after my father thwarted the Whisperer. The violence of Dhuul's arrival and expulsion had opened all kinds of ruptures.

"Brigit charged me with finding the Black Earth druids and returning them to her fold. The next day, I moved to the city, to this hotel. But their master conceals their doings well. It is only when they conduct certain magics that vestiges of the old connection come through. But the city is busy, and they've been efficient in their work."

I nodded, knowing the feeling. "You haven't been reaching them in time."

"No."

Though her story sounded plausible—and was consistent with Jordan's tracking spell—I searched for chinks. Were there any other reasons she would want to collaborate? Nefarious reasons, specifically?

When my magic didn't unfurl any red flags, I nodded some more. "It's tricky what they're doing, but I think I've figured it out," I said. "They're using the victims to summon demonic beings. They spirit them away, then summon a second, inconsequential being for people like you and me to discover."

She considered the idea. "I fear you're right. It fits."

"Any idea what they'd be doing with demonic creatures?"

She stared at me for an uncomfortably long moment, as though scrutinizing my motives as I'd just done hers.

At last she said, "I believe a second coming of Sathanas in the modern era is imminent."

17

"A second coming of Sathanas?" I repeated. "The demon lord?"

Though I said it skeptically, an uncomfortable heat spread over my face while a bitterness soured my mouth. Petra shifted her gaze to the star chart she'd taped above the desk and indicated one area with her wand.

"Do you see this?"

I angled my head at what seemed a random assortment of points. "Not really."

She uttered something, and several of the stars glowed like tiny sparks of fire, not unlike on my mystical map. "This is the pattern that served as our guide for centuries. It signifies the return of Sathanas. That moment has come and gone. Until you look over here."

She moved her wand, dimming the first set of star points and lighting up another. "This pattern has taken newer shape. Do you see the similarities?"

I looked between them and nodded. "A rhyme," I muttered.

"Yes," Petra said, "to a second return of Sathanas."

"But... I don't think that's possible."

"Why not?" she challenged.

"One, I banished him. We sealed the hole. And two, if he were so close to returning, my Order would know. I mean, getting a demon that size into our world would be like trying to smuggle a humpback whale into the local waterpark."

But though the comparison felt apt, doubts rattled me. A demonic being *had* hijacked the Black Earth's god. The druids *were* calling up infernal beings. And then there were all the similarities to the Demon Moon case.

"This pattern differs in one significant way," Petra continued, tapping a faint star in the center of the echo pattern. "We call this *Puer*, the Child. It is rising, suggesting an important and growing role."

Find the child.

"The boy they took?" I asked.

"I believe he possesses a unique power, one that properly released and channeled, will bring about Sathanas's return."

I thought about Edgar's rare genetic condition as well as how I'd found him at Grace Cathedral: strapped to a pallet, burn marks inflicted on his brow and chest. "So the idea is to sacrifice him?" I asked sickly.

"Very likely, yes."

When I met Petra's severe gaze, I remembered Jordan's claim about the Black Earth druids performing similar sacrifices, even on one of the Raven Circle's young. Whatever thawing I'd felt toward Petra immediately iced over.

How could I collaborate with someone like this?

Sensing the change in temperature, Petra said, "I long believed you to be the enemy, Everson. First, for bearing the taint of demon when I was certain of Sathanas's return. And then later, when I read about your partnership with the city during the campaign to eradicate our kind. So when I saw you at one of the recent conjurings, I followed you. I watched you at your college. I watched your home."

I made a mental note to put Tabitha back on ledge patrol.

"I observed your collaboration with the NYPD. From there, I obtained some police reports from after our first meeting those years ago. I was surprised to read about your rescue of a missing bishop, I admit. I spoke with church officials until I learned the demon lord Sathanas *had* returned, but he'd been trapped inside St. Martin's, invisible to the outside. I also learned that you'd banished him."

"All true, but what's your point?"

"That we shouldn't be so rigid in our opinions."

Was I making the same mistake with her that she had with me? I *had* known Jordan to assert claims before having all the facts.

"Then why the fire attack yesterday?" I challenged.

"The encounter caught me by surprise. Someone else has been tracking the druids, and she's attacked me once already."

"Who?"

"A pale woman."

I stiffened. Mary had spoken of a pale woman visiting her apartment prior to Edgar's kidnapping. And now a pale woman was pursuing the same druids who had the boy in their custody? That couldn't be a coincidence.

"What do you know about her?" I asked.

"She didn't speak, she just ambushed me with her sword. She wields a terrible power, one I've never felt. It nearly overwhelmed Brigit. Thank the stars, I built a target that returns me here." She nodded at a symbol she'd drawn in the corner of the room. "Its use depletes me, but it spared me that day."

I nodded vaguely and drew out my notepad.

"You act as though you know her," she said.

"I've heard of her," I replied, flipping to the notes I'd jotted down when I spoke with Mary the night before. "She was also interested in the boy, before he was taken from his mother two days ago."

I'd assumed the druids had *reclaimed* the boy from my custody, but how could a group with a demonic connection enter a holy sanctuary like Grace Cathedral? No, it made more sense that the first captor had been the pale woman. I'd taken the boy from her, and the druids had taken him from me.

That had me thinking again about the hand imprint and a possible connection between Bashi's White Hand syndicate and the fae. But the more pressing question right now was whether I could ethically collaborate with Petra.

"I need to know if you're still in the business of sacrifices," I said.

"Only if Brigit wills it, and she does not harm the innocent nor the young."

I suspected our definitions of *innocent* differed, but I would have to take her word on the young. Given the potential scale of the present threat, I needed her expertise.

I reviewed my remaining notes and sighed heavily. "All right, let's recap. Something demonic wrested Black Earth from your goddess, and now they're calling up demonic beings. They kidnapped Edgar, presumably as a sacrifice to bring about the second coming of Sathanas. How that part's possible, I'm not sure, but it doesn't change our objective: find the druids and recover the boy. Do you have any info on the first?"

"How did you know where they would be?" she asked.

"Just now? I didn't. I happened to be in the right place at the right time. So I'll take your question as a *no*."

"Like I said, their new master is concealing them well."

"The boy was in Bree-yark's backseat," I said. "We may be able to find some material for tracking him."

She shook her head. "I already looked. Anyway, he'll be inside their protections now."

I stood and paced the room. I could try to recover some druidic material from the most recent conjuring site, perform a hunting spell... But I was still thinking about the pale woman. Who was she, and would she be hunting the boy, too? As I turned to discuss our options with Petra, her eyes canted toward the door.

"Someone's here," she hissed.

I caught a shadow under the door an instant before it exploded inward.

18

I staggered back from the banging door, caught the corner of the bed, and went down.

Petra thrust her wand, her fire scorching the air, but a blast was already incoming. It scattered her flames and slammed her against the wall in a dispersion of dust. The dust shimmered gold and swarmed her—a secondary attack hidden inside the first. Gripping her throat, Petra collapsed to one hand and gasped for air.

I aimed my blade at the hooded figure darting through the doorway, my mind going to druids and the face in Edgar's bedrail. An invocation was halfway from my mouth when a familiar sigil caught my notice.

"Whoa, Jordan!" I shouted, as he swung his quarterstaff toward me. "It's Everson!"

My druid friend hesitated, the sigils on his temples illuminating his raven-like eyes. "Everson?" His sigils dimmed along with the magic warping the end of his staff. He looked from me to Petra, who was still down. "What in the hell's going on here?"

"We're all after the same thing," I said quickly. "If you release her, she'll explain."

The suffocation cantrip was still squeezing the air from her body until only the thinnest gasps escaped her. But Jordan kept his staff at his side, his compressed lips suggesting he was okay with his spell finishing the job.

"Release her," I repeated.

"After everything she's done?"

"Black Earth was infiltrated by a demon, like the one that got into the Raven Circle and possessed Delphine." I was referring to his wife. That was what had originally brought us together as members of the Upholders.

When Jordan remained glaring down at Petra, I prepared a dispersion invocation. But he rested a hand atop my raised staff and made a subtle sign with his own staff. The suffocating dust scattered, and Petra drew a hoarse, heaving breath. As she recovered, I straightened the desk. At last, she stood and stared at her attacker. He stared back, a tension more fierce than fire magic crackling between them.

"Jordan," she said at last.

"Petra," he replied stiffly. "Sacrificed any kids lately?"

"Don't pretend to know what I do," she hissed.

"I don't have to *pretend* anything."

With their casting implements dangerously close to firing positions, I clapped my hands sharply. "Look, there'll be time to sort that out later. Right now we need to get on the same page. Petra, give him a rundown of what you told me."

She continued to glare at Jordan, as though willing him to combust into flames. At last, she lowered her gaze. "Only if he agrees to drop his persecution complex."

"A temporary truce?" I asked Jordan.

He was one of the hardest nuts I'd ever encountered. He

didn't let things go. But in the depths of his eyes, I could see he was still haunted by what had happened to his wife and others of his Raven Circle—possessed and placed in a prison ship in 1776 New York as fuel for the demon Malphas.

"Emphasis on *temporary*," he said.

With that assurance, Petra delivered a succinct account of what she'd told me: the demon incursion into Brigit's realm, the defection of her Black Earth sisters, their new infernal power, and the second coming of Sathanas. She included the info I'd provided as well, about the druids summoning demonic beings. She ended with the significance of the Child star and Edgar's abduction.

Jordan absorbed the info wordlessly, seriously. By the time Petra finished, he was pacing the room, a fist to his frowning chin, brow creased in thought.

"That lines up with my magic," he said, addressing himself to me. "After we parted ways last night, I worked on concentrating the energy I'd gathered from the stone. It led me here, to her"—he afforded Petra the barest glance—"but nowhere else. If their power is tainted, then what I've stored will find no match."

"The demon is concealing their doings," Petra repeated.

Jordan resumed pacing as though he hadn't heard her. More likely, he was actively ignoring her. "There must be a way to track them," he muttered. "Some residue they've left behind."

"Their last conjuring," I said, a sudden realization lighting up my synapses. He and Petra turned toward me. "I surprised them. I didn't think about it at the time—I was too caught up in the understanding they were conjuring demonic creatures, and then too preoccupied with getting back to

Edgar." The empty backseat landed in my gut again. "Anyway, they left behind a casting circle they were in the middle of altering. They tried to clear it away when I arrived but did a sloppy job. I'm betting there's some infernal residue in that circle."

I opened my phone and accessed the photo to show them.

"I see some Black Earth elements," Petra said as she looked it over.

"Where is this circle?" Jordan asked.

I gave him the Chelsea address. "In the alleyway behind the rowhouses."

He turned toward the window and peered from our fifteenth story perch, as though gauging the distance. "I'll meet you there."

Before I understood what he was doing, he drew the window up and leapt out. I arrived in time to see his raven form burst from a scattering of dark magic, surge skyward with a ragged croak, and then veer south.

"Wait!" I called. "The police are there, and they don't know you!"

Swearing, I closed the window on his dwindling form and turned back to Petra.

"Show me where we're parked."

By the time we arrived, a police cordon was blocking the alleyway. I'd tried calling Detective Hoffman en route to warn him of Jordan's coming, but no answer. I twisted around to face Petra in the backseat.

"Stay close. I'm probably going to be on damage control."

"Hey, Everson?" Bree-yark said before I could get out. "Listen, I'm sorry about falling down on the job earlier. Letting myself get enspelled like that."

His eyes were still raw from the one-two punch of the druids' paralysis spell and then being placed under Petra's charm, and he was only now fully coming back to himself. But I felt the strength of his guilt at a gut level. It was the same guilt I'd been carrying ever since realizing I'd lost the boy.

I squeezed his compact shoulder. "Put it out of your head. This is one hundred percent on me."

"Nah, you left me in charge. I should have—"

"Hey, there were six of them," I cut in. "Wielding infernal magic, no less. We'll find him."

With the pledge made, as much to myself as my goblin friend, I led Petra to the police cordon. I flashed my ID, even though most of the officers knew me by now, and quickly signed in for both of us.

The scene beyond was much as I'd feared. Detective Hoffman was standing beside the victim's covered body, thrusting a finger at Jordan, who had planted himself beside the casting circle. Several officers were keeping a close eye on their shouting match.

"So what if I remember you from his wedding!" Hoffman barked. "Unless Croft's here, you're just some schmoe scattering his feathers all over my crime scene. And I'll tell you what, you're lucky they didn't shoot you out of the sky."

"Or maybe they're the lucky ones," Jordan snapped.

"Oh, you wanna put that to a test?" Hoffman challenged, turning to the Squad.

"Hey, it's okay!" I called, waving an arm overhead as I jogged toward them. "I asked for Jordan's expertise."

Hoffman's curdled face let out, but only slightly. "Is he always this much of an—"

"*Enthusiast*?" I panted as I arrived between them. "Yes. He's as anxious as anyone to get to the bottom of this. You could say he'd jump out of windows," I added sternly. "Isn't that right, Jordan?"

He'd gone off half-cocked more than once as an Upholder. But like then, he didn't apologize. Instead, he turned away and brought the end of his staff over the casting circle. I had to remind myself he was helping us.

"What's he doing?" Hoffman asked irritably.

"Looking for traces of the ones who did this." I nodded toward the body.

"His last name's Brody. Lived up there." Hoffman cut his eyes to the rowhouses I'd chased the druids through. "A search turned up the usual spell books and paraphernalia, which doesn't look like a surprise to you." He squinted from me to Petra, then did a double take. "Hey, isn't this the broad I put out an APB for?"

"Oh, yeah. You can cancel that."

"Gee, thanks for getting around to telling me," he grumbled. "I've had officers on overtime trying to ID her."

"I only just found her. Or, rather, she found me. Long story."

He eyed her suspiciously before gesturing around the alley. "Well, why don't you start by telling me what happened here."

I filled him in on the encounter with the druids and the possible implications. His eyes glazed over when I brought up star charts and a demon hijacking a druid god, so I pushed on, explaining the double conjurings that linked all the bodies: the first conjuring to summon a demonic being, the second one to hide that fact. And of course the planted spell books and paraphernalia to complete the deception.

"So these are all frigging homicides?" Hoffman asked.

"Unfortunately," I said. "But at least we have suspects now."

"You mean druids like these two?" He gestured between Petra and Jordan.

"No, not like us," Petra said, speaking up for the first time. "The druids in question are not themselves. The real killer is the demon controlling them. I've been charged with freeing them and returning them to our circle."

"Great, lady. And just what in the hell am I supposed to do with that?" When Hoffman turned to me, a vein wriggled in his right temple. "I've got fifteen bodies now, including the one Trevor and his team found up in the Bronx earlier. I can't just write them off as 'demon deaths.'"

"This has the mayor's seal," I reminded him quietly. "He's far less concerned with what's causing the homicides than that they stop. If Jordan can draw off something from the casting circle, we'll take it from there. We're on top of it."

And I believed what I was saying. A lot had come together in a short period of time. It was a matter now of finding the Black Earth druids, banishing the controlling demon, and returning Edgar to his mother.

Though Hoffman's face remained dubious, his shoulders unbunched enough to restore his squat neck. From a jacket pocket, he produced a bottle of aspirin and shook several tablets into his mouth.

"All right," he allowed, crunching them up. "What can the rest of the task force be doing?"

"A fresh APB, for starters. The perpetrators are working in

groups of at least six. They're all women with facial tattoos, last observed wearing hooded gray cloaks. They're powerful, so no engagement."

As Hoffman entered the info into his phone, Jordan joined us.

"There wasn't much," he said, eyeing the end of his staff. "But enough for me to spin the essence into a fragile spell. Like the one from last night, you'll have to be in close proximity for it to alert you."

As I passed my cane to Jordan, Hoffman looked up from his phone. "Got something?"

I explained it to him in layman's terms. "But it's going to involve us canvassing the city, which will take time," I warned.

"Hey, a lead's a lead," Hoffman grunted, sounding borderline optimistic for the first time.

When Jordan finished the transference, he returned my cane and looked at Petra impatiently. After a moment's hesitation, she relinquished her wand for her share of the spell. As Detective Hoffman stepped away to consult with the arriving techs, I pulled my map from my satchel and spread it over the ground.

"We can divide up the city," I said. Petra reclaimed her wand and hunkered to my left, while Jordan leaned over his staff. I peered across the constellation of conjurings depicted on the map as though something telling might pop out, but nothing did. "There are no obvious patterns, other than that they're accelerating."

"Yes, with the rising of *Puer*, the Child star," Petra said ominously. "It aligns with the Father soon, a moment of great potential."

"When?"

"This Friday at midnight."

I'd been wondering about a deadline and there it was. To capitalize on the power of the celestial event, the druids would sacrifice Edgar when the stars aligned. We had two days to find him, no more.

Petra straightened. "I can begin in the proximity of the conjurings."

"I'll take the northern part of the city and work my way south," Jordan said. "If you want to start south and work north, Croft."

"Sounds good." Already thinking of ways to boost our efficiency, I patted my cane. "There should be enough tracking juice in here for me to infuse a couple golems. Give us more boots on the ground."

Not one to waste words, Jordan nodded and broke into his raven form.

"Call through our bond if you find anything!" I shouted as he flapped skyward. With a shake of my head, I turned to Petra. "Here, let me give you my number."

"I have it. Like I said, I looked into you."

She drew a phone from her pocket, and a moment later, mine buzzed with her number.

"Apparently so," I said, equal parts impressed and disturbed. "Do you want Bree-yark to drive you?"

"I have ways to navigate the city," she replied mysteriously and strode back toward the police cordon. The officers parted, as much from her menacing facade as the power that emanated off her like a heat mirage.

I'd just finished returning the map to my satchel when my phone buzzed: Bishop Sheridan.

"Hey, I was just about to call you," I answered. I was not

looking forward to having to tell her how I'd found Edgar before promptly losing him again.

"Can you come to St. Martin's?" she asked abruptly.

"Of course. Is something wrong?"

"It's Mary. She's dead."

19

"I found her like this right before I called," the bishop said as she led me to Mary's apartment at the church. She drew out a key, but her hand was shaking so badly it took her two attempts to fit it into the keyhole.

"Have you told anyone else?" I asked.

"No, just you."

She unlocked the door, pushed it open, and stood back. As I took in the figure on the bed, I braced for the worst. But except for the fact her eyes were locked on the ceiling, Mary could have been sleeping. My gaze automatically dropped to her torso—I'd seen too many amateur conjurings lately—but there was no blood on her sweater. No blood anywhere, in fact. Just a horrible sense of stillness.

My mind went to paralysis spells, like the one that had incapacitated Bree-yark, but I felt the void where her soul had been. Mary Swal was truly gone.

I confirmed it in my wizard's senses, the astral lines and patterns showing the negative space. A fading light in the center of her brow drew my attention. Snapping my sight back to the physical, I flipped on the ceiling light and leaned over her face. On her forehead was a faint char mark, the size of someone's thumb.

"What is it?" the Bishop asked.

"There was one just like it on her son." I lifted the neck of her sweater and peered at her sternum, but I discerned no handprint.

"You... found Edgar?" she asked in confusion.

"At Grace Cathedral," I said, straightening. "Someone had tight security on a building in the center of the close. I found him in one of the rooms, strapped to a pallet, unconscious. He had burn marks here and here." I touched the center of my brow and chest. "Looked like someone worked him over."

"Goodness," the bishop whispered.

"I got him out and was on my way here, but detoured over to a conjuring. While I was away, a group of druids abducted him. We have a lead on them, but it's my fault. I should have... protected him better."

I'd almost said, *brought him straight here*, but how safe would he have been? Maybe why my magic had urged me to the conjuring instead of St. Martin's. The second would have delivered him to his mother's killer.

"Are these druids the ones who took him from his home?" the bishop asked.

"I don't think so. The pale woman Mary mentioned, the one who visited her apartment before Edgar went missing—I think she's the one who abducted him and left the note and photos. I'm also wondering if she has a connection to the interfaith community."

The bishop stiffened. "In what capacity?"

"She spent time at Grace Cathedral, and she came and went here with no apparent problem." I didn't know whether the handprint on Edgar's chest was meant to be a White Hand insignia or not, but a powerful fae would have needed permission to access the holy sanctuaries, whether by hook or crook.

"I can talk to security and staff," she said. "See if anyone here saw someone fitting her description."

"What about security footage?"

"Electronics don't operate well around the church."

Of course. St. Martin's was only sited on the city's most powerful fount of ley energy. I was still too shaken by the sight of Mary's body—and the sense I was partly responsible —to be thinking straight.

"Why would someone kill her?" the bishop asked.

I considered the mark between Mary's staring eyes. "I believe the pale woman wanted information."

"About what?"

"Who Mary talked to regarding her missing son."

A scenario was taking shape in my mind. When Edgar disappeared from Grace Cathedral, the pale woman went straight to the person most likely to have pursued him—his mother. She'd tracked Mary here, somehow. But Mary withheld what she knew, leading the pale woman to apply pressure.

She wields a terrible power, I heard Petra saying.

"I think it's time you talked to the rector over at Grace Cathedral," I said. "Find out if anyone fitting the woman's description made contact with him or his staff. I'll call in Mary's death to the NYPD."

There was no reason now not to tell them.

Ricki arrived twenty minutes later with a small platoon of officers and members of the Sup Squad. She examined Mary's body, which was starting to take on a gray cast. She then walked the scene and gave instructions to the forensics team.

"Do we have any idea who this 'pale woman' is?" she asked me as we stepped out into the courtyard. The slant of the late afternoon sunlight threw our shadows across the blood-red flagstones.

"There are elements about her that suggest fae," I said. "Her appearance, the control she wields over mortals—she could well have manipulated invitations into the faith houses. Or she has someone on the inside helping her." I'd considered relocating our family to one of the interfaith houses as we had done a year earlier to thwart a demon, but that wouldn't serve us now.

"She also left a handprint on Edgar's chest," I continued, "one that looks suspiciously like the White Hand's calling card. And I noticed that Bashi's henchmen are packing fae-enhanced rounds these days."

"He could have picked those up on the black market."

"True," I said, thinking of my Chinatown supplier, Mr. Han, who carried them, too.

I craned my neck around to Mary's apartment in growing frustration. The more theories I concocted about the pale woman, the more inscrutable she became. For all I knew she was working solo. Which put me no closer to understanding why she was hellbent on getting her hands on the boy.

Ricki rubbed my arm. "What's your magic telling you?"

"Right now?" I swam my hand around to indicate its random motions. "But I'm sure it will talk when it's ready." Past experience had shown me that what seemed like

randomness was my magic setting the stage, placing everything where it needed to be. That was where the faith part
came in.

"What about the Order?" she asked.

"Nothing about the pale woman, but I'll bring it up to
Claudius the next time we talk."

Bishop Sheridan reappeared from the church. "I've
spoken with Rector Rumbaugh at Grace Cathedral. He
denied anyone has been using the buildings or close besides
church officials. And he knew nothing about the security
guards being reassigned to watch the old cathedral house
where you found Edgar."

"Not surprising," I said, given the pale woman's evident
power.

"I can send some officers up there for surveillance," Ricki
offered. "In case she comes back."

"Good idea. As long as they keep their distance and don't
engage." The last thing we needed was for the NYPD to fall
under the woman's control, too.

As Ricki moved away with her phone, the bishop sidled
closer. "No one here saw anyone fitting the woman's description, either. I apologize for being away so long. Finding Mary
like that... It's shaken me. I had to pray on the matter."

"Any insights?" I asked hopefully.

"Just the same sense that opposing forces are converging
and we need to remain strong."

I debated whether or not to share Petra's star reading,
given the bishop's past trauma, but she needed to know. "Listen, a druid I'm working with believes the stars are
portending a second coming of Sathanas in the modern era.
She says Edgar is special somehow, that his sacrifice may be
key to bringing about the demon lord's return."

The bishop blanched, and for a moment, her emotional scars stood from her aura. With Sathanas's first coming, she had very nearly been the sacrificial offering. Her death would have empowered the demon lord while weakening the church's threshold enough to release him into the city.

She tucked her chin, as though forcing her trauma back down. "What do you believe?"

"Honestly? There are a lot of parallels with Sathanas's last appearance, including the conjuring of demonic beings throughout the city. As improbable as it may seem, I think we have to at least consider the possibility."

"Then I'll call a meeting of the Interfaith Council."

"I'd like to attend, too."

I wasn't so much asking as telling. And it wasn't just that I had firsthand experience on the topic. There was the matter of the pale woman and how she'd accessed two powerful sanctuaries, not to mention had known Mary's whereabouts. I wanted to see the council members up close and personal.

"Of course," she said.

"Who else knew Mary was here?"

"By name? Just the two of us. We have a strict confidentiality system in place for those we shelter. No one else knew her identity."

"Not even someone you may have trusted?" I asked.

She smiled tightly. "I take that confidentiality seriously, too."

"I know you do, Bishop. I just have to cover all our bases."

"I understand."

As she left to contact the Interfaith Council, I believed what she'd told me. Which made holding onto my skepticism all the more difficult. But I'd learned my lesson with Father Vick the hard way. Despite his benevolence, he'd been the one hosting Sathanas. Bishop Sheridan could have been playing an unwitting role as well.

Ricki rejoined me. "They're on it," she said, referring to the surveillance at Grace Cathedral. "What's the plan now?"

"Is Tony home from school?"

"Yeah. Mae just texted me."

"Good, everyone needs to stay in the apartment for the time being. I'm going there now to work on the protections."

I'd built my wards to deter dark magic, demonkind, and all manner of night creatures. I never thought I would have to add holiness to that list.

But if the pale woman had elicited a name from Mary, and that name had been mine, she would come looking for me sooner rather than later. And because she'd spent time in two powerful holy sites, I was counting on her carrying that holy energy in her aura—regardless of who, or what, she was.

"What about Edgar?" Ricki asked.

"Jordan and Petra are hunting for the druids who took him. Jordan was able to scrape up enough of their energy at the last conjuring. In fact, I promised him some golems. How much longer will you be?"

"Another hour, give or take."

"Can you have the Sup Squad escort you home?"

I didn't need to tell her to shoot first and ask questions second if they encountered the pale woman or a group of fire druids.

"Will do," she said. "Any word on your wizard help?"

I shook my head. "Not yet."

20

Back home, I went right to work on the wards. I carved new sigils into the door and window frames, infusing them with the holy power I had absorbed into my coin pendant. I then integrated the glowing symbols into the rest of the system, which required a good deal of focus and energy.

Once I finished, I spoke an incantation and watched the fresh wards merge with the protective barrier around the unit. Nothing holy could enter now without permission. Massaging the pressure from my brow, I released a spent sigh.

"Whoa there, Everson!" Bree-yark barked from the living room.

I hadn't realized I was sagging against the doorframe, the new sigils blurring out of focus, until he rushed over and caught me around the waist.

"C'mon, let's get you sitting down," he said, draping my arm across his shoulders.

He half escorted me, half carried my exhausted body to the reading chair, where I sat heavily. The cushions had never felt so divine. Mae tsked and arranged a throw blanket over my lap. Tony pulled my shoes from my throbbing feet and handed them to Buster, who scuttled off with one in each claw. I tried to tell everyone I was all right, but I was so spent, I could barely get the words out.

"What can we *do*?" Mae scolded more than asked me.

"How about a coffee with a shot of invigoration potion?" I managed.

She sighed. "You can't go on like this, Everson. Look at you, you're flat rundown."

From her permanent depression in the divan, Tabitha scoffed. "*Falling* down is more like it."

Though it was Tabitha, her jab struck a rare chord. There was still a ton to do—tracking the druids, finding Edgar, figuring out the pale woman and her affiliations, not to mention stopping a possible return of Sathanas by tomorrow night. The urgency of it all buzzed in my skull. And yet here I was, unable to stand under my own power, much less cast. Between the day's action and updating the wards, I was running on fumes. If Thelonious wasn't so weak, he would have been bar-crawling me through the city.

"She's worried about you, too," Mae said, bouncing Abigail in her thick arms.

When I noticed how serious my daughter's eyes looked above her pacifier, I couldn't help but smile.

"Here," Mae said, setting her in the crook of my arm. "Will you rest for her sake?"

"Maybe just for a minute," I murmured, nuzzling Abigail's head. "Then I'll need to get back to work."

A moment later, Ricki came through the door and announced she was home for the night. For the time being, we were all safe. As Abigail released a contented sigh beside me, my eyelids dropped closed.

"Edgar!" I called.

I was peering into a misty wash of gray, looking for some sign of the boy. When the cold wind picked up, I tasted the salt of a nearby sea. Where I was, I had no idea. I knew only that I had to find him.

"Edgar!" I called again.

Points of light took hold in the far mist, like fire. For a disorienting moment, I thought I was looking at my mystical map of the recent conjurings, but these were the druids, the ones who'd taken Edgar. I was seeing their wands. I broke into a run, arms and legs kicking the surrounding mist into spectral swirls.

Find the child...

But the lights didn't seem to be getting any closer. And then they blinked out altogether.

I staggered to a stop as the mist thinned. I was in a massive courtyard, ornate cathedral domes looming ahead. I knew this place. I was standing in St. Mark's Square in Venice, facing the main basilica. I'd been here once, years earlier, when I was a graduate student. I'd come here to research...

I paused. What in the hell had I come here to research?

No, that hadn't been me, I realized. That had been my probable self, my shadow. This is where he'd died.

I felt an icy fist close around my heart as I stared up at the basilica. I tried to will my shadow's memories into my own—I had to know what had happened. Like a haunted invitation, the main doors creaked open. Though every instinct begged me to run, a magnetic force latched onto my soul.

A force as strong as Fate.

It pulled me forward until I was passing through the doorway into the basilica's vast interior. Mist drifted in beside me, washing out the holy statues and centuries-old gold mosaics. I jumped when the doors slammed closed behind me. But I continued onward, the force drawing me down corridors and stairwells, until I was standing in what looked like a cave. I was in an old and secret part of the basilica.

"Kneel," a booming voice ordered.

Before me, a massive, winged figure took shape. The same being I'd encountered when I'd opened myself to the power of the whip against the Greek monster, Typhon. But the angel had a name now: Faziel. No face, no distinct features, he remained an impression in the mist, enormous wings rising to either side of him.

I wanted to stagger back, to flee, but Fate held me firm. Or maybe it was my own morbid fascination, because there was something about this place, this being, that transfixed me, even as his presence reduced my bowels to water. With a roar of white fire, he drew a sword and raised it overhead.

"Kneel," he repeated.

I dropped to my knees—and nearly collided with a body that had been at my feet, hidden by the mist. He was wearing a tweed jacket, leather patches at the elbows. I seized his shoulder and drew him toward me. His head, oddly angled, was slow to follow. As it rolled toward me, I saw it was severed.

I also saw that the young, staring face was my own.

As fear shrieked through me, I shot my eyes upward. The angel Faziel was no longer standing over me, but the pale woman, her white hair lashing around a pitiless visage, and we were back in New York.

With a cry, she brought her sword down.

I jerked awake, heart hammering in my ears, my hand clutching the back of my neck.

As the terror of the dream released its hold, I realized I was still in my reading chair in the living room, a blanket over my lap. I brought my hand around in front of me to check. No blood, I hadn't been cut.

"Well, damn, bro," someone said. "Happy to see you, too."

Opposite me, a man with stonewashed jeans and a leather cowboy hat stood from the couch. Silver light shrank into the wand he'd been showing Tony as he slid it into the pocket of his vest.

"James?" I said. "James friggin' Wesson?"

"The OG, baby. Straight outta Grimstone."

"He got here an hour ago." Ricki entered the room, bouncing Abigail in her arms.

"An hour?" I repeated. "Geez, how long was I out?"

"About two," she said.

I checked my watch as I pushed the blanket from my lap and stood. "Why didn't someone wake me up?"

James laughed. "Bro, if you were any more out of it, I would've had to jab a resurrection potion into your right behind."

He swallowed me in a bearhug and lifted me from my feet. Though we were about the same six-foot height, he had a good twenty pounds of muscle on me, and he flexed all twenty. He clapped my back several times before setting me back down.

For an awkward moment we just grinned at one another. It was partly the ridiculous adventures we'd shared out West. And *ridiculous* barely began to describe half of them. But it was more that we were the closest thing to a brother the other knew, and all the good, bad, and occasional ugly that entailed.

"You don't know how stoked I am to see you," I said at last.

"Hey, that goes double for me. And you've bailed this dude out enough—it's high time I returned the favor. We've got you."

Mae, who was preparing the table for dinner with Bree-yark, looked over with a proud smile.

It took a moment for James's words to register. "Wait, *we*?" I asked him.

"He was not the only one who was called," a woman with a Greek accent said.

I turned to find Loukia Kouris emerging from the bath-room, a headscarf drawing her thick black hair from her sun-freckled complexion. I'd met the fellow magic-user of the Order three months earlier in Athens. She was a fearless caster and frighteningly good with her enchanted blades.

I broke into appreciative laughter. "Man, the Order *really* came through."

Her stern brown eyes softened. "It is good to see you again, too, Everson."

As I hugged her and exchanged kisses, James said, "We bumped into each other outside JFK."

Loukia frowned. "Yes, I caught him giving me the 'up and down' at ground transportation."

"But then we recognized each other's magic," James quickly interjected. "Found out we were headed to the same place. We ended up splitting a cab."

"You still owe me twelve dollars," she said.

"Hey, I'm good for it. Tell her, Croft."

"Yeah, he pays his debts. Eventually. So I take it you've both met everyone."

"Sure have," James said, looking around before his twinkling gaze settled on Ricki. "You've done well for yourself, Croft. Damned well."

Though he'd toned it down some, James remained an incurable womanizer. He'd consulted for Ricki years earlier when she and I had been on the outs. She wasn't having it then, and she wasn't having it now. Returning a bland look, she hiked Abigail up her hip and left to help Mae and Breeyark.

James clapped his hands once. "So, Croft-man. What are you needing from us?"

"*After* dinner," Mae called from the kitchen. "And it's all ready, so wash up if you haven't already."

21

I brought everyone up to speed over Mae's meatloaf special with baked mac and cheese and fresh string beans. As I was finishing up, I received updates from Jordan and Petra on their citywide search: no hits on the Black Earth druids yet.

"So you are needing golems?" Loukia asked me.

"That's right. I can transfer the infernal energy from my staff to a set of amulets for them to wear, but I'm afraid that's all I'm good for right now." Though the two-hour nap had cleared my head, my magic remained in a state of recharge. Thank heaven my fellow spell-slingers turned up when they did.

"Hey, just show us the clay and stand outta the way," James said with a smirk. He turned to Ricki, who was feeding Abigail. "Have I told you how much motherhood agrees with you?"

"Twice already," she said. "Any updates from the Order?" she asked me, referring to the possibility of Sathanas's return.

"Claudius called while I was washing up," I said. "He said the senior members had to respond to an emergency rupture in an outer plane. Doesn't sound like it's related to this, but he'll keep me posted."

Ricki was the only one at the table I'd told so far about Sathanas's second coming. I didn't want to say anything in front of Tony, of course. Neither did I want to alarm Mae and Bree-yark, not until I knew more—all I had was one druid's star reading. But my dream with the angel Faziel got me thinking about the bishop's vision of opposing forces. Angels and demons fit that bill. And I'd had prophetic dreams in the past, especially after combining a high volume of casting with a lack of sleep.

But just how prophetic were we talking?

I turned to Tabitha, who was crouched in front of a pile of meatloaf in her food bowl. Though she made noises of revulsion, she was on her second helping and would no doubt accept a third—grudgingly, of course.

"Hey, Tabby," I called. "How have you been feeling lately?"

In the past, major doings in the Below had upset her. The last time, she'd downed half a bottle of whiskey. If a second coming of Sathanas were imminent, she would feel something. She was my canary in the demonic coalmine.

I waited for an answer, which involved her chewing as slowly as possible, then taking a good half minute to "choke down this offal." But I also noticed she batted Buster's claw away when he stretched it cautiously toward her bowl. At last, she pounded her chest twice with a curled paw and hacked.

"Did you say something, darling?" she asked.

I repeated the question with exaggerated patience. "*How have you been feeling lately?*"

"Besides nauseous?" She shrugged a shoulder. "Peeved, annoyed, borderline depressed."

Her usual self, in other words. So either she'd become less sensitive to demonic doings, courtesy of her additional poundage, or nothing seismic was happening. That was slightly reassuring. She scowled at the meatloaf before going in for another bite.

"While you guys are building golems," I said to James and Loukia, "there's somewhere I need to go."

"Where's that?" Ricki asked.

"Bishop Sheridan texted me," I said, patting my pocket with the phone. "The emergency meeting of the Interfaith Council is happening tonight. I'm hoping someone there will know something about the pale woman. The one who originally kidnapped Edgar and then"—I cut my fingers across my throat where Tony couldn't see—"his mother. Now that the wards are up, I want to get a jump on her."

I could tell Ricki didn't like it—she'd seen Mary's body up close, and the preliminary cause of death was a massive brain hemorrhage—but she understood that it beat waiting for the pale woman to come to us. "She hasn't been back to Grace Cathedral tonight," she offered. "That's according to the Sup Squad."

"Could be hiding out in another interfaith house," I said, thinking aloud, "using the holy energy for cover."

"Also, when one of the security guards left for the night, a couple of officers followed him," Ricki continued. "They buddied up at his local bar, bought him a drink, talked shop, but he didn't have any info for them. Just acted like it had been another day on the job. Nothing about a pale woman."

That had me thinking fae again. Powerful fae.

The Interfaith Council Center, or IFCC, was in a squat fortress-like building in Midtown not far from St. Bartholomew's Church. Bree-yark had insisted on driving me, and as we pulled up, I spotted Bishop Sheridan getting out of a dark sedan.

"You're welcome to come in," I told Bree-yark.

"Actually, I was planning to drop the seat back and catch a little shuteye. I missed my afternoon nap, and you don't want me nodding off in there. If you've never heard a goblin snore, it's a tractor convention."

"All right, I shouldn't be too long."

I got out and met Bishop Sheridan, who'd stopped to wait for me. She was wearing an official black robe, a long white stole draped around her neck.

"This came together quickly," I remarked.

"We have a special provision for emergencies, and I felt this met the requirement."

As we passed between a pair of hired security at the door, I checked them in my wizard's senses. They didn't bear the same single-minded aura of the guards at Grace Cathedral, but their armed presence put me on edge, especially when they locked the glass door behind us. Procedure, of course—they were responsible for the Interfaith Council—but I snuck a look back anyway to make sure.

"Any updates?" the bishop asked.

As the power of the building mitigated my casting abilities, I hustled to catch up to her.

"I have some friends combing the city for the druids who took Edgar. I'll join them after the meeting. As far as the pale woman? Nothing yet." I still had the cover I'd cut from the cushion, but if I was dealing with a powerful fae, any exploratory magic was going to take time to set up in order to perform safely.

Maybe I would learn something here.

I followed the bishop into a round conference room at the building's center. Its walls were ringed in flags, each one bearing a religious symbol that, collectively, made up the Interfaith Council. Judging from the full table, we were among the last to arrive. I recognized most of the members' affiliations by dress alone, which included Sikh, Afro Caribbean, and Native American denominations. I joined Bishop Sheridan at the table, pulling up a chair, and scanned all of their nameplates.

"Swami Rama is running late," she announced to the room, gesturing to his nameplate before an empty seat. Though I'd never met him, I recalled his kind, bespectacled face from the papers. The executive director going on a decade now, he frequently spoke on behalf of the Council. "He asked us to begin without him."

Bishop Sheridan introduced me as an ally of the IFC, then proceeded to explain the growing threat, starting with the conjuring of the demonic beings.

As she spoke, I opened my wizard's senses. As representatives of the faiths of thousands to hundreds of millions, the members' patterns were potent but unique to each. Images sprang from their auras, everything from crosses to a great eagle. Though interesting, I focused past them, alert for hostile energies and telltale signs of deception.

Not only had the pale woman gained access to two of the city's most formidable faith houses, she'd tortured a boy in the first and killed his mother in the second. Having an enabler on the Interfaith Council made a lot of sense.

"We believe this may all be leading to the return of a

powerful demon known as *Sathanas*," the bishop was saying. "Many of you were on the Council the last time he came, four years ago. Fortunately, he didn't emerge fully into the world and his presence was short-lived—thanks to Mr. Croft here."

She turned to me, her nod offering me the floor.

I cleared my throat as I stood. "I didn't succeed alone. The power of St. Martin's, bolstered by the collective faith, contained the demon lord. And when I destroyed him it was by tapping into that same power. Father Victor, the demon lord's host and victim, lingered in spirit long enough to help me channel that power."

As happened every time I thought of Father Vick, I saw Sathanas bursting through his body as if it were an overripe fruit. But I also remembered how Father Vick had held my prism together. Without him, that raw energy would have blown my mind to pieces and Sathanas would have been loosed upon the world.

A few solemn murmurs sounded from those who had known the late vicar.

I took a moment to compose myself. "This is all to say that the power of the interfaith community and its members is as vital now as it was then. It must remain strong and inter-joined. And we must be *very* careful about who we allow in."

"He's right," Bishop Sheridan said. "To that end, Swami Rama and I are proposing a schedule of focused prayer."

She glanced over at me, hesitating when she saw I hadn't sat back down. When I'd said the part about being careful who we allowed in, one of the members had dropped his eyes and begun fidgeting. He was middle-aged, with dark, wiry hair and thick-rimmed glasses. The nameplate identified him as Rector Rumbaugh of Grace Cathedral—the same campus where Edgar had been held and tortured.

Rumbaugh had denied knowing anything to the bishop, but his agitated energy suggested otherwise.

"I'm sorry," I said to Bishop Sheridan. "I don't mean to interrupt, but I have to ask the room. Has anyone here been in contact with a pale woman? She's on the young side of forty with an unusually pallid complexion and white hair to her shoulders."

Questioning murmurs went up and heads shook. But I remained focused on Rumbaugh, whose auric layers were pulling in now. When he saw me watching him, he blinked his raw-looking eyes and affected a concerned expression.

At last, he licked his lips. "It might help if we knew who she was."

"I was hoping one of you could tell me," I replied, not shifting my eyes from his. "She's extremely manipulative. She's also extremely dangerous. She's a suspect in a child kidnapping and now a murder investigation, and there's evidence she was recently active on the Grace Cathedral close."

He was opening his mouth when gunshots cracked outside, and a cry sounded. I snatched my cane and spun toward the door.

"Everyone stay inside!" I shouted as I took off.

22

I broke into the corridor outside the conference room. Gunfire continued to crack, but now only from one weapon —then that broke off abruptly. As I raced toward the front doors, I strained to see beyond the glass before realizing it was blood-streaked.

The hoarse cry sounded again, an older man's.

I reached the doors and pulled one open onto a scene of carnage. The two guards who'd let us inside were down, their weapons scattered, bodies savaged. Ahead, a man I recognized as Swami Rama, was on one knee, blood pouring from a hand he clamped to his forehead. In his other hand, he held out a necklace of mala beads, power radiating from it in a halo that I felt from the doorway.

He cried out again and swung his necklace to his other side. A creature materialized from the darkness, something large and black with scaly wings and a gargoyle's face, the fangs glistening with blood.

A demon!

Its taloned foot snapped closed, just missing the swami's

bloodied head before it lifted off again. The power in the beads had thwarted the demon, but only just.

I thrust my cane up as I hustled toward the swami and shouted, "*Protezione!*" The air overhead crackled into a shield that I infused with banishment power.

"Are you okay? Can you walk?" I needed to get him inside the sanctuary.

He stared up at me, his expression vacant from shock and blood loss. When he adjusted the hand pressed to his head, part of his scalp shifted.

"C'mon," I said, lifting him under an arm. "Walk with me."

I did most of the work getting him to his feet, but once there, he managed his own precarious steps. I peered through the shield as we staggered toward the door and its powerful threshold. The night sky was still—until it wasn't.

From seemingly nowhere, the demon dove in again. Talons furrowed my shield, spilling sparks over us. The pain from the contact arrived an instant later, like barbs gouging the length of my soul.

"*Respingere!*" I managed, partly doubled over.

The power of the shield gathered and released in a bright pulse. The creature reared up, disappearing back into the night. I pulled Swami Rama the final few feet to the door, opened it, and set him inside.

"We need medical attention!" I shouted toward the conference room before closing the door again.

With both hands available now, I pulled my cane into sword and staff. As the pain of the demon's attack faded to a dull searing, my senses heightened to a shimmering readiness. It seemed there was only one demon—and that was plenty, especially with its apparent resistance to holy power.

The swami's necklace and my banishment energy had deterred it, but the creature hadn't acted hurt.

Is this what the druids are conjuring? A more resilient breed of demon?

I had no time to consider the question. The nightmare creature was coming in again. I released another pulse, knocking it sideways before it could sink its talons into my shield. To end it, though, I was going to have to send my blade through it. But first, I needed to get a visual on the damned thing.

"*Luminare!*" I cried.

From the opal end of my staff, a ball of light spun into being and shot skyward, blowing open the night.

It exposed the demon, its black wings slicing through a backdrop of Midtown skyscrapers as it cut around for another attack. I raised my staff, preparing to enclose the creature in a sphere of hardened air, when a fresh burst of gunfire sounded. Rounds ripped through the creature's wings, sending it into a reeling spiral. It crash-landed on a parked sedan, flattening its roof and blowing out the windows.

Bree-yark came hustling up, an automatic rifle in his two-handed grip.

"Nice shooting," I said as we arrived at the car together. "Composite rounds?"

"Damned straight." Bree-yark grimaced as he looked over the demon. "What in thunder is that thing?"

It had landed on its back, one wing nearly touching the scale-littered street. I eyed the shape and pattern of the creature's obsidian horns, the way its serrated fangs extended past both upper and lower jaws.

"A pitch demon," I said grimly.

Pitch demons were similar to shriekers, but with more tools for ripping souls from bodies and flat-out killing. At least shriekers gave some warning they were incoming. These things were silent as death. Throw in resilience to holy power, and the Black Earth druids had gone next level with their army.

As I glanced over at the fallen guards, the demon shuddered. The rips and perforations Bree-yark had inflicted were closing. Gesturing my partner back, I prodded the demon with my staff. When it jerked toward me, I thrust my sword through its chest, the blade sheened in banishment light.

"*Disfare!*" I shouted.

The demon twisted its head back and forth in a silent scream. I kept pushing, struggling to overcome the infernal bonds holding it together, even in its damaged state. At last, the demon bubbled more than exploded into a black ichor that oozed, steaming, down the sides of the smashed vehicle.

Clouds edged my vision as I stood back.

"Was that all of them?" Bree-yark asked, scanning the sky.

Blinking my eyes clear, I did the same. "Yeah, at least for now."

I pulled out my phone and called Ricki.

"Hey, how's the meeting going?" she answered.

"We're going to need the Sup Squad."

"Why? What happened?"

"Demon attack outside the IFC Center. The director, Swami Rama, escaped with a bad head wound, but a pair of security guards weren't so lucky. An ambulance is probably en route, but I'd feel better if they had a Sup escort out of here. In fact, all the members should have them." The target may have been the IFC's director, but the entire Council contributed to the city's powerful protections. "We might even need to arrange round-the-clock detail for them."

"I'll see what I can do," she said. "Are you all right?"

"Yeah, fine."

"You don't sound fine."

She knew my inflections forward and backward. The truth was, I was bothered by the amount of energy it had taken to banish the pitch demon. Was I still weak from updating my wards at home, or had the demon been that powerful? Also, I couldn't remember the last time my vision had begun to cloud like that.

"Just a little shaken," I hedged. "It's a grim scene."

Beyond the fallen guards and blood-streaked doors to the IFC Center, I could make out a small group gathered around the swami.

"I'll start making calls," Ricki said. "Let me know if you need anything else."

"Will do. I love you."

"I love you, too," she said forcefully.

When Bree-yark and I entered the IFC Center, Bishop Sheridan was pressing her folded stole to the swami's head. It was already soaked, sending dark rivulets down the side of his face and into his robe.

"How's he doing?" I asked her.

"The bleeding's bad and he's in shock. We called for an ambulance."

As I filled her in on the encounter, she peered past me at the fallen guards and crossed herself.

"I think this was a preemptive strike," I finished. "If we *are* looking at Sathanas's return, he knows that weakening the power of the Interfaith Council is his best chance of breaking into the city. Tonight he went right for the head." I nodded at the downed swami. "But I believe the entire Council is at risk."

"And there are more demons," she said, remembering the conjurings.

"Yeah, at least a dozen. We're arranging special protection for all of you."

"I'll ride to the hospital with him," she said of the swami. She squinted at the opposite wall, as though gauging the distant storm again. "This means our collective faith is more important than ever. I'll tell the others."

Bree-yark took over care of the swami as Bishop Sheridan and I returned to the conference room. The members who'd stayed inside were all standing, speaking solemnly. They remained standing as the bishop explained what had happened, their faces resolute and compassionate to the last. When the bishop reinforced the call to bolster the power of the Interfaith Council, they bowed their heads in prayer.

But one of them was missing.

"Where's Rector Rumbaugh?" I asked before the prayer could begin.

Heads turned. A few questions sounded until the Native American council member spoke up. "I saw him go out that way." She pointed to a door that led from the back of the conference room.

I shifted to my wizard's senses as I ran out the same door, picking up the rector's trail immediately. It proceeded down a corridor, past a bathroom, and out an emergency exit that led onto an alleyway. From there, it continued toward the street.

Did the attack scare him off? Or had it been my earlier interrogation of him?

Back in the conference room, I shared my findings with

the bishop. "I sensed his guardedness, too," she said. "Let me handle him. You have enough to do."

I was already overextended, and trying to chase down Rumbaugh was one job too many. The question of whether or not I could fully trust Bishop Sheridan remained, but I'd have to roll those dice. She was my only ally on the Council, and she knew its members much better than I did. Already, my thoughts were turning to the druids, Edgar, and the pale woman. When my magic nudged me toward the last, I nodded.

"Okay," I said. "There's someone I should go talk to."

23

"Right here," I said, pointing out a spot along an affluent stretch of East Seventieth Street for Bree-yark to park. It had taken a bit of searching to find the townhouse with the emerald-green door, thanks to a powerful enchantment.

As he backed in, I drew a pair of stoppered potions from a coat pocket and activated them. Bree-yark knew the drill and followed my example, glugging down the one I handed him. They were neutralizing potions that would protect us from incidental contact with the townhouse's defenses.

As the potion took effect, I closed my eyes. We'd stayed at the IFC Center long enough for the ambulance and Sup Squad to arrive. I filled Trevor in on the type of creature I'd put down. While two of the squad escorted the ambulance to the hospital, he worked out a plan for the rest of the Squad to keep tabs on the council members.

Bishop Sheridan had given me a final reassurance that she would follow up on Rector Rumbaugh. In her own stoic way, she was asking me to trust her.

I opened my eyes and turned to Bree-yark. "You ready?" I asked.

I led the way up the townhouse steps and rapped on the door. The contact sent out faint tendrils of magic that explored us before thinning away. As I waited, I considered my visits here in the past. The first time, I'd come looking for Caroline Reid, my former colleague at Midtown College, only to learn she had married a fae prince. The other times, I'd been in search of special assistance—twice to access New York's past.

I was reflecting on that history, gazing up the narrow edifice, when Bree-yark cleared his throat. I started, realizing the door had opened. From the shadow beyond the entrance, a pair of gray eyes glimmered.

"Osgood!" I blurted out.

The butler stepped forward, his parted silver hair and formal attire as impeccable as ever. He bowed slightly. Despite his small build and servant's manners, he was one of the most powerful fae I'd ever met. As he straightened, his calm face gave off the barest hint of humor, as though he'd been expecting me.

"Mr. Croft," he said in his refined voice. "And Bree-yark."

"I don't think we've seen each other since my wedding," I said. Prior to that, he'd helped the Upholders and me access a time catch, then assisted in subtle ways when his kingdom was infiltrated by a demon.

"We have not," he confirmed. "And how are you and Mrs. Croft?"

"We're super, thanks. We have a little girl now."

He smiled affably. "That's splendid."

"And you?"

"I'm just fine, Mr. Croft." He folded his gloved hands

primly at his waist. Now that we had completed the niceties, he was ready for me to get to the point.

"Listen, I'm sorry to just show up like this," I said. "But I have a question."

He peered back into a parquet entrance hall, too large for the narrow townhouse, before stepping forward. I caught the tittering contrails of pixies as he closed the door behind him.

"Of course," he said, as though not wanting someone to overhear.

I had earned massive points with the royal family a year earlier for helping rid their kingdom of the aforementioned demon and saving Caroline's husband in the process. Though the kingdom had repaid me in gifts, I sensed they were still indebted to me; otherwise, I wouldn't have come. The fae didn't dole out favors, not even to allies. In the past, either Caroline or I had paid the price for their assistance.

"There's a woman operating in the city," I said, "someone powerful who might be from Faerie. She has white hair and pale skin. She kidnapped a child and killed his mother and can cast deadly magic inside the faith houses. She was working out of Grace Cathedral for a time. I'm wondering if the family knows her?"

"Are you certain this being is one of ours?"

The way he asked suggested he might have known something. "No," I admitted. "Just happens to tick a lot of boxes."

I studied his eyes, but they simply peered back into mine. "I'm afraid Mrs. Caroline and Mr. Angelus are away on diplomatic business," he replied after a moment. "I'll have to await their return to consult them."

"I understand," I said, hiding my disappointment. "Oh, here, let me give you this." I drew out a plastic evidence bag that contained the cloth cover I'd taken from the old cathedral building where Edgar had been held. I'd been saving it to cast on, but my magic was urging me to hand it over, and I was learning to heed these rare moments of clarity. "It may hold some of this woman's essence."

"Yes, very good," he said, accepting it. "Was there anything else, Mr. Croft?"

"That was all. Thank you, Osgood."

He remained staring at me long enough for the moment to verge on uncomfortable. At last, he blinked and nodded. "I should return to my duties, then. Good evening, Mr. Croft. Bree-yark."

We echoed his farewell. He held the bag up before disappearing through the doorway. Subtle but powerful protections grew back over the door, sealing off the fae house and its many, many mysteries.

Back in the Hummer, I showed Bree-yark a hand. "Hey, could you give me a minute before we take off. That bit of exposure to Faerie left me woozy, even with the potion." I wondered if my exertion against the demon—hell, my exertions that entire day—had made me more susceptible to the realm's magic.

"Yeah, it's pretty concentrated up there," he said, probably to be nice because he looked fine.

As I gripped my cane and tried to stare my rotating vision steady, Bree-yark peered toward the enchanted townhouse, then angled his neck in a way that told me he was having a hard time finding it again. At last, he shook his head.

"So how d'ya think that went?" he asked.

I blew out my breath. "Honestly, I was hoping Osgood

would break rank and just tell me. I think he knows who the pale woman is."

"Picked up on that too, huh?"

"Yeah, but I trust he'll follow through."

Which felt a lot safer than exposing myself to the pale woman through spell work. The fae would either provide info, or they would do what I was hoping for but hadn't dared ask: take care of her themselves. If she *were* a powerful fae, she was bucking tradition. The fae had cultivated influence in the city, all the way back to its founding, in part by not drawing negative attention to themselves.

Bree-yark punched my knee. "Ready to roll, buddy?"

With my wooziness steadying, I nodded. "Yeah, I should get back to the apartment."

The golems James and Loukia had been working on were probably ready to deploy, and I would need to coordinate their search grids with the druids, Jordan and Petra.

As Bree-yark pulled out, I drew my map from my satchel and unrolled it across my lap. With a Word, I lit up the conjurings sites from the past weeks. Petra was canvassing the areas around those, while Jordan was performing a low-flying search for the druids' infernal energy from north to south.

As I scanned the map, my wooziness returned in a flood.

I was suddenly back in my dream, chasing the druids' fire through the mist—more vision than memory. I allowed the vision to play out... entering the basilica, seeing the angel Faziel, finding the body of my shadow, and, finally, cowering as the pale woman brought a sword down on my neck.

My thoughts turned to Mary's body and the thumbprint glowing in the negative space of her departed soul. My magic moved meaningfully. The map returned to focus. But instead of looking at the lights, I shifted my attention to where they *weren't*—the negative spaces. The largest one was Chinatown.

My heart double-thumped. Was that where the druids were hiding?

One man knew the neighborhood better than anyone. Before I could second-guess my magic, I dug into a pocket, retrieved the card I'd been given the night before, and punched the number into my phone.

A man with an Asian accent answered. "Everson Croft."

"I'm ready to meet with Mr. Gang," I said.

24

"You sure about this?" Bree-yark asked as he idled in front of a restaurant in the heart of Chinatown.

My call to Bashi's henchman had resulted in him hanging up. He called back a short time later with an address along with a threat that I'd better show up. I eyed the armed guards bracketing the dark doors of the chic-looking restaurant.

"No," I admitted. "But you remember how Osgood stared at me after asking if I needed anything else and I told him no? I think he saw that I was after the druids, and he gifted me some sort of fae vision to intuit their whereabouts. If the druids *are* operating in Chinatown, Bashi will know."

"Well, I'm going in with you."

Bree-yark's readiness to have my back anytime, anywhere moved me, but this was no meeting for a temperamental goblin.

"Tell you what," I said. "How about you park nearby? If I get into trouble, I'll, ah, scream."

I expected him to balk, but he nodded thoughtfully. "Just

make it high-pitched enough for my goblin hearing. I'll come in fully loaded."

Under different circumstances, the idea of mimicking a dolphin in distress would have made me laugh, but I was too preoccupied as I shed my coat and packed it beside my cane and satchel in the footwell.

"What are you doing?" he asked.

"They're going to check me at the door, and I trust you to safeguard my things a lot more than I trust them."

I removed my coin pendant and ring last—invaluable heirlooms. If I had to, I could invoke through my body. Recalling the enhanced rounds Bashi's henchman had been packing last night, I took down another neutralizing potion. It wouldn't spare me from the bullets themselves, but it would soften their magic.

I gave Bree-yark a tight smile. "Wish me luck."

The armed guards pivoted toward me as I approached the front doors. In my wrinkled slacks and stained shirt, sleeves shoved to the elbows, I didn't fit the profile of a fine diner. More like a fine mess. Before I could explain my summons, a slender man in a black suit and headset emerged between them.

"Professor Croft?" he asked in a clipped voice. When I nodded, he said, "Right this way."

He led me into what looked like a cross between a coat closet and an interrogation room, where another armed guard was waiting. Mr. Headset stood to one side and observed as the guard patted me down.

"Carrying any weapons?" Headset asked.

"No," I replied. *If you don't include my magic.*

When the pat-down was complete, Headset looked me up and down, then across the shoulders, and said something into his slender microphone. Minutes later, a woman delivered a black dinner jacket.

"Fix your shirt," Headset ordered me.

He waited, holding the jacket by the shoulders, while I straightened my sleeves and tuck-in job. When I finished, he helped me into the jacket. Though heavy, it fit surprisingly well. It was only when he adjusted the tails that I felt my magic withering. The jacket was infused with lead meant to stunt my casting.

"Hey, man," I said.

"Keep it on," he snapped, reappearing in front of me. "Mr. Gang is waiting."

Last night I'd considered how Bashi hadn't controlled Chinatown this long by being a dolt, but the extent of his preparedness in this case surprised even me. As a test, I called a quantum of power to my mental prism and sent it down my arm. The invocation fizzled out before it even reached my elbow.

Grumbling, I followed Headset into the dining area.

We passed tables of Chinatown's elite: most of them graying men with women half their age and younger, swan-like necks glittering with expensive jewelry. Waiters moved among them with cloth-wrapped bottles and sizzling platters. The aromas were mouth-watering. If this hadn't been Bashi's domain, I would have considered bringing Ricki here for our anniversary.

At the back of the dining area, Headset opened a door to a sumptuous private suite where six men sat at a table arrayed with platters of food. Wang "Bashi" Gang sat in the center, facing the door. He was bedecked in a blinding white jacket and designer shirt that contrasted with his black spike cut.

This was my first time seeing him in the flesh since our

encounter almost four years earlier. And the *flesh* part was apropos. His basketball-round head looked as though it had been given several extra pumps while his multiple chins had proliferated. Sagging man breasts rested on either side of his overflowing plate.

The last few years had been good to the crime boss, evidently.

"Mr. Croft is here," Headset announced with a lowered head and promptly retreated from the room, closing the door.

Bashi squinted at me from behind a pair of yellow-tinted glasses. I raised a hand in greeting, my stomach taut with nerves.

To Bashi's right sat the bleach-haired henchman he'd sent for me the night before. I noticed some bruising below his eyes. That plus his nasty glare suggested he'd been punished for failing in his mission.

I assumed the rest of the men to be members of Bashi's inner circle—until one with his back to me turned and pushed a cowlick from his pudgy brow. I stared back at him, my mind scrambling to make sense of his presence opposite Manhattan's deadliest mobster.

"C'mon on over, Everson," Mayor Lowder said, angling out the chair beside him. "We all need to talk."

"Budge?" I finally managed. "What in the—what are you doing here?"

Bashi slapped the table hard enough to make the dishware jump. "Sit down!"

God, I'd almost forgotten about his screechy voice. I walked over and lowered myself beside the mayor. As I scooted my chair in, he clapped my shoulder as though to say *Hey, I know how this looks, but it'll all make sense shortly.*

As anxious as I was for it to make sense now, I had to remain focused on my reason for coming: to learn if the druids were operating out of Chinatown. Any connection with the pale woman would be a bonus. I took a calming breath and opened my hands to Bashi's corpulent form.

"All right," I said. "I'm here."

He squinted at me some more, making no attempt to disguise his loathing. He clearly hadn't forgiven or forgotten my recent trespasses. I still wondered why he hadn't sought retribution, but maybe the answer was sitting right next to me. Had the mayor been shielding me from his wrath this whole time?

When Bashi resumed shoving greasy noodles into his mouth, Budge launched into his pitch.

"Okay, Everson. As you might have noticed, Chinatown's been growing. Which is great for Manhattan," he hastened to add. "The developers are picky about the parts they're willing to restore, you see. They'll build here, renovate there, but they won't touch the gray zones. Not without the right incentives, and we don't have the budget. But having Chinatown grow into some of those areas... it really helps the city." He sounded as if he had to force out that last part.

Though Bashi continued to eat loudly, I sensed that his small ears were attuned to every word. The rest of the table was pin-drop quiet.

"But we've, ah, run into a little snag," Budge continued. "One we were hoping you could help us out with."

"Oh, yeah?" I said, as confused as ever.

"There are a few blocks just north of Chinatown, near Grand Street. Real eye sore, but Mr. Gang here has a mixed use proposal that would tie it all together nicely: apartments, restaurants, small businesses. He's even offered to maintain the park over there, which really helps us out."

"So, what's the problem?" I asked thinly.

Budge pulled out his phone and accessed a map that showed the zone in question, the blocks proposed for development shaded in yellow. He zoomed in on the one building highlighted in red.

"Problem's right here. We've tracked down all the other building owners and gotten them to accept cash offers. All except this one. An old hotel purchased under an LLC about two years ago. Never went back into operation, and we can't track the principals down—contact info's no good. They still pay their taxes, though, regular as clockwork."

"I'm sure the city can find another excuse to kick the door down," I said.

Budge chuckled nervously. "Yeah, we tried that. Thing is, it's protected by magic."

I stiffened. "Magic?"

Maybe I didn't have to ask Bashi about the druids. Maybe he'd just told me exactly where to find them.

25

"What kind of magic?" I pressed.

"Well, when a couple of our city marshals tried to ram the door, a fireball wiped them out," Budge said. "We've had surveillance on the building—well, Mr. Gang has—and his men report no comings or goings."

A veiling, like the one in the alleyway that afternoon, could have explained the apparent dearth of activity. Throw in the fireball, and these were sounding *a lot* like our druids.

"Needless to say, that's where we could really use you," Budge finished.

As I eyed the building on his phone, I remembered Jordan's criteria for their homebase. Proximity to nature? Check—it was one block from the aforementioned park. Rooftop with a view of the stars? Another check—no adjacent skyscrapers to block out the sky. In addition to veilings, the druids could have used other magics to keep the building vague for the past couple years. It was only when Bashi and the city locked in on the area that the building popped up on anyone's radar.

But even with the mounting evidence, I took special care to keep a poker face. Bashi had not only delivered me the druids' whereabouts, but also the chance to ask for something in return. As desperate as I was to raid the building and recover Edgar, I couldn't let this opportunity slip past.

"I'll help you," I said. "But I'd like something in exchange."

Bashi choked on his next swallow and stabbed his chopsticks into his dish. "*Exchange? How about not putting a bullet through your head?*" He stopped to cough violently, sending bits of noodles spraying across the table. "*Or your family's?*"

My protective instincts spiked at mention of my family, but I stared back as though I wasn't fazed. "Since you bring it up," I said, "I want lifetime immunity for us. I'll promise to stay out of your business if you stay out of ours."

"It is too late for you to stay out of my *business*," he seethed.

The mayor wrapped an arm across my shoulders and chuckled nervously.

"Do you, ah, mind if I speak with Everson in private for a moment?" he asked Bashi.

The mob boss grunted and made a dismissive gesture with his ringed fingers. He glared after me as I got up and followed Budge to the side of the room.

"*What are you doing?*" Budge whispered harshly.

"What do mean, 'what am I doing?' What in the hell are *you* doing, working with him?"

He sighed. "C'mon, Everson, we've had this conversation before. Your job is straightforward: find the bad guy—or thing—and stop it. As mayor, I don't have that luxury. I have to work with the hand I'm dealt, and right now, it means people like him. And look, he does keep the crime stats low in Chinatown."

"Yeah, 'cause he has the monopoly," I muttered.

"And listen," he said over me, "people like him don't take kindly to being strong-armed, especially in front of their subordinates. Let me handle your protection. Who do you think's kept him off your back all this time?"

Guilt straddled my conscience as he confirmed my earlier guess.

"And I'm not gonna be mayor forever," he continued. "Just tell him you'll help, and I'll make sure you never have to deal with his type again."

I considered what Budge was saying. I also considered that if Bashi wanted my help, he probably didn't have a powerful fae in his service. Which meant the White Hand must have gotten their ammo on the black market, as Ricki suggested, and the handprint on Edgar was coincidental. I'd committed the very human fallacy of seeing a pattern where none existed. No connection between pale woman and White Hand.

But as for the druids, I was certain this was them.

I refocused on Budge. "All right, but I'm gonna hold you to that."

"Have I let you down before?" He quickly showed his hands. "Okay, don't answer that. I know we hit a bump with the waterfront, but I did go into that shadow realm for you. My hospital stay wasn't the worst part of it, either. Did I tell you I'm seeing a shrink? Turns out spending time in a *parallel version* of yourself can rattle a few screws. And the sessions aren't cheap, Everson."

I gave a grudging nod. He *had* come through for us in the

shadow realm, big time, earning his redemption for the waterfront. "All right," I said. "But I'm not kidding about protection for my family."

"I know you're not, buddy. And that's what I like about you. You know your priorities."

With a companionable hand on my back, he escorted me back to the table. "He's in," he announced, grinning like a politician, for which he'd had some practice.

But Bashi's expression remained surly. "When?" he demanded.

"You're in luck," I said. "It just so happens I have a team around me. We'll be able to move tonight. I just need—"

"Team?" Bashi cut in. "No team. Just you!"

I squinted at him, at an honest loss. "Why? What's the problem?"

"*You or no one!*"

I turned to Budge, who nodded for me to acquiesce, but there was no way I was going to confront a dozen Black Earth druids, not to mention their demons, solo. It had taken all I had to put down the one at the IFC Center.

"Permission to approach the bench?" I asked Budge.

"This isn't making me look very good," he said when we arrived back at the wall. "I assured him of your cooperation."

"Listen," I whispered. "If the occupants of that building are who I think they are, it has to be more than just me. The police task force on the conjurings? Turns out a group of druids are behind them. They're calling up powerful demonic beings, and they kidnapped a boy for a ritual sacrifice. It gets better. The druids are under the control of a major demon, possibly to summon a demon lord."

"Geez." Budge dragged a hand through his hair. "And

here I was worried about the city budget. Is that all as bad as it sounds?"

"Put it this way, if they succeed, this development project is going to fall down your list of priorities faster than you can say 'big-time apocalyptic shit.' We need to do this right. I have people around me who can help, powerful druids and magic-users. This could be our best shot to shut them down."

"Look, I hear you." He paused to lick his lips. "Thing is, Mr. Gang wants to show he's in charge. The minute you subdue the occupants, he's going to send in his enforcers—you know, to 'finish the job.'" He air-quoted the words. "Make it look like it was his operation all along. He'll expect you to play ball, and that's where you'll get your immunity. But the minute you start bringing in other people..."

"The narrative gets harder for him to control," I finished for him. "Then let's make him understand the stakes." Bashi was a lot of things I didn't want to say out loud, but at least he was open to the supernatural.

Budge let out an aggrieved laugh. "Unfortunately, he's gotten less rational with age."

I followed his gaze to where Bashi was shrieking at one of his subordinates. The man kept his head bowed, even as Bashi hurled his glass at him. It nailed him in the forehead, cracking and dumping ice water all over his plate. Two White Hand enforcers entered the room, yanked the man from the table by his jacket and hair, and dragged him out through a side door. Muffled screams sounded beyond.

"He'll do a lot worse than that if you cross him," Budge whispered ominously.

I swore under my breath. On top of everything else—battling a circle of demon-possessed druids, rescuing Edgar, preventing Sathanas's possible return—I had to worry about propping up Bashi's main-character complex. But the clock was ticking. Something had to happen tonight, with or without a team.

"All right," I sighed. "Let me see what I can come up with."

26

"Here's what we're looking at," I said to my team, spreading the hotel's blueprint over the island counter in my basement lab.

While Budge was arranging to have the blueprint delivered to me from the Department of Buildings, Jordan had checked out the old hotel in his raven form. He'd had to coast low, but on his second pass he picked up veiling magic—and beneath it, a match to the energy he'd absorbed in the alleyway.

Huge score, but it didn't make the next steps any easier.

"Every entrance is going to be warded and mined with infernal magic," I began, circling them with a red pencil.

Bree-yark dragged over a footstool for a better view, while James, Loukia, and Ricki pressed to both sides of me. Jordan hung back, his dark eyes glinting beside the top of his planted quarterstaff. He was still keeping his distance from Petra, who watched from the other side of the island.

"Inside, I may be up against as many as a dozen druids," I

said. "Bashi wants them all 'subdued.' Same with any demons. And if they're like what I faced at the IFC Center, that's going to mean more banishment energy than I can probably summon. Once past them, I need to find Edgar, who's likely in one of these basement rooms. I'll have a better idea once I'm in."

We'd struck gold in the backseat of Bree-yark's Hummer, locating a fragile filament of the boy's reddish hair. A hunting spell had produced nothing, which wasn't a surprise. The building was covered in concealing magic. But on the other side of those concealments, I was counting on my spell to kick in.

"Then I need to get him out of there without any obvious outside help," I said, looking up. "I'm not trying to make this sound like *Mission Impossible: Druid Reckoning*, but those are the facts. Thoughts?"

"Why not just use one of Claudius's portals to pop in and out?" Bree-yark asked.

"He's been having some problems with that," I replied, wondering if he'd located his missing magic-user yet.

"There will also be dislocation cantrips," Petra put in, repeating something she'd told me earlier. "Attempts to portal in or out will send you to Brigit knows where."

"And given the druids' demonic sponsorship," I said, "'Brigit knows where' is likely to be the nastiest pit in the Below. So no shortcuts, unfortunately."

"Well, you're not doing this alone," James said, adjusting one of the holstered revolvers under his leather duster and cocking back his hat. "Loukia and I didn't come all this way to kick dirt on the sidelines."

"Yes, who is this Bashi person, and what can he actually do?" Loukia asked.

I grunted a laugh. "A lot, actually. Not only is he ruthless, but he has access to supernatural weaponry."

I glanced over at Ricki, who returned a solemn face. We both knew that our family was between a boss and a bullet. If I didn't play by Bashi's rules and conduct this mission solo, I would lose our immunity of the last four years. I thought of the subordinate who'd been dragged off at dinner. I didn't know what the man had done, but he'd whimpered a couple more times before going disturbingly quiet.

"Then maybe we should take care of *him* first," Bree-yark barked.

"That would involve another operation entirely," I said. "And we wouldn't be taking on one person but an entire criminal organization." I patted the blueprint. "C'mon, let's all stay focused on this."

"The Raven Circle is on standby, you know," Jordan said, referring to his fellow druids. Before I'd told him about my deal with Bashi, he'd been ready to storm the hotel with overwhelming force. In part, I suspected, to exact retribution against the Black Earth druids, something Petra picked up on now.

Her eyes smoldered. "Your circle isn't going anywhere near my sisters."

"Your sisters are the reason we're staring down the barrels of Armageddon," Jordan shot back. "With your pagan *god* worship."

"A demon infiltrated your nature circle, too," she seethed.

"Guys," I called. "You're arguing over nothing because no one's going in but me." I took a moment to collect myself. "Look, I keep thinking about how much this mirrors a case from a few years ago. But one important difference is that in the lead-up to my fight against Sathanas, I had no one. Ricki and I were closing in on the same person, sure, but we weren't exactly working in concert."

Sathanas had stressed that point in the ossuary under St. Martin's. *Alone,* he'd taunted, a word that struck more deeply than the barbed tail he would spear through my shoulder. *The poor wizard is all alone.*

The daunting memory was broken up by a dry scoff. Jordan stepped aside to reveal Tabitha, who was overspilling a chair seat, her eyes hooded at me in contempt. "Aren't you forgetting someone, darling?"

"Oh, right," I said. "I wasn't completely alone. I, ah, had you."

"Yes, who tipped you off to the demon moon and then sank her teeth into some of the foulest flesh I've ever tasted to save your pathetic self. Sometimes I wonder if I would have been better off letting events take their natural course."

"Indeed," I said. "Tabitha, ladies and gentlemen."

A smattering of applause went up.

"Ungrateful ass," she muttered.

"The point is, I have all of you now." I looked around at them emotionally. Two magic-users I had been isolated from for more than a decade. Two druids, one with whom I'd butted heads and another who had wanted me dead. Trusty Bree-yark, whom I'd met while he was housesitting for Gretchen. And, of course, my wife, who had brought me into the NYPD's fold, not to mention her intimate trust.

"Even if you can't fight alongside me," I said, "I can't do this without you. And look, you each have a lot to contribute. James and Loukia, we can repurpose your golems." I gestured to the beings they'd created for the hunt, the two of them propped like mannequins against the near wall. "Bashi may have forbidden us from going in as a team, but he didn't say anything about using animated clay."

"Remote ass-kicking," James said thoughtfully. "Yeah, I can work with that."

I turned to Jordan. "You've installed magic in my staff. You can do it again. You too, Petra, and you know your sisters better than any of us."

They glanced over at one another guardedly before returning nods of agreement.

Bree-yark, who was studying the blueprint from above his propped fists, grunted. "You know, Everson, I think I just found a way in for you."

I clapped his thick back. "You see?"

That just left one teammate. I turned to Ricki. She had proposed the Sup Squad as a standby force, but with Bashi's informants inside the NYPD, we had to nix the idea. Still, I needed an evacuation plan, and preferably several.

"Think you can arrange a passing helicopter?" I asked.

"Oh, is that all?" She smirked. "I'll see what I can do."

"Excellent." I patted the blueprint and waved the team closer. "Now let's take our combined assets and hone them into one kickass breach-and-rescue plan."

27

From my magical perch outside a window on the hotel's second floor, I studied the druids' ward. The fire symbol had been etched between the window and frame to detect entry. It was part of a building-wide network, and it looked much as Petra had sketched it: advanced, but not especially sophisticated.

With a steadying breath, I consulted my watch. The golems would be lumbering toward the front of the hotel about now, behaving just strangely enough to attract attention. The city's recent attempt to breach the hotel had undoubtedly put the druids on edge, something we planned to jujutsu to our advantage.

As the second hand on my watch ticked past midnight, I nodded to myself. *Go time.*

I slid the tip of my sword's blade into the side of the symbol and spoke an incantation. A tiny white flare erupted, draining off the infernal energy. I spoke another Word, infusing the symbol with replacement energy that Jordan had drawn from the druids' circle and made harmless. This would fool the network into believing the ward was still intact, even while it lacked any protective properties.

I released the latch lock with a simple invocation. Then, I wedged my blade under the window and pried until it budged. Wincing, I slid the window the rest of the way open. No fireballs or signs of an alarm. I stepped from my platform of hardened air into an empty room, leaving the window open a crack.

If everything went to plan, I'd be coming out this way.

Stealth magic vibrating from my coin pendant, I peered around for additional wards or tripwires. Nothing. Bree-yark had suggested the entry point, correctly recognizing it as a dummy room that hotels sometimes used to test different styles and decors. The absence of a bathroom had tipped him off.

Point one to Team Good Guys.

I accessed the hunting spell I'd cast on Edgar's fragile hair. Now that I was past the outer defenses, the magic latched onto something. My staff wiggled weakly toward the floor, possibly the basement, stoking me with relief. That increased the odds Edgar was not only in the hotel, but alive.

I peered into a dim corridor from the room. No druids in sight. At corridor's end, I drained another ward and replaced the energy before opening the door. The faint light of my staff illuminated the top of a staircase.

This is where I have to be really damned careful.

The building's electricity consumption suggested the druids weren't riding the elevators—Budge doubted they were even operational. Which meant that for vertical transit, the druids were using these narrow stairwells at either end of the building. I would be at my most vulnerable inside them.

I descended quickly, the stealth magic that radiated from my pendant silencing my pattering footfalls.

At the main floor, I paused to listen at the door. A group of voices murmured beyond. Not close enough to make out, but I imagined them discussing the spectacle of the two blocky figures shoving each other on the sidewalk out front, courtesy of James and Loukia.

Keep 'em busy, I thought as I resumed my downward journey.

The final flight of stairs ended at a thick steel door. The pull of my staff turned horizontal, confirming that Edgar was in the basement. I defused the door's ward and was about to test the handle when I paused. And thank God. Amid the patterns of energy, I caught a second ward pulsing from the other side.

Expelling my breath, I wedged the tip of my blade into the door's seam to access the symbol—and came an inch short.

Well, crap.

I checked my watch. With the building's outer defenses frustrating my ability to communicate with teammates, we'd timed everything out. We spaced the events such that I wouldn't feel rushed, but that I wouldn't have to impersonate a sitting duck, either. Translation: I had time to crack this second ward, but not much.

Producing a tube of ice crystals from a pocket, I thumbed off the lid and directed a blast of subzero frost up and down the doorframe. I just needed that extra inch of slide. Operating on the principle that cold contracted, I inserted the tip of my blade into the frostbitten seam and wedged it forward until...

Gotcha!

I incanted, breaching the edge of the symbol, draining it of infernal energy and replacing it with the ringer.

I then swapped the empty tube of crystals for a vial with a brush built into the cap. The potion turned a luminescent silver as I activated it and began painting it beside the door handle. The outer layer of metal appeared to dissolve away, but I was actually applying a remote viewing potion that worked across inches. Within moments the potion "broke" through the door, and I was squinting through a peephole into the corridor beyond.

A pair of druids in gray hooded cloaks stood watch beside a closed door. I checked the hunting spell again. It was twitching like a compass needle gone haywire, the chaotic energies down here making it difficult to get an exact reading. Still, the odds were good that Edgar was behind the door.

And I had about five minutes to recover him.

Enveloping the hinges in my pendant's aura of stealth, I pressed the handle. The door released soundlessly. I slipped my staff through the opening, tapped into Jordan's spell, and took aim at the druids.

"*Liberare*," I whispered.

The freed magic impacted the cement floor between them, sending up a dusty cantrip. Before they could bring their wands into casting positions, the druids stiffened from the powerful paralytic magic. In a burst of pink, a second cantrip detonated from the first, this one dropping the druids off to sleep.

I gave Jordan my silent thanks as the guards toppled to the floor.

I sealed the stairwell with locking magic and hurried over to the druids. Grabbing their wands, I stored them in a bag of neutralizing salt. I then defused the door they'd been guarding and opened it onto what the blueprint had labeled a laundry room. But one sniff told me it was no longer in the business of washing dirty linen.

Large metal containers lined the room—pill-shaped coffins that gave off a putrid smell, like rotting shrimp. Tubes ran from old washer hookups to the containers, while a red ball of thermal magic hovered overhead, heating the space to sweltering and sending sweat trickling from my hairline.

To my left, a wall of shelving held dozens of fluid-filled jugs and open cages. A closer look at one of the cages showed sigils etched into the metal: obfuscations to hide the box's contents. The cage was about one foot by two, the same dimensions of the covered object the druid had been carrying from the alleyway that afternoon.

I turned back to the metal coffins.

If that was a baby demon, this must be their incubation center.

One of the coffins stood open, empty save for a puddle of dark fluid. I followed a dribbling trail from the coffin to an open ventilation shaft where the hotel's industrial dryers would have been. Dollars to demons, the liquid contained some sort of growth formula along with a homeopathic dose of holy essence to immunize them.

This must have been the path the creature had taken en route to attacking Swami Rama. Fortunately, I was looking at the only open container and trail in the room. None of the other demons had been released yet.

A low squelch sounded, making me start. It had come from a container to my right—a demon shifting in its soup. I felt a sudden urge to open all the containers and blast their occupants from existence, stealth be damned.

Instead, I blew out a shaky breath.

The priority was to find Edgar and get him to safety.

Denied their child sacrifice, the druids couldn't summon
Sathanas. With Armageddon off the table, I would subdue
the remaining druids, undo the hotel's defenses (allowing
Petra to recover her Black Earth sisters incognito), banish the
casketed demons in situ, and then turn the hotel over to
Bashi, all of his conditions having been met.

But a check of my watch showed I was running low on
time. The golems would be attacking the hotel's front doors
soon, which would distract the druids and give me the opportunity to escape with a child I'd theoretically have in my
possession.

I took a final, baleful look at the demon incubators. Then,
adjusting my sweat-soaked grip on my staff, I tuned into the
hunting spell.

Still no clear pull, I thought, *but he's not in the incubation
center.*

Back in the corridor, I stepped around one of the slum-
bering druids and began counting doors, aligning them with
the floor plan. We had ranked the basement rooms by the
likelihood they were holding Edgar, but the count was off. I
was preparing to start again when the door to the stairwell
shook.

28

When the stairwell door shook again, I picked up voices like the ones I'd heard upstairs. I blocked them out to focus on the corridor. I started my count a third time, pairing each door to a basement room on the building's blueprint.

There!

Focusing on the blank wall opposite the incubation chamber, I uttered, "*Rivelare.*"

The cement wall wavered, and the outline of the door to the missing room took shape. The druids hadn't just been guarding the room at their backs—they'd also been watching the one before them. A bathroom, according to the blueprint.

As the veiling dissipated, the hunting spell in my staff surged to life, yanking me forward. I dispelled another ward and pushed the door open.

I stopped and stared at the crib before me. Little Edgar lay inside, clad in diapers and curled up in a ball. He wasn't physically restrained, but I sensed an aura of incapacitating magic around him. Petra had anticipated this, and I was relieved to see that he was breathing, his frail ribs rising and falling in a rapid rhythm.

Hell. Yes.

As I accessed Petra's spell, I glanced around the rest of the bathroom. A portable shelf held blankets, wet wipes, packs of disposable diapers, cans of toddler formula. By all appearances, he'd been well cared for.

Yeah, until you consider the druids were preparing him for a demonic sacrifice.

A bright pain compelled me to tune into my locking spell on the stairwell door. The magic of the arriving druids was colliding against it now.

I quickly lowered my staff into the aura surrounding Edgar. Petra's magic sizzled red, absorbing the druidic elements of the incapacitating spell and scattering the rest. Edgar stirred in his sleep.

"It's okay, buddy," I whispered. "I've got you. For real this time."

I opened my coat, revealing an ergonomic toddler carrier strapped to my front. It had been a baby shower gift from Ricki's oldest brother and his wife, though it wouldn't fit Abigail for at least another year.

I lifted Edgar from the crib, struck again by how little he weighed, and took a moment to study his energy signature. Yes, the lines and color patterns were a match. And I could still make out the lingering thumbmark on his forehead. Confident I had the actual boy and not an illusion, I lowered him, facing me, into the seat. I adjusted the neck support to secure his large head and strapped him snug.

I left the bathroom and turned toward the stairwell door opposite the one under assault. Best case, the druids had been coming down for a shift change. Even so, they had to know something was off by now. And once they took a closer look at the wards, they would see the fake magic and work backward, leading them to the cracked-open window. That made my planned escape route too risky.

Fortunately, we'd worked out a backup.

I checked my watch. A bit behind schedule, but they were seconds I could make up.

Edgar's legs jostled below the carrier as I jogged toward the far stairwell. I was nearly there when my locking spell failed. The stairwell door behind me burst open. I spun and took in a pair of cloaked druids. I'm sure I looked as absurd to them as I felt, but the point of the carrier had been to free up both my hands.

With no time to access another of Petra's spells, I thrust my sword and shouted, "*Vigore!*"

The force blast expanded as it rocketed the length of the corridor. But the lead druid arced her wand, incinerating the invocation in a flash of sulfuric fire. Unlike the basement sentry, I hadn't caught these two by surprise. Not only that, they looked seriously pissed off.

"Return the *Puer!*" the lead one screamed, fire growing from her wand.

Petra had been right. Edgar was their *Puer*, or Child, whose star was to align in the next twenty-four hours.

"*Protezione!*" I cried, willing a shield into shape.

Gleaming with banishment energy, it caught the druid's infernal blast, reducing it to an explosion of smoke and ashes. With another Word, I sent back an arrow-shaped force from my protection. But once again, the lead druid dispersed it with the slash of her wand, scattering its impact.

Two fireballs roared back this time.

Can't do this all night, I thought, grunting from the balls' one-two punch against my shield. They weren't giving me a chance to access the stored spells in my staff—or even to dispel the wards on the stairwell door at my back.

And the damned seconds were ticking further and further away from me.

With the prospect of more druids arriving, I reinforced my shield and reached back for the door handle. My best option now was to trigger the door's incendiary traps and try to absorb them like a champ.

I hesitated when I heard a surprised cry. Through the dispersing ashes of the last fireball attack, a hulking figure came into view. The figure was missing an arm and half of its head. One of our golems!

"Bro, I can't keep this up forever," James called in a deep, moaning voice. He kicked one of the druids into a wall and dropped his fist on the other one's back. "Same goes for Loukia. She's trying to block them from your end."

"I owe you, buddy!" I called back, quickly draining off the two wards and pulling the door open onto the stairwell.

"A blunt would be nice," he replied. "Big, fat one."

I stole a final look back in time to see his golem form explode into clay rubble. He'd surprised the druids, but their magic had overwhelmed his already damaged form. I slammed the door closed against a stream of fireballs, wincing from the blasts of heat through the metal.

"We're still good, buddy," I said, rubbing the curve of Edgar's back.

I bounded up the stairs, taking two and three steps at a time. As I reached the first floor landing, I could hear the sounds of battle coming from outside: Loukia's golem versus the druids. She and James must have broken into the hotel to slow the stampede toward the basement. We'd added magical resistance to the golems, but as a hail of debris rang against the door, I knew hers had just reached its limit.

Footsteps echoed in the stairwell below as the druids began to climb. Thanks to my recent spate of casting, my pendant's stealth magic was depleted. I was making a racket. Although I had a one-flight lead, I would need to open the final door to the rooftop, and a one-flight lead wasn't enough time.

For the past three months, I had resisted using my blade's third rune, the one that Hermes had imbued with his magic. I'd wanted to save its power for my attempt to visit Alec, the son of my shadow. But times were desperate, and I struggled to steady my raised blade long enough to focus on the rune.

The rune's edges glinted green, and I felt the Hermes atoms in my system gather and oscillate. At first, I thought nothing was happening—my speed seemed to remain constant. But then I noticed the sounds of the pursuing druids getting fainter. I slowed abruptly as I neared the restricted door at the top of the stairwell, feeling woozy. As my head cleared, it sounded as if my one-floor lead had grown to four.

I drained what I prayed would be my final ward of the night, hurried up a set of metal steps, smashed through a push-bar door, and broke out onto the rooftop. The night air chilled my sweaty skin. I sealed the door with a locking spell and checked my watch, panting out a surprised laugh. I was a little ahead of schedule.

As the Hermes magic left my system, I turned toward the sound of rotary blades. It wasn't an NYPD helicopter, but one of TV20's traffic helos. Ricki had cultivated a good relationship with the producer, and she had called in a favor: a flight path over the hotel at this precise time. Our backup plan.

As the helicopter came in low, I palmed the back of Edgar's warm head and readied an invocation to catch our ride out.

The druids were at the door to the final stairwell, and I could feel their infernal magic colliding against my locking spell. But I would be up and away before they broke through. Jordan was waiting at the TV20 heliport with a basket of druidic protections and any healing magic that Edgar might need.

"You doing alright, buddy?" I whispered, giving the boy a small jostle. "This is almost over."

His legs kicked below the carrier, and he emitted a soft cry. Good—signs of life. I manifested a shield of hardened air around us, then extended it toward the helicopter's landing skids as they passed overhead.

Got you!

My feet lifted from the gravel rooftop. I brought my hand to the back of Edgar's head to steady him, then jerked it away.

Hot, hot, hot!

I looked down, alarmed to see his carrier breaking into flames. And then a fireball erupted around us.

29

The force of the fiery blast threw me against the rooftop's retaining wall. I lay there for a moment, stunned and broken-feeling, potions leaking from my jacket. Beyond my splayed legs, a field of flames swept the rooftop. Its tar was already starting to bubble, casting up noxious black smoke. Above the hellscape, the helicopter was veering away, a jacket of flames rip-roaring from its tail rotor.

Find the child...

I pawed for Edgar, but the fire had torn the carrier open. I encountered my coin pendant instead, its protections having spared me the worst of the fire blast. When I craned my neck, I expected to find the Black Earth druids bursting onto the rooftop, wands ablaze, but the door remained shut and sealed.

"Edgar!" I called hoarsely.

The wind shifted, blanketing me in smoke. Eyes burning, I dug into a pocket in search of my ice crystals, but their tubes had shattered alongside the others. Hacking, I gained my knees—chest hurting like hell—and recovered my staff and sword. Using the retaining wall, I pushed myself the rest of the way up.

Man, *everything* hurt like hell.

"Edgar!" I tried again, listening for a cry, a cough, something.

Ignoring my pain, I raised my blade and concentrated into the second rune. The etched lines glinted red and white. I pulled, willing the flames into the symbol for fire, drawing down the inferno over the rooftop. When it was done, I staggered against the wall, searching the smoke for the boy.

"Everson Croft," a rakish voice said.

Out in front of me, a figure took form. He was tall with sunken cheeks, round shades, and blazing-red hair slicked back from a narrow brow. His collarless shirt was buttoned to his throat, while a trench coat batted around a pair of snakeskin leather boots. He sauntered forward in a way that suggested our matching coats was a deliberate taunt. But where mine was tattered and crispy, his was inexplicably pristine. This had to be the demon who had hijacked the druids' god and taken control of Black Earth.

"Where's Edgar?" I demanded, willing power to my blade's rune for banishment. "Where's the boy?"

A knowing smile creased the demon's thin lips.

"You killed him?" I growled.

He laughed. "So presumptuous. I *am* him."

When he shook his right leg, a set of small toes, charred and brittle, spilled from his boot onto the smoking gravel. In disturbing flashes, I saw Sathanas breaking from Father Vick, splitting and incinerating the shell of his body until it fell to pieces around him. The demon before me grinned with a perfect set of white teeth.

"We grow up *so* fast, don't we?"

I looked wildly around. There had been no ceremony, the Child star had yet to align. I'd recovered Edgar in plenty of time. We'd frustrated the demon and druids' plan. This didn't make any goddamned sense.

"I would ask if you were surprised, but that much seems evident," he said.

His smile turned vicious as he ground the husk-like toes underfoot. I narrowed in on his shades, black voids that absorbed rather than reflected the light from the pockets of fire around him. He was one hundred percent demon.

But was he *the* demon?

"You're not Sathanas," I said under my breath, as though declaring as much would make it so.

"Well, no and a little bit yes." He assumed a contemplative face. "I'm his son. You can still call me Edgar, in fact. But patrilineage operates differently in our world. My father can express himself through our connection."

I stared, still stuck on the "I'm his son" part.

He laughed harshly, sounding more like his father now. "You didn't think I put my entire chip stack on strong-arming my way out of that church those years ago? No, no, no, no. I'd had too long to plan, my friend. Centuries. When your silly vicar tried to exorcise me from those old bones, he granted me more than just the use of his body. I also claimed his *influence*. Yes, all it took was a suggestive whisper here, a 'come hither' look there, and a pretty young thing like Ms. Mary was only too eager to avail me of her womb."

I suddenly felt ill to my stomach.

Mary had said the father had never been a part of Edgar's life. Very true, because he'd been Father Victor. Father Victor, whose room was right there on the church grounds. Father

Victor, under the control of the demon lord Sathanas. Father Victor, gone too soon, months before Mary would give birth to their child.

"And here I am," the demon spawn said with a small curtsey.

Now it all made sense. The Black Earth druids had never intended to sacrifice Edgar. They had been protecting him until he could come into his own. But having just arrived, how powerful could he be?

Only one way to find out.

I'd been concentrating into my blade's banishment rune as he talked, summoning the power of the collective. It arrived now, softening the burns and bruises over my body while priming me with its raw power.

"Now that we've completed the introductions," Edgar said, "I believe we have some unfinished business." Though his voice continued to gloat, I sensed the rage that smoldered under every word. He was a demon prince of Wrath, after all. And he was addressing the one who had banished his father.

"Not for long," I growled, tearing the incinerated toddler carrier from my chest and thrusting my sword.

The blade crunched above his glistening belt buckle and through his stomach, all the way to the first rune. Perfect shot, right through the core. Banishment light sang from the blade, enveloping his demonic form. At the same moment, the door to the rooftop burst open, and the Black Earth druids came pouring out.

Are you freaking kidding me?

But despite being skewered, Edgar raised a hand, signaling for them to stay back. Why, though? And why wasn't he counterattacking? I may not have understood his confidence, but I couldn't allow it to undermine my own. My whole-souled job was to rid him, and his father, from the world once and for all.

Driving the gathered power of the collective into the blade, I shouted, "*Disfare!*"

I winced from the surging light, and Edgar arched his neck back. The entire rooftop shone like a star. But when the light faded, the demon prince was still standing in front of me.

What in the hell's holding him together?

"Oh, Everson," he said, his laughter jostling my sword as he straightened again. "You really must take me for a fool."

Grunting, I redoubled my grip on the sword hilt.

"That's right, try again," he said. "I have another surprise for you."

As I set my shaking legs and gathered every available joule of power, he angled his head to the side and mouthed something.

"*DISFARE!*" I bellowed.

My remaining reserves stormed through my casting prism and out the banishment rune. With the strength of the collective containing me, I didn't hold back. I became an open dam, a pure channel, a mighty vessel.

I'm a magic-user of the Order, goddammit...

My entire body quaked with the torrent of raw power. Surely this would end him.

But Edgar continued to resist. I strained for a decisive surge, the one that would overwhelm him once and for all, but my power faltered, then flagged. As the light faded from my blade, creamy waves rushed in. They arrived from all sides, pummeling me like the surf.

No...

As I fell, I heard a voice—a strong, bass voice that I'd hoped never to hear again. It was my incubus, Thelonious.

Ooh, yeah, he purred.

30

The creamy light of Thelonious's realm rolled over me, layer upon layer. I struggled to swim up against it, to hold onto my consciousness, but the throb of the realm's baseline grew stronger as I was dragged ever deeper. At last, I was shoved into a dazzling space of diffuse light and inchoate forms.

"Everson, baby," came a rich voice.

Though everything was indistinct, the place had the feel of a palatial nightclub.

Ahead, the light thickened around a massive, reclined figure. But this wasn't the Thelonious I remembered. Years earlier, the demon-vampire Arnaud had tortured him for info, reducing him to a wrecked spirit and his realm to a cheerless shadow. I'd likened it to a convalescent home, where I was the only visitor. And every time I'd visited, Thelonious appeared more withered and frail.

In fact, I'd been hoping to get out of our bargain by him simply dying.

Now, the sheer power of the light and constant bass note, as well as his rich voice, spoke to his former glory—and then some. A harem of sensuous forms streamed around his corpulence, attending to his every need. I was standing in party central. The only thing missing was a glittering disco ball.

"Thelonious?" I asked to be sure I had the right incubus.

"Indeed, indeed," he replied with a pleasant laugh. "Welcome back, young blood."

"What the hell's going on? What am I doing here?"

"That's why I brought you down, to explain everything. But first, how are you liking my new digs?"

"You've gotta send me back," I said desperately. "I'm getting butchered up there."

I imagined some combination of Edgar, the Black Earth druids, and the summoned demons flaying me open and flame-broiling my insides. I had let everyone down. My family and friends, the Order, the city...

But Thelonious chuckled some more. "Relax yourself, young blood. You're nowhere, remember?"

He was right. I was in a parallel plane, outside space and time.

"Now just sit yourself down and listen." He cocked his head, prompting several of his harem to stream toward me.

One pressed her hands to my chest and pushed. Titters sounded as I wheeled my arms around to stay upright, but I landed in a cloud-like recliner that had been positioned behind me. I resisted the urge to thrust myself back up. I needed to stay cool, study my hand, work the cards to my benefit somehow.

"You've been good to me, Everson," Thelonious said in his rumbling voice. "You kept your word about visiting when I was a big, fat zero and no one would touch me with a ten-foot pole. You could've stopped coming, and I couldn't have done

a damned thing. You're a stand up cat, and I appreciate that."
I didn't like his somber tone—it was like he was preemptively
apologizing.

"So what's going on?" I was already starting to assemble
some pieces, so his answer came as little surprise.

"This big-time player paid me a visit."

"Sathanas," I muttered. Or one of his hench-demons.

"Thought he had come for the same thing as that last one,
the one who broke me. So I told him, 'You want to split this
old beggar's wig, go right ahead, 'cause I don't have a thing for
you, and I'll probably be better off.' But the cat only laughed
and said I had it all wrong. Said he'd come to bestow a gift."

The minute Petra had mentioned Sathanas's return, I
should have taken stock of my vulnerabilities, my bargain
with Thelonious topping that list. But I hadn't taken his
return seriously enough. I allowed reason to intrude. I
thought him too immense to enter our world undetected. It
never occurred to me that the demon lord had already seeded
his return the last time he was here. Very literally.

"Yeah, he knew about our bargain," Thelonious
confirmed. "Said he could give me back my mojo, make it so I
could take you over whenever the mood struck. But there was
a string." His voice turned contrite again. "Whenever he gives
the word, I *have* to take you over, whether I'm in the mood or
not."

That must have been what Edgar had mouthed on the
rooftop, the word that bonded them.

"But listen here, young blood. I couldn't not take that
deal. My entire reason for being is to groove on the fairer sex,
and I couldn't make a single move in my sorry shape. It's been
so lonesome. That cat showing up like he did, telling me
what he could do for me..." He released a rumbling laugh,

deep with pleasure, before catching himself. "Anyway, I felt I owed you the whole truth."

"I'll be sure to nominate you for a Ridenhour," I grumbled.

He showed his hands. "Hey, I am what I am. I've never claimed different."

As desperate as my situation had become, he was right. Thelonious was an incubus. He hadn't tricked me into summoning him in Romania—I'd done it of my own free will. In fact, I was *alive* because I'd summoned him. And despite all the compromising situations he'd put me in over the years, often without pants, he had never hurt me.

I got that some small part of him regretted putting me in this position. The question now was how much mileage I could get from that regret?

"What does he want with me?" I asked.

"A big shot like him?" Thelonious tilted his head in thought. "Probably to show you're nothing more to him than a toy. Not only that, but you're so insignificant, he's delegated playtime to yours truly." He shook his head in an unconvincing show of sympathy. "I'm telling you, those demons are all kinds of wrong."

I stood from the recliner and paced the creamy space that shook with each bass note. Edgar had been confident on the roof, even with my blade coming out his back, but in that contact, I'd felt Sathanas. I'd felt vestiges of his banishment under St. Martin's, the agony of being blown into a billion particles and cast back down.

He feared it could happen again.

"That could be part of it," I replied, "but there's another reason he's keeping me alive."

"Well, I don't know anything about it," Thelonious said,

which was no doubt true. Sathanas may have pumped him full of super unleaded, but Thelonious was only a means to keeping me powerless. The incubus was as insignificant to the demon lord as... well, an incubus to a demon lord. He wouldn't have shared his motives.

I leveled my gaze at him. "What will it take for you to release me?"

Thelonious shook his head some more. "Sorry, young blood. Can't happen. And not just 'cause I'm back in black. The fat cat made it so if I try to junk our bargain, I'll die sure as I'm luxuriating here."

I had known releasing me was out of the question. I wanted to compromise down, get him to make another concession, however small.

"Look, I'm a family man now," I said. "I'm married and we just had our first baby. It can't be like before, you using me to... you know. If you're truly sorry about this, tell me what I can do to keep you from taking me over."

Though I was still asking a lot, Thelonious's silence unnerved me.

"You seem pretty well off down here," I pressed. "And like you said, you're not always in the carousing mood."

"Hmm," he said at last. "That cat made me pretty potent. But you've gotten plenty strong yourself. I'm not sure I can come barging in when your mind's sharp and your magic's topped off, but it's not like you're gonna stop casting."

And there it was: *stop casting.*

How, I had no idea. With Edgar's arrival and Sathanas's second coming more imminent than ever, I couldn't just close up shop. Not unless the Order was en route. But the more I thought about it, the less I liked what Claudius had said about the senior members responding to a massive rupture in an outer plane. It was too reminiscent of the Harkless Rift, where they'd become trapped by a major demon.

"And you have no idea what Sathanas is planning?" I asked. "There's nothing you might have picked up?"

"Not a thing, young blood. Not a thing."

He signaled to his harem. They streamed away and reappeared with what passed for food and drink in his realm. They teased and tickled him as they served his boundless appetite. The space shook with his contented laughter.

"So now what?" I demanded.

He smacked his lips. "Well, it's after midnight in your city. Once I'm good and fed, I'm gonna go check things out. Been a minute since I was last up there, and there are some ladies who've been missing me. But how about this? I promise to just look this time. Come morning, I'll let you back in your body."

I didn't trust his promise to "just look" any farther than I could throw him.

"How about you skip to the 'letting me back in my body' part," I suggested.

He laughed. "You've got bigger problems than me right now, young blood."

A charge went off in my chest. "What do you mean?"

"You'll see." He heaved himself up, sending his harem streaming away. "Come morning, you'll see ..."

"Hey, wait!"

But his giant form was already fading away, the creamy waves of his realm lapping back over my consciousness.

31

I inhaled sharply and cracked my swollen eyelids to complete darkness. By the feel of things, I was sitting propped up in a corner. By the smell of things, it was nowhere good: sickness, dank mildew, and something astringent.

I dragged a hand through my stiff hair and clamped my throbbing temples. "Sweet Jesus," I rasped.

When Thelonious had said he planned to play catchup, he wasn't kidding. The last time I'd been even half this hungover was with James out in Grimstone County. I shifted from one bruised butt bone to the other, sending up a scent of smoke and liquor from my clothes and detonating a small acid bomb in my gut. I mewled pathetically and twisted the front of my shirt until the pain diminished.

What in holy hell had Thelonious gotten up to last night? More importantly, *where* in holy hell had he gotten up to?

Beyond my extended legs, I noticed a weak bar of light. A door space. It illuminated my extended shoes, the glint of an opal stone (the end of my cane, thank God), and the edge of a rolling mop bucket.

Must be in some sort of janitorial closet.

Cane clutched to my chest, I shimmied my back up the wall until I was standing. Everything spun, and a throbbing mask opened over my face, suggesting I'd been hit a few times.

I still had my coin pendant and Grandpa's ring. Good. Among the shattered potions in my coat pockets, an intact vial of dragon sand remained. I also had my keys and my wallet. Not bad for a Thelonious visit.

More than anything, though, I needed my phone. Needed to call home. Ricki would be as worried for me as I was for her. When I found it in my coat's inside pocket, I grunted with joy, then disappointment. While the indicator showed enough battery, there was no signal. The time read 6:05 a.m. Friday.

What had Thelonious said?

You've got bigger problems than me right now, young blood. Come morning, you'll see.

I'd wanted him to explain, but wasn't it obvious? Sathanas's son was in the city going on six hours now, plenty of time to wreak havoc. I tried calling Ricki anyway, but my phone returned the dreaded double-beep of no signal.

I stumbled against the door and wrenched the handle. Locked. I was girding myself for a force blast when I remembered something else Thelonious had said. With his incubus powers at full tilt, my best chance of blocking him was to keep my own power topped off. No casting, in other words.

All right, basic physics, then.

With a grunt, I threw my weight against the door and crumpled from the impact. I drew the vial of dragon sand from my pocket and pressed it to my aching forehead in thought. Activating the sand would require only a fraction of the energy of casting an invocation. Would that leave me a full-enough tank?

Only one way to find out.

I pushed two granules into the keyhole and croaked, "*Fuoco.*"

The trickle of power fed the sand, igniting it in a growing hiss. But as the lock began to smoke, creamy clouds crowded my vision. I pushed against them, pleading for Thelonious to give me a break. By the time the lock's metal began to boil, the clouds relented. With a gasp of relief, I shoved the door with a foot.

That had been too damned close.

The door yawned open onto a dim corridor. I followed it into a large room with cocktail tables clustered around several spaced-out stages. Spangled curtains hung from the walls.

Surprise, surprise, Thelonious took us to a strip club.

Lines of LED lights illuminated a path to the front door. As I broke into a shamble, new parts of me ached and protested, but nothing felt permanently damaged. Good, because I wouldn't have been able to heal myself.

"If you like your head intact, you're gonna back away from that door."

I stopped and turned to find a musclebound man with a tight shirt and a mane of dark hair standing from a chair beside the nearest stage. As he stalked toward me, he raised a shotgun.

"Look, man," I said, too busted-up to feel threatened. "I'm just trying to get out."

He squinted. "It's *you.*"

"Me, who?"

"Mr. Hands."

Based on the venue, the nickname made it easy enough to guess what had gone down last night. So much for Thelonious's promise to just look. "Hey, whatever happened, I'm sorry. I was out of my head."

"Yeah, that's what they all say by the time I'm through with them," the bouncer snarled. "If it weren't for Casey, you would've eaten much more than the stock end of this thing."

That explained the state of my face, as well as my presence in a locked closet. I tongue-probed a loose molar and swallowed a fresh trickle of blood. "Be that as it may, I've learned my lesson. Can you put that down now?"

"Not until you back from the door. All the fucking way."

My fist tightened around my cane. Normally, I would have encased myself in a shield and sent this joker sailing the length of the room, pieces of shotgun trailing behind him. But thanks to Thelonious's resurgence, just attempting to use my wizard's voice felt dicey, never mind invoking.

"C'mon, man," I said. "The night's over. I just want to leave."

"Well, that's not happening, and I-I'm not gonna warn you twice."

His voice had caught mid-sentence, and as he glanced past me, I caught a flash of fear in his eyes. This was less about detaining me, and more about maintaining the integrity of the door.

Remembering again what Thelonious had said, I asked, "What's happening out there?"

He must have heard my honest concern because he lowered the gun to his waist. "I-I didn't see." His voice was really rattling now. "Casey got the best look. I only heard what happened when the place emptied out. And—and the aftermath."

"What did you hear?"

"Screaming, mostly. And ripping, like limbs being torn from sockets. Some of the crowd made it back inside. The rest?" He shook his head in a way that said he didn't want to know what had become of them.

The floor had been sticky when I crossed it—from what, I hadn't wanted to imagine. But now I made out a stampede of bloody shoeprints. I pictured the demon pods back at the hotel. Had the druids released the rest of them? Were they out in the city now, hunting and plundering souls for Sathanas?

I checked my phone again, but it was still signal-less.

"Do you have a working phone in here?" I asked him.

"Lines and cell signals are all dead. Power, too." He nodded at the LED lights. "Those are running off battery."

He tensed when I approached the door, but I only wanted to press my ear against it. I didn't hear anything beyond the metal, not even the droning of traffic or the blare of a car horn. Unusual for the city at six a.m. on a weekday.

"I thought he told you to get away from there."

A tall, ginger-haired woman entered the room, her white slacks and gold jacket glowing through the gloom. As she came closer, I could see that both were smeared with blood. Streaks had also gotten onto her face. She must have been tending to the wounded. Her shrewd eyes, heavy with age and dark liner, regarded me coolly.

"You must be Casey," I said distractedly. "I'm Everson."

"I know who you are. Guess you don't remember me."

I was readying my lines about being out of my mind last night, and apologizing for anything I might have done, when her features suddenly lined up with a face from years earlier. And then a name.

"Casey Lusk?" I said. "You danced at that club for—what was his name? Sonny?"

Memories of tackling Sonny to the floor after he'd threatened her returned all at once. Ricki had been there, too. We were pursuing a trail of leads after Arnaud Thorne had kidnapped her son, my now stepson.

"If you mean that lowlife, piece-of-shit vamp, yeah," Casey replied. "The place was called *Seductions* back then. Now it's *The Kitten Club*." She nodded at a suggestive pink sign over the bar. "An improvement in more ways than one."

"You work here?"

"*Own* here. Thanks to whoever ventilated Sonny."

Though I was glad she'd moved up in the world of after-dark entertainment, there were more pressing matters at hand.

"What in the hell happened last night?" I asked.

She rubbed at a streak of dried blood on the back of her hand before looking up. "It was closing time after a pretty meh night. Most of the patrons had already left. One was back in the closet, detoxing after drinking his weight in bourbon and getting fresh with the girls." She narrowed her eyes at me.

"Gabe here had gone to see if you could stagger home on your own. We have a two strikes rule, and you were still on your first. That left me to lock the main doors. That's when the smoke came storming in. Smelled like a chemical fire and so thick you couldn't see a damned thing. I heard cars smashing up, and then people screaming. Couldn't make out much, 'cept for this big shadow that swooped down and grabbed someone off the sidewalk. Ralph, I think—one of our regulars."

That seemed to conform to my demon theory.

"Only seven made it back in before I managed to get the door closed against that thing. The girls and I have been doing everything we can to stop the bleeding. We can't reach 911, not even on the emergency line, and we've already lost one fucker. Another's looking pretty bad."

She conveyed everything matter-of-factly, befitting someone who'd spent most of her adult life in the city's underworld, but she couldn't have understood the scale of what was happening. Sathanas's son loose in the city... Demons ripping souls from bodies... A city covered in infernal smoke and fire...

The enormity of it all made me dizzy. To spare my mind, I focused on what was most important to me at the moment.

"Listen, I'll send help, but I've gotta get home," I said. "Is there a car I can borrow?"

She cast her eyes to the side in thought. "Dwayne is back there, another one of our regulars. Drives a giant Silverado. Compensating, if you ask me, but not for much longer. I'll be surprised if he makes it till noon."

I nodded guiltily. "That'll work."

When Casey left, I noticed that the bouncer had returned to his chair—a safe distance from the door but still close enough to cover it with his weapon. He was wide-eyeing it as if expecting the drawbar to snap at any moment. Casey returned and handed me a keychain with a thick rubber fob.

"Quickest way to the parking lot is out back."

She led me past what must have been the changing area. I picked up the urgent voices of several women and a distinct scent of blood. I wanted to help, but without my magic I'd just be another body. Plus, my stomach was still deciding whether or not to eject its sloshing contents. I repeated my promise to Casey to send help.

The door in back was smaller than the one in front, but featured more bolts. Casey unsnapped them one by one, then paused, her fingers on the lowest bolt.

"Are you sure about this?" she asked. "Because once you're out, I'm not gonna open this door again. I barely got the main door closed."

"I understand. How long can you hold out in here?"

"There's enough food to last a couple days, and we've been storing water. What's coming from the faucets still looks clear."

"Good. Whatever you do, don't go outside."

"After what I saw? Wasn't planning on it." She smiled tightly. "Good luck, hon."

She patted my arm in a way that said she didn't expect to see me again and opened the door onto a smoke-filled lot. I made out the vaguest impression of a vehicle's front end a few feet away, and that was all.

Alert for demons, I ventured out. Behind me, Casey slammed the door closed and snapped the bolts home in a rapid line.

32

The smoke carried a hellish-yellow cast and a foul bite that felt as if it were stripping the membrane from my throat. No wonder Casey had thought it was from a chemical fire, but this smoke was demonic.

I lurched into a fast walk, glancing skyward as I clicked the vehicle's alarm button. Muted chirps sounded from the smoke. I hooked an arm overhead as I weaved around parked cars that seemed to rear up right in front of me. A pair of orange smears appeared, blinking in time to the chirps: Dwayne's truck.

Hallelujah.

I broke into a run, certain a demon was going to skewer my neck and yank me, flailing, into the thick haze. I was so used to summoning protections at will that lacking the power amplified my sense of vulnerability.

By the time I reached the truck, I was wheezing, but I'd made it, cervical spine intact. I locked the doors and sat back in the high cab to let my heart slow and my stomach settle. When I coughed into my handkerchief, it left spots of blood

—whether from the smoke or Thelonious's visit, I had no idea.

I swapped the kerchief for my phone, but it remained bar-less. The smoke wasn't just smothering sounds, but signals, apparently.

Dammit.

I dropped the phone in the center console, then paused to consider the faint white lines on the side of my hand. The Upholders sigil connected me to Jordan, but it also required power to activate—and there was no guarantee I could even reach him. I couldn't risk it, then, not with Thelonious so close.

Any discretionary energy will be for emergencies, I decided.

The truck's engine roared to life and settled into a muscular idle. I'd been worried it would be as dead as every-thing else. I played with the headlights until I found a low-beam setting that gave me the best visibility—about fifteen feet.

Baby steps, I coached myself.

I reversed from the space at a crawl, still managing to bang into something, and pulled from the back lot. First step accomplished. Now it was a matter of advancing a block at a time until I reached home.

I hadn't thought to ask Casey the address, but I remem-bered the old club being in Midtown, close to Times Square. As I pulled forward onto the empty avenue, I recognized an entrance to the Port Authority Bus Terminal. With my loca-tion pinned, I pulled up a mental map and worked out the fastest route to the apartment.

Manageable, I thought of the thirty-odd blocks between here and there. *Very manageable.*

Taking a left, I rolled the truck forward. The headlights

created an otherworldly orb ahead of me, like I was navigating the peaty depths of Loch Ness in a submersible. I weaved around one stalled car, then another, trying not to fixate on their shattered windows. But I couldn't kid myself, either. Even in a truck this size, a quarter inch of laminated glass wasn't going to protect me from a demon attack.

I scanned the smoke on all sides. *So this is what letting in a major demon looks like*, I thought sickly. *We had a pretty good streak going, too.*

But why hadn't Sathanas killed me on the rooftop?

I was happy to have a pulse, don't get me wrong, but the question bothered me. Was the idea to keep me alive long enough for him to gloat over his victory? Staying my execution seemed super risky, considering I'd banished him once already. Or did he have a plan in mind? The year before, the demon Malphas had tricked me into gathering essential elements for his arrival—and it had nearly worked.

A large shadow drifted beyond the reach of my headlights, knocking my heart off rhythm. I stomped the brake.

It was only when I lurched to a stop that I saw the intersection ahead. The shadow was a passing vehicle. I couldn't tell whether it was official or civilian, and it didn't slow. As it trundled under the flashing stop lights, I was tempted to honk, to advise them that the interfaith houses offered the best refuge. But with no way to know whether these were good guys or bad, I couldn't take the chance.

Being an impotent wizard sucked.

I continued forward, keeping a silent count to the next intersection. It ended up being one hundred eighty-four seconds, just over three minutes. At that pace, it would take ninety minutes to reach home, and that was on top of the

more than three hundred sixty I'd already been away. Baby
steps or not, that was too damned long.

I nudged the accelerator, trembling the needle past five
miles per hour.

The stalled-out cars arrived faster. I clipped a fender, my
truck's mass knocking the entire vehicle aside. And then I
was coming on my first body. I swerved around it, studying
the afterimage in my mind. A vagrant, judging from the ratty
clothes. He'd been ripped open, his face locked in a scream,
bloody holes for eyes.

My stomach churned some more as I imagined a demon
hooking its teeth through the man's orbital bones to rip out
his soul.

As much as I was trying to focus on the hazy globe of visibility ahead of me and nothing else, I wondered how far the
smoke extended, how much of the city it encompassed, and
how many victims it had claimed. I reminded myself that my
family and friends were in a protected space. They were also
armed with magic and magical implements. There were few
safer places in the city.

"That's right," I whispered. "You'll see when you get
there."

I locked eyes with my reflection in the rearview mirror.
There was a gash through my brow that I hadn't even felt, and
bruising around the bloodshot eye on the same side. It wasn't
my first beating, and it wouldn't be my last, but something in
my battered visage made me reconsider what I was doing.

Was I putting my family and friends in *more* danger by
going home?

I eased off the gas, dropping the needle back down. I'd
been so preoccupied with keeping Thelonious from taking
me over that I hadn't considered a more serious problem.

With Sathanas controlling the incubus, he could use our bond to find me whenever he wanted, wherever I happened to be.

And if I happened to be with my family and friends...

I rolled to a stop. Maybe I was better off going to one of the interfaith houses. The IFC Center was only a few blocks away. Safely inside, I could try to reach Ricki and the Order, take better stock of the situation.

With a decisive nod, I turned at the next intersection and set a new course for the IFC Center. I didn't bother consulting my magic. We would have that talk when I arrived. I'd done what it told me—I'd found the child. And where had it gotten me? In the middle of an infernal shitshow with a major demon on the loose and his minions ripping out souls willy-nilly. Oh, and I'd also been rendered powerless.

I hammered the steering wheel in frustration.

"I know, I know," I said from a clenched jaw. "Magic operates in its own dimension and on its own terms, beyond logic and intellect, blah, blah, blah. A magic-user has to go to it, not vice versa. The key is *faith.*"

I punctuated the word with another blow to the steering wheel. Because at that moment, my faith felt a world away. I took a deep breath and exhaled slowly.

Maybe another reason to stop at the IFC Center.

33

Three blocks, and a few more bodies later, I pulled the truck onto the sidewalk in front of the IFC building. Though the smoke was paling with the morning, it remained as thick and oppressive as ever.

Using my handkerchief as a breathing filter, I got out and tried the building's front doors—locked. Blood still covered the glass from the demon attack earlier, but I could feel the threshold's radiance, a promising sign that the city's faith was holding up. Thank heaven the IFC leaders had Sup Squad escorts.

I knocked hard. "Hello? Anyone here?"

A shadow appeared from the conference room, withdrew for a couple seconds, and then hustled toward the door. It took me a moment to recognize the pale, dark-haired man because he was no longer wearing his thick-rimmed glasses. It was Rector Rumbaugh of Grace Cathedral, the one who'd fled the meeting.

At the blood-streaked door, he cupped his hands to the

sides of his smallish eyes to peer out. He flinched when he realized someone was right on the other side.

"It's Everson Croft," I said. "A friend of the Interfaith Council."

For a second I thought he might retreat. But he unlocked the door, opening it just enough for me to enter. I stepped past the guards' blood from earlier and over the dripping trail Swami Rama's head wound had left.

"My God, how long have you been out there?" Rumbaugh asked, quickly locking the door behind me.

I noticed that no infernal smoke had followed me inside, the powerful threshold holding it back like an invisible membrane. And everything sounded loud suddenly, as if my ears had been unplugged.

"Long story," I replied brusquely, pocketing my kerchief. "Is anyone here besides you?"

He shook his head. The energy patterns in the space seemed to confirm his claim. "I kept expecting others to arrive," he said. "But after a couple hours, I accepted that it would only be me. Is this the threat you mentioned at the meeting?" he asked in a hoarse whisper. "The return of Sathanas?"

"The early stages," I replied. "You ran off earlier. Why?"

For some reason that felt as important as the smoke suffocating the city.

Rumbaugh blinked rapidly and peered past me. "Do you mind if we get away from the door?"

I gave a grudging nod and followed him to the conference room, where votive candles illuminated the space. Otherwise, the room was how we'd left it, the nameplates arranged around the table as if another meeting might convene at any moment. I didn't know what I was walking into, if anything, but I had enough dragon sand to turn Rumbaugh into a human torch if he tried to get cute.

"I've been alternating between praying and trying to reach my family," he said. "We have a place in Morningside Heights, but I haven't had any luck getting a signal. I've tried everywhere inside the building."

When he checked his phone again, I snuck a look at mine. The absence of even a single flickering bar dashed my hopes of reaching Ricki. When I finished here, I would have to take my chances and go to the apartment.

I put my phone away, but Rumbaugh continued to hold his inches from his face, the screen's glow amplifying his concern for his family. That softened my stance toward him slightly, but far from entirely.

"What happened to your glasses?" I asked.

He looked younger without them on. "Oh, I lost them on the way back here," he said, blinking over at me. "It's a long story, too."

"Why don't you start from when you split."

He put the phone away and bowed his head slightly. "I know how that must have looked—especially in the middle of the chaos. But I left in search of something and planned to come right back."

I circled a hand for him to keep going.

"You'd asked about a woman with pale skin and white hair during the meeting. Bishop Sheridan called me about her yesterday. I told her I hadn't seen anyone like that—I checked with my head of security as well. But when you brought it up at the meeting, and cited her crimes, I remembered an odd letter that arrived in my office a few weeks ago. No name or return address. It was the type of letter we receive occasionally—End Times speculations—but I held onto it for some reason."

He reached into his coat and offered me the folded letter. I opened it and turned it around to read the typed message.

Father Rumbaugh,

A storm gathers over your city. A malevolent storm where hooded ones breed evil, and ten thousand souls scream and plead for an end to their torment, where fire is breathed, and smoke is swallowed, and where right action is nowhere to be found.

There is still time, for I am a Chosen One. I see the crouching son of Satan, an ill child to an ill mother. I see the child as Satan himself, and the ten thousand souls who scream and plead as ten million and more. I've seen these in Guiding Dreams, and so far the Dreams have led me true.

I can draw off the evil and prevent the storm. This is my promise. But I will need a place of sanctuary. I ask it of you and your holy house. To grant it, you have but give the word silently and then aloud.

Search your faith, Father, and you will find truth in what I tell you.

I await your word.

I brought the letter to my nose. It didn't carry the mothy scent of the other one, the medium was different—typed versus written—and the wording more extravagant. Still, the "ill child to an ill mother" bit told me that this had to be the pale woman. It was also disturbingly prophetic, a skill some fae were known for…

"I believe similar letters were sent to other members of the Interfaith Council," Rumbaugh said. "That was why I didn't bring it up. I didn't want to risk any ugly accusations, not with the unity of the interfaith community paramount right now. But I didn't like the thought of that unity being undermined, either. I planned to give you the letter discreetly. I understand you have powers of perception? I don't judge you for them," he stressed. "I have my own sensitivities, namely to holy energies. I can identify every interfaith house in the city by feel alone. They're like colors to me."

I reread the letter and nodded. "You did the right thing."

"I pray so." He glanced at his phone before pocketing it again.

"Who else could have granted this person access to your close? To St. Martin's?"

"Technically, anyone on the Interfaith Council," he replied. "That's the way this works. Through the Council, we all have the keys to the others' houses, both literally and figuratively. Risky, perhaps, but it's shored up our institutions against the various evils that have appeared in our city over the years."

I held up the letter. "Can you think of anyone on the Council zealous enough to have run with this?"

As he squinted in thought, the lines around his raw eyes made him appear thoroughly depleted. He shook his head. "Our faiths may differ, but all the members believe strongly in consensus when it comes to IFC matters. That's been my observation in my two years on the Council, anyway."

And yet someone had given the letter-writer access.

Someone who knew such a move would be controversial, and so kept it to themself.

I thought about Bishop Sheridan's premonition of gathering forces. If she had received a similar letter, might she have felt enough resonance with the message to have allowed an outsider access to the city's holy spaces?

"I know this doesn't really help," Rumbaugh said, "but I was certain someone was following me on my way back here. More a feeling than anything, but it gave me such a scare that I ran for the door. I didn't even stop when my glasses fell off. The feeling lasted until I was inside. That was when Bishop Sheridan called to inform me of the demon attack. She was at the hospital with Swami Rama. I remained here to pray. The smoke moved in not too long after, and I became stranded."

"There are more demons out there," I said. "So you should—"

I was interrupted by loud banging on the glass doors.

Gesturing for Rumbaugh to stay put, I returned to the front of the building. At the door, I peered out between streaks of blood, much as Rumbaugh had done earlier, but I couldn't make out anything in the smoke. I unlocked the door and eased it open, remaining in the threshold's protective aura. If this was a survivor, I didn't want to strand them outside.

"Hello?" I called.

I stepped forward. The threshold's resonance climbed in pitch, as though in alarm. A tall figure appeared from the smoke, circling the back of Dwayne's truck. Not a demon, but maybe something worse.

Curtains of white hair fell to the figure's shoulders, illuminating a pallid face with colorless lips but the piercing green eyes Petra had described. She was younger than I'd pictured, but fae beings were good at hiding their years.

"Hello, *friend*," the pale woman said.

As she advanced through the hellish smoke, she produced a sword from under her long white coat. The threshold behind me ratcheted up to an ear-splitting pitch. Wincing, I drew my cane into sword and staff.

34

"Who are you?" I demanded, having to yell over the stifling effect of the smoke.

She advanced, sword overhead. White fire hissed along its length, evoking my dream of St Mark's Basilica. In a look of fanatical resolve, her lips crushed together as she brought the sword down.

Criss-crossing my blade and staff overhead, I cried, "*Protezione!*"

Pent-up energy crackled through my mental prism. Her sword rang against a dome of hardening air, releasing a fierce flash and concussion. I grunted to one knee, head ringing. The pale woman staggered back, circling her sword arm for balance. By the time she'd set her feet, I realized what I'd done.

Oh crap...

I braced for the creamy waves to come crashing over me, drowning out my will and carrying in my incubus. But the waves never arrived. Not so much as a current. If anything, I felt Thelonious diminish further.

As I pushed myself back up, my rear heel knocked against the glass door, and Thelonious's no-show made sudden sense. The threshold. Proximity to its holy energy must have been keeping him at bay.

Okay, so just a matter of keeping the fight right here.

As I faced the pale woman, my relief at having discovered the loophole was quickly replaced by anger.

"Who *are* you?" I repeated. "What the hell do you want with me?"

She continued to wield the heavy looking sword one-handed as she stalked forward, but she appeared a little less confident now. Probably not accustomed to seeing her enchanted blade rebuffed like that. When she remained mute, I pushed my threshold-and-Thelonious theory further by thrusting my own blade.

"*Forza dura!*" I shouted, releasing a giant force blast.

She swung her sword around. Instead of slicing my invocation apart, her blade hoovered it up. The white fire along its shimmering edge dimmed as she brought her other hand to the grip and braced the weapon before her. Eyes narrowing, arms trembling, she squeezed the energy out again, returning the attack in a violent flash.

But while she'd been absorbing and squeezing, I'd been shaping a sphere of hardened air around her. My fresh invocation not only absorbed the released magic, but used it as additional fuel.

Surprise, surprise.

She peered around her shrinking enclosure, then tried to attack it with short sword thrusts. But my invocation held, making me wonder just what kind of a fae I was dealing with. Potent enough to operate in the faith houses, but unable to overcome the invocation of a midlist magic-user after a heavy night of drinking?

I funneled more power into the sphere, intent on two things: keeping her from getting out and getting some goddamned answers.

When there was no room left to thrust, she brought her sword against her body and closed her eyes, as though preparing herself for burial. Was she surrendering?

No, she was concentrating her energy, drawing it toward her core. Her eyes suddenly opened onto voids of white light, and the energy discharged like a thermonuclear suitcase, thrashing her hair and coat. My shield shook violently, but I battened it down, absorbing the blast. Barely. The diminishing power rattled the struts of my soul.

She blinked, restoring her irises. Then she peered around as though surprised to find she wasn't free. Careful not to show how close she'd come—or how badly my lungs wanted to hack up more blood—I straightened.

"What were you doing to the boy?" I growled.

She stared past her enclosure and met my eyes. "He was no boy."

Confirmation she *had* been the original kidnapper, the one who'd held him at Grace Cathedral. I thought again of the thumbprint on his forehead, the handprint on his chest. "What were you doing to him?" I repeated.

"Drawing off the evil that envelops us. But someone *interfered*."

Even in her accusation, her voice was clear and declarative, as if she were asserting some God-given truth.

"Is that why you went after his mother?"

She stared back at me. "I was chosen to stop him."

"And that merited a death sentence? What the hell was her crime?"

I remembered Mary picking at her cheap sweater the day we'd talked—confused, guilt-ridden, scared for her child. But whatever mistakes she had made, she'd loved and cared for Edgar the best she'd known how.

"Do you believe one life is worth more than the millions that might have been spared?" the pale woman asked. Amid the hellish smoke, her voice shimmered like a guiding light. I resisted its call to follow and abide.

"I believe *every* innocent life is worth saving," I replied.

"Then you're not only tainted, Everson Croft, but stupid."

"How do you know my name?"

"Mary spoke it."

Of course. The torture session that had led to her death.

But there was no guilt in the pale woman's confession. Her piercing eyes were candid, hard for me to hold. They seemed to stare into my being, weighing my Thelonious-tainted soul and finding it lacking. But something she'd said disturbed me so much more.

"Millions are dead?" I asked hollowly.

"By *virtue* of his son, Satan now has access to this world. He beclouds the air and smothers the city with his foul evil. The hooded ones creep about like ghouls, feeding innocents to the newly spawned. Demons patrol the skies like nightmare birds of prey, hunting souls and seizing them at will."

She spoke as if she were holding a tent revival in Middle Earth. By "hooded ones" she must have meant the druids. And "Satan" and "Sathanas" were interchangeable at times, depending on the belief in question, but this wasn't the time to polish my PhD. My heart was going hard enough to hurt my chest.

"Are millions dead?" I repeated.

White light filled her eyes again, making it appear as if they'd rolled back and she was seeing another reality entirely. "Not until the son becomes the father. Then the ten thousand will become the ten million."

Ten thousand dead wasn't exactly a relief. In fact, the notion made my head spin so violently I wanted to sit. But it beat ten million. It beat ten million by a lot. And the son becoming the father sounded like the celestial event Petra had described, scheduled for tonight. Meaning there was still time.

"Where is he now? Where's the son?"

"He hides behind fire outside Chinatown."

Still at the hotel, then. But I was helpless to do anything that involved casting, given my Thelonious problem.

"How are you planning to stop him?" I asked.

"I am preparing myself for the Contest, as is he. Naturally, we seek to disadvantage the other. For me that will mean destroying all who have and might yet enable him. This includes you, Everson Croft—for giving him to the hooded ones. Your folly hindered me once. I'll not let it happen again."

"Getting a little ahead of yourself, don't you think?" I growled.

She eyed her enclosure before returning her blunt gaze to mine. "You asked and I answered."

True enough, but I was still struggling for why a fae would be involved. I couldn't recall a time in my lifetime or lore when they'd given two sparkly farts about our beliefs. They had their own complex dogmas.

"What's the Contest?" I asked.

"I'll answer no more questions."

"How did you get into the churches? Who let you in?"

She remained silent.

"So what am I supposed to do with you?" It wasn't a rhetorical question. Sathanas may have been her enemy as much as mine, but she was also intent on killing me in preparation for this so-called "Contest."

She surprised me by responding. "That decision will be out of your hands shortly. They're coming."

"Who's coming?"

In an excruciating burst of sparks, a figure collided into the sphere. I staggered back. Talons ripped at my invocation, trying to get at the pale woman. Another damned demon.

Still reeling from the violent contact, I backed toward the threshold and hissed out an incantation to reinforce the enclosure. But when a second demon joined the first, I hadn't a prayer in hell of holding it together.

Gathering my remaining power, I shouted, "*Respingere!*"

The sphere detonated, blowing the demons into the smoke and raining spent magic over me. Freed, the pale woman made no move to escape or seek cover. She remained standing in the open, sword rotating back and forth from an arm she'd extended to one side, as if willing the demons to return.

A moment later, she got her wish. Wings sliced in on her blind side, kicking up sparks in the smoke.

"Look out!" I shouted, my drive to protect overriding my instinct for self-preservation.

But her sword was in motion before my message could have registered. I caught the afterimage of a dazzling arc, and then the demon fell to the ground in two pieces, each one writhing independently of the other.

"Holy shit," I breathed.

I called power to my blade's first rune. Before I could decide which half of the demon to banish, they burst into pillars of black ichor that splashed across the walkway, then sublimated into the smoke from which the demon had appeared.

I looked from the woman's sword to her person. Her face was tilted skyward, watchful for the other demon. I only realized I'd strayed from the doorway of the IFC building when Thelonious stirred.

His voice arrived like a rumble of thunder: *Now's your chance, young blood. Run her through before she turns that thing on you again.*

As my gaze fell back to her sword, I recalled the horrific image of her preparing to decapitate me. Dream or prophecy?

Demonic wings slashed here and there in the smoke, kicking up more sparks. The pale woman adjusted herself and her sword, compelling the demon to lift off in search of another opening. And then her back was to me.

I redoubled my grip on my sword and eyed the spot behind her heart.

I could end whatever threat she posed to me and my loved ones right here and now.

Do it, young blood, Thelonious urged. *Or she'll fix your wife like she did that young mother...*

Gunfire erupted. A figure appeared through the haze, bulky with Sup Squad armor. He angled his weapon upward and fired again, shuffling back as the second demon plummeted to the walkway.

Another figure, this one wearing a hooded cloak, drove a long staff into the demon's core. Power exploded from the contact, and the creature burst apart, a clawed foot tumbling to a stop beside my right shoe. As the grotesque appendage dissolved into smoke, the cloaked figure turned toward me.

"Is that Everson?" he called.

"Jordan!" I cried, staggering toward him.

When I arrived, he seized one of my arms and looked me over with his raven-dark eyes. "Are you all right?"

"Fine," I said, even though I felt anything but. "How the hell did you find me?"

He gripped the wrist of my staff hand and rotated the Upholders sigil into view. Even with our proximity, the bond remained too weak for communicating, but he must have been able to use it as a locator.

"Is everyone else safe?" I asked.

"Yes, they're all back at the apartment," he said. "Come."

His confirmation sent a massive wave of relief toppling through me. Beyond him, I could make out the dim lights and idling engine of an armored personnel carrier. But I hesitated. "Where did the pale woman go?"

Jordan followed my searching gaze. "What pale woman?"

In the place where the clear light of her sword had just shone was a confusion of infernal smoke. She was gone.

35

"Buckle up," Jordan said, taking the seat beside mine.

I fastened my three-point harness as the carrier rumbled into motion. The Sup Squad carriers were equipped with radar and real-time maps, allowing the driver to accelerate well beyond what I'd attained in Dwayne's truck.

When I shared my concern with Jordan about returning home, he helped me reason out that if Sathanas could locate me through Thelonious, he could use the bond to acquire my address. My family was at risk whether I was home or not. Not the assurance I'd wanted, but he was right—I was being overly cautious.

With another carrier dispatched to pick up Rector Rumbaugh and reunite him with his family, I sat back and pulled several painful breaths of filtered air into my lungs.

Jordan handed me a small flask. "Drink some. It will help heal your insides."

A taste of bitter grass and earthy roots filled my mouth when I sipped. It soothed my raw throat as it went down and then warmed my stomach with druidic magic. The burning in my chest eased by degrees.

"I was afraid we'd lost you," he said as I returned the flask.

I wiped my mouth. "The boy we rescued? Turned out to be Sathanas's son."

"No shit?"

I proceeded to give him the full account, from finding Edgar to the demon prince's fiery manifestation to my descent into Thelonious's realm and how I'd ultimately come to arrive at the IFC Center.

"I saw the explosion from the helipad," Jordan said. "I flew to the hotel as a raven, but the entire structure was walled off in infernal flames, smoke blowing out in all directions. I couldn't get close enough to search it. I tried to reach you through this"—he patted the Upholders sigil on his hand—"but no luck. I flew to your apartment, barely able to stay ahead of the smoke. It swallowed the building the moment I landed. The power failed shortly after and all communications went down."

"But everyone's all right?" I asked, needing that reassurance again.

"Yes. They're worried about you, of course, but fine otherwise. Thinking you were still in the hotel, we were planning on how to extract you. That was when I received my first hit through the bonding sigil. It told me you were no longer at the hotel, but somewhere farther north."

"Midtown," I confirmed. "Courtesy of my incubus. But how did you hook up with the Sup Squad?"

"Ricki found a weak signal on her radio for the Office of Emergency Management. She was eventually able to reach a Sup Squad leader to arrange for an armored carrier. By then, you'd started moving. My connection to you was shaky, and I was afraid the others' magic would interfere with my attempts to track you if they came. Oh, and your goblin friend was... well, a little too hot-blooded to offer steady backup. I eventually convinced them to remain behind." The shake of Jordan's head told me there had been pushback. "You have some devoted friends, Everson."

"That I do," I chuckled. "What else do we know about this?"

"Manhattan is covered in an infernal dome. The smoke extends as far as the Hudson, Harlem, and East Rivers, where flames have been seen. Nothing seems to be getting in or out. Demons have attacked some police units, and there are reports of bodies in the street, but no telling the numbers right now."

Ten thousand, or approaching it. But I was still too sick to tell him.

At least I don't have to bother canceling my classes, I thought darkly.

Closing my eyes, I pictured the scene from the air. I saw our oblong island as a smoky chrysalis. One that was scheduled to break open at midnight, releasing Sathanas, demon lord of Wrath.

———

Fifteen minutes later, the carrier arrived at my apartment building. I'd picked up scraps of conversation on the vehicle's radio en route. Sup Squad units were beginning to coordinate patrols to help those caught outside. I told the driver about the wounded at the Kitten Club. I also advised him to deliver the uninjured to one of the interfaith houses, and to go there themselves if they felt threatened.

Every innocent we spared would be another soul denied
Sathanas.

As Jordan and I entered the apartment building, I felt the
hum of additional protections—my teammates had been
busy. Their magic helped to keep the smoke outside while
Jordan's light illuminated our way to the top floor.

I unlocked the three bolts and opened the front door,
grateful as the smells and feel of home rushed around me.
Ricki, too. She met me with a full-body hug, legs wrapping my
hips, arms squeezing my head, neck, and upper back as she
mashed her cheek against mine, then kissed me aggressively.

I smiled as I set her down, my relief equaling hers. "I'm
really sorry for the scare—and my godawful stench. Other
than that, I'm good. Are the kids...?"

"Sleeping," she said, still overcome.

"But we're not," Bree-yark barked.

He stood from a couch with Mae, who was clutching her
hands to her chest and openly weeping. I embraced them
both, spending additional time with Mae to assure her I was
truly back and mostly unharmed. Buster scrambled around
my legs, clacking his lobster claws and chirping happily.

Bree-yark chortled. "Yeah, we thought you were a goner,
buddy."

"Oh, don't say that." Mae swatted his bottom while
sponging her cheeks with a fistful of tissues. "We were just
concerned, but we never doubted you for a moment, hon. We
knew you'd make it back here safe and sound."

"Ugh," Tabitha moaned from her divan. "You should have
heard them carrying on. You would've thought the queen
herself had died. It was torture, darling, and there was no
refuge for me *anywhere*."

"I'm sorry for your suffering," I deadpanned.

"Yes, well, when you're debating whether asphyxiation is the better option, it's gone way beyond simple torment." She craned her neck enough to peer out the bay window, where the yellow-tinted smoke hung like a toxic fog. She appeared ready to say something more, but then angled her head at me.

"There's something different about you, darling," She squinted her eyes. "Is that your incubus?"

No longer being irradiated by a holy threshold, Thelonious had ventured back out. A good reminder that I couldn't risk casting—hell, I could barely risk *coughing*—without him claiming me again.

"Unfortunately," I sighed.

Tabitha grunted in disgust. "The creep. Did I ever tell you what he tried to do to me that one New Year's Eve?"

I cut my fingers back and forth across my throat, suggesting now wasn't the best time, but she didn't take the hint.

"*That* would have been a new low for both of us," she said.

Ricki came up beside me. "Wait, what's this about Thelonious?"

"He's back in the picture," I said, speaking quickly to preempt Tabitha from painting a more graphic picture. "But it connects to what happened last night, and everyone should be here when I tell it. Where are the others?"

"Loukia and James are in the lab, trying to contact your Order," she said. "And Petra is up in the loft taking a rest."

The druid's tattooed face appeared above the railing. "I'm awake now."

Even in the dimness, I could read her concern for her Black Earth sisters and what was happening in the city.

"Let's all meet now, then," I said. "I need to fill everyone in on the latest."

"I'll get the others from the basement," Jordan said, allowing Petra the barest glance. Though they'd collaborated with me on the hotel mission, the tension between the two druids remained palpable.

"Well, we're going to need some breakfast," Mae said, bustling past me toward the kitchen. "You can't plan anything on empty stomachs. We should probably start on the perishables. Are eggs, sausage links, and fried potatoes going to be enough?" She was already firing up the gas burners and pulling food from the dark fridge.

"Yeah, I'll help you," Bree-yark said.

"Don't forget the goat's milk," Tabitha called. "And then move my remaining bottles to the freezer. The minute it starts to sour, it's absolutely dreadful, no good to me at all." Then, under her breath: "I fucking hate turned milk."

Facing Ricki, I lowered my voice. "How are we fixed for food?"

Back among my loved ones, and with powerful protections buffering the apartment, my overtaxed and underslept mind was at risk of getting comfortable. Something I couldn't afford, not with Sathanas on the verge of emerging. If we were going to spare New York, we had to start with ourselves.

"Mae made a store run recently," she replied, "and she tends to over-purchase."

"How about the water? Still running?"

"As of now. We filled both tubs and all of our spare containers. Bree-yark made a to-do list. He knows about sieges from his time in the goblin army. The next time you have six hours, you should get him to tell you about them."

Her flat expression made me snuff out a laugh. "I'll put it on my calendar."

As she rubbed my arm, her lips tensed. "It happened, didn't it?" she whispered. "Sathanas's return?"

I saw the demon prince crushing the blackened baby toes under his boot. I recalled the fire and smoke and the threat of winged demons. But mostly I thought of the ten thousand screaming, pleading souls becoming ten million—and more. I drew in a breath, pushing back hard against the thoughts, and nodded.

"He's part way here, but not all."

"How much time do we have?" she asked.

"About sixteen hours."

When Ricki's eyes widened, I nodded grimly. Less than a full day to either escape the city or put the Sathanas threat down for good.

36

I gave the team the blow-by-blow of the hotel operation over breakfast. Voices of alarm met my bombshell about Edgar being Sathanas's son. They only grew when I explained that Sathanas could also operate through him.

I wasn't trying to craft a supernatural thriller. Last night did that all by itself.

"So, he's here?" James Wesson asked, gesturing to the windows, where the wards bent the tainted smoke beyond. "This is him?"

"*Partly* him. His son is his own demon, but he's also a conduit to his father. A narrow conduit now, but enough for Sathanas to call the shots. Tonight at midnight, when the Child and Father stars align"—I nodded at Petra—"Sathanas will arrive fully formed. Not to be Captain Obvious, but we can't let that happen."

"Told you," Tabitha called from her divan.

It took every fiber of my willpower to ignore her, but then I turned toward her anyway. "Told me what?"

"That the wretched thing in those photos wasn't a boy."

"Fine, but you didn't know he was a demon lord's son."

"Says the *expert*," she yawned, sedated from the quarter gallon of goat's milk in her belly. "I had my suspicions."

I knew better than to believe her, but I also knew why she hadn't been reacting to events in the Below. There *were* no major events happening in the Below. Sathanas still ruled the roost, and even were he to claim his ten million plus souls, God forbid, that would only consolidate his command.

"What about the kids?" Mae whispered, glancing toward the bedrooms. "Should we try to get them to an interfaith house?"

"Well, the houses are only as strong as the collective faith that supports them," I said, having already discussed the option with Ricki. "Should that falter, all bets are off, and Sathanas has already targeted the IFC's director. Plus, there's another threat out there, someone who can access holy spaces and isn't above claiming innocent lives." I told them about my encounter with the pale woman. "I still don't know who she is, but we have protections against her here."

"Damn," James said, shaking his head. "Was she good looking, at least?"

Loukia scowled at him before addressing me. "Why didn't you destroy the demon boy when he was in front of you?"

"It wasn't for a lack of effort, believe me. His stomach was eating my blade, but he resisted banishment."

Possibly because Mary had unwittingly inoculated him, carrying him in and out of St. Martin's while she was pregnant. Edgar's human half could have buffered him from the full weight of the holy energy while his demon half developed at least some resistance. The demons in the time catches had done something similar.

"When I upped the wattage, he empowered my incubus,

and that was it." I snapped my fingers. "Next thing I knew I was in Thelonious's realm, and he was back to running my body like a timeshare."

Ricki raised an eyebrow. "Oh, really?"

"He didn't touch," I said, before remembering my encounter with the bouncer and the stock end of his weapon. "Well, not much, anyway. But the real issue here is that with my incubus back, I can't risk casting anything beyond simple activations. Not unless I'm in the proximity of holy power."

Loukia squinted as she adjusted her head scarf. "But why did Sathanas let you live in the first place?"

"Great question. Something I'm still trying to puzzle out."

"What's there to puzzle out?" Bree-yark barked. "Let's go back there and stomp that little twerp's head in!"

"He's not so little anymore, but hold that thought," I said. "I want updates from everyone."

Ricki, who continued to monitor her radio, started with the Sup Squad. They'd been finding smashed vehicles and plenty of bodies. Team members were still posted up with the IFC leaders, including at Manhattan General with Bishop Sheridan and Swami Rama. Rector Rumbaugh had joined them as well, possibly to bolster the IFC's faith. No more demon encounters, making me wonder if Sathanas had called them off to avoid the Squad's firepower and focus on soul hunting.

I pushed my breakfast aside, no longer hungry. "Any word from the mayor's office or city officials?"

Ricki shook her head. "Nothing."

"How about from outside Manhattan?"

"We had brief contact early, but nothing since. With fire ringing the island, there's no getting in or out. Not even by the subway tunnels. A unit explored that option and the lead man's suit burst into flames."

Great. I turned to James and Loukia. "Any luck reaching the Order?"

"The lines are still down," Loukia replied, "so we sent some messages the old fashioned way. Silver cups and oil crystals."

James curled his fingers and thumb into a circle. "Big, fat goose egg."

"The messages went out, though?" I pressed.

"Mine, yes." Loukia narrowed her eyes at James. "But with his strange accent, there is no way to know."

"Hey, that's how we talk out West. Right, Croft?"

"You're from Brooklyn," I reminded him, then nodded at the silver cups arrayed across the kitchen counter. "We'll just need to keep an eye on them. The minute a message comes back, let me know."

I refused to believe the Order had gotten themselves trapped again. But then where in the hell were they? And why hadn't our magic tipped them off to Sathanas's son? He'd only been in the city for the last three years.

I relaxed my shoulders and breathed. *One thing at a time.*

"Have you been in contact with your circles?" I asked the druids.

Jordan, who never seemed without his quarterstaff, moved it to the other side of his chair. "I've tried reaching them, but the infernal energy is too thick."

Petra simply shook her head, not raising her eyes from her picked-over plate. If I had to guess, she was still coming to terms with the fact her possessed sisters had delivered us to this point and she'd been powerless to stop them. I knew the feeling. I'd done her one better by handing Edgar to them all but wrapped in a pretty bow.

Then the ten thousand will become the ten million...

"So we have communication with the Sup Squad and IFC leaders," I said in summation. "And SOS messages went out to the Order." That put us in a slightly better position than I'd been hoping for as far as resources went.

"And you've got us," Bree-yark said.

"Don't get too excited," Tabitha warned from the divan. "He'll make a point of forgetting every helpful act you've ever undertaken, even ones that imperil your life."

"Hold on, let's go back to this pale woman," James said. "Is she on our side or not?"

"She predicted most of what's happened so far—I'll give her that," I said. "But she also has a gargantuan messiah complex. And not the pious, 'give me your suffering' kind. She thinks she's a Chosen One, and she'll kill anyone who suggests otherwise. She's gunning for Sathanas, yeah, but it's a solo act."

"Hmm, I don't like the sound of that," Mae said.

"But she did say something that's got me thinking," I added. "She referred to an event called 'the Contest.'"

Mae retracted her head. "The Contest?"

I nodded at Petra. "Does that mean anything to you?"

She cleared her throat, but her voice still came out faint. "I can only convey what the movement of the stars foretell, and that's the alignment of the Child and Father. It wields the power of predestination. Regardless of what 'the Contest' signifies, we're still up against a force as old as Creation."

Bree-yark chortled dismally. "All right, now let's hear the *bad* news."

Instead of responding, Petra lowered her gaze, as though

submitting to the very predestination she'd referenced. Jordan looked over at her like he was going to say something but kept it to himself.

"*The Contest,*" James repeated. "Why does that sound so danged familiar..." He snapped his fingers suddenly. "I was hitting the library this past summer. It was slow, and there's this chick over there named Myrtle. Looks *nothing* like her name, right, Croft?" He correctly interpreted my Ricki-like stare as him needing to get to the point.

"Well, anyway, I had her bring me anything she could find on battles of good versus evil. Thought it would make me look erudite, like the Prof here, but also a little edgy. I was flipping through a book on Milton—his unfinished manuscripts—when I came across a poem that was left out of *Paradise Lost.* It's a second battle between the angels and Satan, long after he's been cast out of Heaven." He jabbed the table with his finger twice for emphasis. "Milton called it 'the Contest.'"

"How did it end?" I asked.

"Don't know." James shrugged. "It was unfinished."

As I regarded him in thought, a magical resonance I'd been feeling since his arrival kicked up a notch and we both began to nod slowly. As James caught on to what was happening, his eyes lit up.

"Whoa, is that what it feels like?"

Though he'd had more practical training than me, James was still struggling to hear his magic. Loukia, too. She'd even given me crap over it in Athens, suggesting I was the Order's favored child. But I was too busy considering what James had shared that had gotten our magic so excited just now.

"You know," I said, thinking out loud, "there are plenty of stories of angels and demons facing off for world domination.

That happened briefly in our own history, before the Creator replaced the Avenging Angels with the First Saints. Sathanas still carries that history in his makeup. With the alignment of Child and Father empowering his arrival, I think a counter-force is responding."

James squinted at me. "You mean like angels?"

"One angel in particular," I replied, apprehension gripping my gut. Because what did that say about the identity of the pale woman?

A knock sounded on the door.

I turned to Ricki. "Were we expecting anyone?"

She shook her head, eyebrows drawing down. As I got up, the others moved in behind me. Ricki with her service weapon; James palming a revolver; Loukia wielding both glowing blades; Jordan bearing his quarterstaff; Petra clutching her smoldering wand; and Bree-yark with his fists raised in a boxer's stance.

"Oh, do be careful," Mae whispered.

Tabitha peered over at us blandly from the divan before dropping her head again.

I stooped toward the peephole. "Holy hell," I muttered.

37

I released the bolts and opened the door. A tall woman stood beyond the threshold, her eyes glowing with familiarity as they met mine.

"Hello, Everson."

"Hi," I said, still in mild shock.

She had been Caroline Reid once, my friend, colleague, and former crush at Midtown College. Though she'd taught urban history, she would cover my classes when I was late, which was embarrassingly often, in order to spare me Chairman Snodgrass's power trips. She'd left Midtown College—and Manhattan, for that matter—to marry a powerful fae prince. Our contact since had been spotty but hugely significant. She'd helped me outwit and destroy the vampire Arnaud Thorne. Later, we collaborated in the time catches to recover the Upholders and stop the demon Malphas.

I'd last seen her at my wedding, which felt like a lifetime ago. A lot had happened since, but being in the presence of a powerful fae also altered time calculations.

Remembering myself, I stepped back. "Please. Come in."

Ricki had moved up beside me, and I sensed the others jockeying for a view from behind us. Though technically half fae, Caroline radiated the power and possession of royalty. Parted blond hair framed a smooth face and fell behind the shoulders of her long coat, its collar draped with a mauve scarf. If not for the infernal storm raging outside, I would have thought she'd been out for a stroll.

"Thank you, but I can't stay long," she replied, peering down the corridor as if a bevy of royal attendants might arrive at any moment to escort her away.

I told my friends we'd just be a few, and Ricki and I stepped out. As I closed the door, Caroline greeted my wife sincerely, and Ricki returned the sentiment. Ricki knew I owed my life to her—a couple times now. But I was still puzzling over why she'd come.

"We're leaving the city," she said regretfully.

She didn't need to explain. Decisions came from higher up, and the fae rarely intervened openly in human affairs. Defiance on Caroline's part would only land her in their byzantine, and often brutal, system of court justice.

"No, I understand," I said.

"Osgood told me of your visit."

"Oh, right. About the pale woman."

"This woman you seek isn't fae, nor is she from Faerie."

"No?" I said, though I'd already suspected as much.

"We were able to glean some information from the material you left Osgood. Her name is Emma. She's from Los Angeles. She arrived in the city recently, but spent time in Venice, Italy just prior."

A jolt hit me. *Venice.*

All in a moment, I recalled the dream of St. Mark's Basilica: the angel Faziel commanding me to kneel before his sword, the fallen body of my shadow, the pale woman poised to deliver the decapitating blow. It wasn't until Ricki nudged me that I realized Caroline was awaiting some response.

"Does this information help you?" she asked.

I nodded. I knew with certainty now who the pale woman was.

"I don't believe I need to tell you that she does not mean you well."

"No," I agreed with a dismal laugh. "I sort of got that impression."

"She also carries something powerful. What that is, we don't know. It's not something we've encountered before."

The enchanted sword? A weapon I'd effectively parried and contained inside a shield invocation? If so, it only added to her mystery.

"What can we do about her?" Ricki asked.

Caroline squinted slightly, as though reading something in the pattern of fae light surrounding her. "I don't know, but Everson will," she replied at last. "I'm very sorry that I cannot stay and help."

I sensed she was also apologizing for not offering us refuge. Though she'd likely requested it, their royal court had been undermined by demons once before, and they weren't willing to chance a second infiltration. Her head tilted regretfully and in a way that allowed me to glimpse the Caroline Reid of old.

"We understand," I reiterated.

"Thanks for coming to tell us this," Ricki added.

Caroline embraced my wife and kissed her cheek, then did the same to me. Her fingers touched the coin pendant around my neck, stirring up a subtle dance of fae magic. As she stepped back, her eyes peered meaningfully into mine. She'd imparted a gift with that touch. At what price to herself, I didn't want to know.

"Angelus and I believe in you," she said, telling me the gift was from both of them.

And then she left. Ricki and I remained staring after her, even after she'd disappeared into the stairwell, both of us slightly fae touched. At last, I coughed into my fist and Ricki blinked the glassiness from her eyes.

"Wow, I'd forgotten about that," she said.

"Yeah, even a little bit of exposure can pack a punch. If you wondered what got Carlos dancing at our reception, there's your answer." Her stiff brother hadn't touched a drop of alcohol that night, but with fae royalty seated nearby, not to mention a pair of prankish pixies zipping about, he hadn't had to.

Ricki faced me in the lingering fae light. "You know who the pale woman is, don't you?"

I nodded and leaned a shoulder against the doorframe. "At dinner the other night, Claudius and I discussed my angelic line. He said that others would have the blood, too, but in such diluted quantities it would be unlikely to express itself except in the most mundane ways. Well, this Emma begs to differ."

Ricki's eyes widened. "She has angel blood?"

"Enough of it to give her powers and direct her here."

It probably also explained her raging narcissism, believing she was a Chosen One authorized to dole out justice and punishment, innocents be damned. And here I'd been anxious to meet another of that blood line.

"She was in Venice before coming here," Ricki said. "Isn't that where your shadow…"

"Yeah," I replied, so she wouldn't have to say it. "My magic's telling me there's a connection. I'm just not sure how yet."

I thought again of the letter to Rumbaugh. Driven by apocalyptic visions, Emma must have left her home in Los Angeles and gone to Venice. Then she came to New York, seeking to use one of the holy spaces for her work.

That last part made sense. An invitation would not only have given her access, but enhanced her holy powers. Powers she planned to use on Edgar to "draw off the evil." Powers she used to pressure his mother for information after I'd taken him, causing Mary to stroke out, then leaving her for dead.

"Caroline said you'd know what to do about her," Ricki said. "Do you?"

I considered all that my magic had already done and arranged: alerting me to the demonic conjurings, pairing me with Bashi, then Petra...

Where I'd gone wrong was imposing reason on my magic. Trying to create a connection between the pale woman and Bashi where none existed. Even insisting the pale woman was fae in the first place, blinding me to her true nature. Worse, I'd reasoned myself out of taking Sathanas's return seriously.

At no point had my magic steered me wrong. I'd steered wrong from my magic.

Well, no more. Especially now that it was talking again, pulling in other elements.

"I'm starting to see some solutions," I said, turning back to Ricki. "And I may not even need to cast."

Back at the breakfast table, I held up a finger and concentrated into my coin pendant. The subtle whispers Caroline had instilled changed direction. Like Osgood the night before, she had seen a need in my eyes and gifted me its solution. In this case, an obfuscation enchantment. The magic would disguise my thoughts and deeds from Thelonious, allowing us to plan freely. I explained this to the group before filling them in on Caroline's visit about the pale woman.

"Emma is heeding an Avenging Angel," I concluded. "She's acting as his stand-in for the Contest."

Bree-yark looked around. "Is that a bad thing? I mean, if she wins, problem solved, right?"

"Or bigger problem," I replied. "The other night, Claudius said the Order is concerned about what might prompt the angel to take form. They don't think it will take much. If Emma wins, we'd be rid of Sathanas, sure, but we could also be looking at the angel's return. And this is a violent, vengeful angel we're talking about. I've seen the aftermath of his coming in a parallel realm. It's grim."

Mae made a noise of concern as she stroked Buster, his lip tentacles undulating serenely over her shoulder.

"So we have to defeat this Emma before we defeat Sathanas?" Loukia asked.

"I'm thinking we *beat* her to Sathanas," I said. "She's preparing herself for midnight tonight, and so is he. So, we get to him early and take him by surprise. Once he's banished, Emma will have nothing to fight for. The Contest will already be over."

"Oh, that's genius," Bree-yark said, rubbing his hands eagerly.

But Jordan's visage remained dark. "Your banishment didn't work the last time."

"I have something more powerful," I said, heeding what my magic had been showing me. "There's a weapon in my warded safe, an angelic whip. I used one like it to destroy Typhon, a major monster from the Greek myths. I think it would do even worse to Sathanas's son, given that he's truly demonic. The best part? It originated in the shadow realm, meaning Sathanas probably doesn't know it exists, much less that I have it."

"But you just said you can't cast," Loukia said.

"Sathanas may have crippled my power as a descendant of a First Saint, but he didn't touch my Avenging Angel blood. I don't have a lot, but it's enough to power the whip."

"And that won't risk calling up the angel?" Ricki asked.

I'd had the same question, the anxiety of it returning in a ripple of pins and needles, but I'd made a promise to myself out in the corridor: no more deferring to reason.

"This is coming from my magic," I assured her.

"We're going in as a team, though, right?" James said, returning to pass around mugs of cowboy coffee he'd prepared on the stove. "None of this remote fighting crap. That clay golem was as slow as a crippled turtle."

Bashi's ultimatum had kept us from going in together the last time, but to say circumstances had changed was putting it mildly.

"If everyone's agreeable?" I offered.

"Hell yes!" Bree-yark shouted, looking surprised I'd even put it out there as a question.

"Why do you think we came all this way?" Loukia added.

"There's still the matter of Sathanas's infernal protection," Jordan said. "I could not have penetrated the hotel last night."

"Right," I muttered. The pale woman had said it too, *he hides behind fire.*

"It's shaped by druidic magic," Jordan added, shifting his gaze to Petra.

The fire druid had been studying her hands for the last several minutes. She looked up now, her eyes meeting ours for the first time. They hardened in a way that suggested her dark ruminations had led to a decision.

"I mentioned that I feel vestiges of my old connection to my sisters when they cast," she said. "That's because we're still bonded by our original vows. As their former priestess, I can attack them through it, debilitating them and disrupting their fire-based spells. That should allow us access to the hotel."

"Why haven't you done it before?" I asked, sensing a catch.

"Because it could harm them," she said. "Maybe kill them. And for that, Brigit would punish me severely."

That explained the looks Jordan had been giving her. He'd known she possessed that power, but he'd been reluctant to out her. Perhaps he was thinking of our confrontation with Malphas and whether he would have been willing to take the same risk with his Raven Circle. The table fell silent as we watched her.

"I'm willing to try," she said at last.

38

From the aisle of the personnel carrier, Petra's breaths sounded like a bellows feeding a furnace. She sat in a tray of potting soil, druidic symbols etched around its metal lip. What should have been an absurd sight was as serious as sin. With each breath, the symbols glowed a fiery red, reflecting off the tattoos mapping her bowed head.

Jordan and I watched from the edge of our seats, while Bree-yark fussed with a shotgun beside me. James and Loukia were outside, maintaining protections around the vehicle.

We'd arrived, our staging area a parking lot four blocks from the druids' hotel. We could all hear its cocoon of fire roaring in the near distance. The very protection Petra was preparing herself to bring down.

She drew another sharp breath, tattoos glinting bright red, then grunted in pain.

Jordan shifted uncomfortably—not from her show of distress, I gathered, but from watching her parlay with her fire god, something that still struck him as unnatural. But we both knew that getting inside the hotel depended on Petra's ability to access the old vows that bound her to her sisters.

Petra looked up, sweat dripping from her face.

"I have them," she said, moving her wand to her other hand. "I'm ready."

"Would you like one of us to stay with you?" I asked.

"No." Her voice trembled, as though she were trying to hold back a dozen horses with a single rope. "This is my task."

"Let's go," Jordan said brusquely.

I waved for Bree-yark, and the three of us climbed out. Before closing the door, I looked back. Petra's body shook now, steam billowing from her sweat.

"Thank you," I said, then closed the door, wishing I could have conveyed more.

We gathered around the rear of the vehicle: Jordan, Bree-yark, James, Loukia, and I. Mae had been frank with me: "Normally I'd insist on helping, but I'll only slow you down. Besides, there's no way I'm leaving your babies." I was openly grateful. Between her nether-whispering, Ricki's supernatural ammo, and the plethora of wards, my children were as secure as anywhere in the city.

For Tabitha's part, she'd slept through our planning, only stirring to ask when lunch would be ready.

"Petra's locked in," I whispered. "Let's go."

As we took off through the smoke, I peered back. The Sup Squad driver and escort stood guard. One returned a thumbs-up: they had their end covered. I returned the gesture as the haze swallowed them and the carrier.

"Petra's a tough cookie," Bree-yark said to reassure me.

He was dressed in his favorite action outfit: a flak vest over an army-green tank top and a pair of cargo pants. The canvas slings crisscrossing his torso held a sawed-off shotgun and an overloaded tactical bag.

"She is," I agreed, though I had very conflicted feelings about her undertaking. What could help us could also turn into a sacrifice—the lives of her druid sisters, as well as her own. But up until grounding herself in the tray of soil, she had remained insistent on doing this. I could only respect her commitment.

When she cried out, we kept moving. She'd warned us things could get vocal.

As we headed east on Grand Street, James cast a fine meshwork of silvery magic through our protection to filter out the worst of the smoke. It worked. Breathing freely, we picked up our pace. Jordan sent out cantrips to alert us to any approaching demons.

The demons were clearly active, something the smashed vehicles and occasional ravaged body attested to. Hopefully the pale woman was keeping them busy elsewhere, but I remained watchful for her as well.

To keep myself from casting, I'd left my sword and staff at the apartment. My jostling coin pendant glowed with protective enchantments, including the one Caroline had installed. For offense, I was counting on one weapon. I reached into a coat pocket and gripped the duct-taped handle nervously.

I'm trusting you, I told my magic as much as the whip.

At Broome Street, the hotel glowed into view, a pulsing nova through the smoke. Petra had explained that the protection was outward-facing. The hotel itself suffered no damage from the heat we could feel from about a block away now. It wasn't the kind of heat that peeled paint, either, but scorched souls.

"Here it is," I said, directing the team to our waiting spot —a subway entrance.

We descended several steps as Loukia grew her protection over the opening above. We were all breathing hard when we turned to watch the hotel's glow through the smoke, waiting for it to dim.

Instead, it exploded.

"Holy thunder!" Bree-yark exclaimed.

We crouched low as flames roared over the entrance like a thousand fiery hoofbeats. They then reversed just as violently, returning to the hotel, where the whole show seemed to collapse in on itself, casting the street in sudden dimness.

The five of us ventured up and out, weapons readied. The nova was gone. Petra appeared to have done her job.

"That's our cue—" I started to say.

Gooseflesh rippled over my body as a scream speared the smoke from behind us. It was Petra's, but it wasn't like her scream from earlier. This sounded like she was being skewered on a molten spike. She'd warned us that if she pushed too hard, if she hurt her sisters too badly, Brigit would demand her pound of flesh.

I spun to go back, but Jordan seized my arm.

"C'mon, man," I said, tugging against him. "She's our goddamned teammate!"

"I'll go."

I stopped struggling and met his serious eyes.

"I have magics that can protect her," he said, "heal her, if need be. I'll join you when she's stable."

Jordan helping Petra? He released me and took off into

the air, the smoke swirling behind his raven form. I let him go.

"Can you two fill in Jordan's part?" I asked James and Loukia.

They returned affirmations, and we surged on. As the front of the hotel materialized through the haze, we didn't slow. With the druids out of commission, so went their protections. No fire wards to drain. James thrust his wand, manifesting a cannonball of silvery energy that smashed down the front doors.

We poured into the lobby, each of us covering a section.

Druids littered the space like crash test dummies, all limp extremities and staring eyes. When Bree-yark panned his weapon across them, I showed him a hand. We'd promised Petra the opportunity to restore them.

"*Cercare*," Loukia hissed, slashing her enchanted blades apart.

The invocation released a wave of crimson sparks. They blew across the lobby, disappearing into adjoining rooms and under closed doors. When they faded, they left a pulsating line that led down the corridor ahead of us.

"Either there is an orgy of demons back there," Loukia whispered, "or it is him."

I took the lead, the whip slick in my grip. It was still a two-foot length of steel cable, but I could feel a crackling synergy taking hold between the weapon and my blood. James and Loukia flanked me, a silver wand and the red-glowing blades in their respective grips. Bree-yark backed up, watching our rear.

The searching spell led us to the end of the corridor, where a door stood ajar. Piano music filtered out in a somber melody.

"Sounds like Chopin," James whispered.

Loukia scoffed. "What do you know about Chopin?"

"Can't stand classical," Bree-yark grunted.

I signaled for them to keep it down as I eased forward, shifting to my wizard's senses. No traps, but my whip was starting to talk in spits and hisses. Our final battle was on the other side of that door.

With everyone in position, I pushed it open.

The large space was the hotel's dining room. The Chopin-playing piano was in the far corner, though no one appeared to be sitting at it. Tables and chairs were amassed to one side of the room, while two figures danced a slow waltz around the parquet square in the room's center. Edgar wore a black tuxedo with a long tailcoat and a blazing-red shirt that matched his slicked-back hair. His partner was one of the paralyzed druids. Her toes brushed the floor under her cloak as he carried her like a mannequin.

"What in thunder?" Bree-yark muttered.

Great question. I'd anticipated a lot of things, but not this.

On his next turn, Edgar seemed to notice us. Beneath his void-like shades, his mouth spread into an arrogant grin.

"Welcome!" he called. "Why don't you pair off and join me?"

And then Edgar was turning into his next step and slide, showing us his back. His confidence would have been troubling had it not been for Caroline's obfuscation enchantment. He thought he had the jump on our next move.

He didn't.

"*Now*," I grunted.

Bluish-white bolts shot from Loukia's blades and impacted the parquet floor at either end. The magic spread, turning the wood a frosty white and flash-freezing Edgar and his dance partner in a pillar of ice.

Meanwhile, James produced a jar from his leather duster and underhanded it. He snapped a pistol from his holster and squeezed twice. The shots blew the jar open, scattering hundreds of copper washers. As they bounced and slid over the frozen parquet, Loukia was already incanting, gathering the copper into a circle.

Unable to cast, I could only nod ardently.

Edgar reduced his confinement to a hissing column of steam and spun his partner away, sending her crashing into the tables. But when he tried to follow, he collided into something. He looked from the invisible wall to the floor. A powerful pattern encircled him, its coppery light gleaming from his dance shoes.

"Devil trap, sucka," James announced, reholstering his pistol.

Edgar tested the column with his hands, then hammered it twice with the sides of his fists. It shuddered slightly, but held. The piano continued to play in the corner—until Bree-yark knocked it off key and half mute with a shotgun blast.

"Told you I can't stand that stuff," he muttered, his next blast silencing it altogether.

Meanwhile, my whip was growing and splitting into branches. As I stalked forward, they skipped over the floor and trailed grooves of white smoke. My angel blood simmered hotter, stoking my rage centers.

"Oh, be reasonable," Edgar said. "Let's talk about this."

"Let's not," I growled, and lashed the whip forward.

The tendrils snapped around him, wrapping him from ears to ankles. White fire hissed from the contact, followed by a ragged whine. As smoke plumed up around him, the whine turned into a full-throated cry.

Now it was my turn to smile. Because this was more than ending a threat. This was inflicting as much pain as possible on the vile spawn before casting his wrecked and shrieking essence back to the Below.

But I caught myself.

Just finish him and be done with it, man.

Concentrating through my angel-hot fury, I yanked back on the whip. The cord broke through Edgar's form, severing his scream and dropping him into smoking pieces over the circle trap. The pieces erupted into flames and then, like the flash paper magicians use, vanished into the barest mist.

Abracadabra, asshole.

As the anger drained off me, I lowered the dimming whip and gave it a light flick. The branching cords retracted, becoming a short length of steel cable once more. I held still, listening for the sounds of trumpets or angel wings or whatever else might herald the arrival of the angel Faziel. Though I trusted my magic, I whispered a prayer of thanks all the same when he didn't swoop in.

My teammates looked from the demon trap, where a thin coil of smoke lingered, to the rest of the room.

None of us had expected the encounter to end that quickly, but a major threat didn't always have to mean a major finish. Sometimes you were just on your Annihilation A-game, and I had my teammates, solid planning, and a damned powerful weapon to thank. My magic, too, for showing me the way.

We would still need to clear the hotel, ensure the demons were gone. But as went Edgar, so went the connection to the

Below. There was no more infernal energy to sustain demons or command druids.

A series of *tsks* sounds. "And he was *so* young."

I spun to find a respawned Edgar leaning in the doorway to the dining room, shaking his head.

"A fine dancer, too," he added. "Does anyone have anything they'd like to say in his memory?"

39

Edgar was back in his attire from our first encounter, a collarless white shirt buttoned to his throat and a trench coat that matched mine. But screw all of that. The version of him dancing hadn't been an illusion. Loukia's detection spell singled him out. Not only that, but I'd *felt* him through the whip.

The hem of the trench coat slid to the ankles of his boots as he straightened. "Self-duplication is *really* underrated."

With a Word, James thrust his wand, spinning a silver net from the air that snared Edgar.

Loukia, meanwhile, was gathering the copper washers from the dance floor with her magic and relocating them to the doorway. Before she could complete the trap, though, the net dropped, scattering into silver sparks.

"The hell?" James muttered.

"Yoo-hoo!" Edgar called.

He was sitting on the ruined piano now, swinging a leg. Great, so we could add teleportation to his list of abilities. I guessed that was what ten thousand souls and a demon lord for a father got you.

"And that's not all," he said, as though divining my thoughts.

When he snapped his fingers, a giant roar sounded. Hellish light filled the doorway he'd just vacated, but it was coming from the blown-open doors to the hotel. He'd resurrected the fiery enclosure Petra had taken down. As I shook my whip out, I glanced over at Edgar's former dance partner.

"Oh, you thought I still needed them for protection?" he asked with a laugh. "No longer, but since it could get lonely…"

He snapped his fingers again, and the druid he'd spun off into the tables lurched upright, an infernal glow in her eyes. I picked up more shuffling in the lobby. Just like that, he'd restored all the Black Earth druids.

"And it doesn't stop there."

He wiggled his fingers. James and Loukia, who'd been working furiously to rebuild the trap around him a third time stopped suddenly. They lowered their casting implements and began jittering into spastic fits. The red of demonic possession came and went in their eyes. They resisted, teeth gnashing with effort.

I gathered my breath for a dispersion invocation, then stopped.

Despite carrying holy power in my pendant, I'd felt the inrush of clouds that heralded Thelonious's arrival. As the clouds thinned to a gray, mind-fogging haze, I looked to my whip, but it wasn't the branching, crackling beast of just two minutes earlier. It was a dull, two-foot length of cable.

I shook it again, trying to stoke the angel fury back to life.

Loukia collapsed to her knees, while James toppled onto

his side, one of his fists alternately striking out at the air and mashing into his own face. Something told me Edgar was toying with them, that he could send them into full possession any time he wanted.

"What the hell do you want?" I shouted, still hazy from my near miss with Thelonious.

"An appropriate turn of phrase," Edgar replied. "We'll get to that in a moment, but first I—"

Ka-blam! The shotgun blast threw the demon prince into a half twist. He turned back in time to receive a second blast, this one flattening him against the piano lid with a discordant *jang.*

When he came upright, smoke drifted from a face that had been ripped open.

"More where that came from," Bree-yark grunted, pumping the action again.

But when he took aim this time, his weapon blew apart. He staggered back, blood glistening from his shoulders and brow where the exploding shell had struck him. Worse, the haunting glow of infernal light was taking hold in his eyes, too.

Snorting like a bull, he set his stout legs and stared back at Edgar. The demon prince fixed his skewed glasses and extended a hand, upping the possessing power. But Bree-yark's resistance held fast. The muscles in his face clenched, and his snorts came faster, as though he were trying to squeeze out his available oxygen. The hellish glow in his eyes dimmed by degrees, then went out altogether.

"Tenacious little shit," Edgar muttered, showing anger for the first time.

He drew back his hand, freeing Bree-yark, who fell forward with a gasp. But the demon prince hadn't stopped moving his fingers, as though sifting around for something. His puckered lips molded into a grin over his healing face.

"Ooh, I see you've been demon-attacked before."

He was referring to the 1776 time catch, when Bree-yark had battled the demon Forneus. Ravaged by infernal fire, Bree-yark had been mortally wounded, on the brink of death. It had taken Elder-level magic to restore him, and even then, his full recovery had required another year.

"The thing about demonic wounds," Edgar continued, sounding philosophical, "is that they never really heal. They just get smoothed over."

He sliced his fingers now, as though ripping through stitching and scar tissue. Bree-yark released a crazed cry, as if all the pain he'd endured during Forneus's attack were landing back inside him at once. The sound scattered the last of my mental haze.

"Stop!" I shouted.

I dug into my coat pockets for something, anything, I could use in lieu of the whip.

Edgar smiled sadistically. With the demon prince's next gesture, Bree-yark's cry ended with a dry grunt, and he toppled forward. Smoke gusted from his body as he landed face down—just as I'd found him in the time catch.

I abandoned my pockets and rushed to my friend's side.

His mouth hung open, showing the tips of his lower teeth. His dull, empty eyes stared past mine.

"*Bree-yark*," I said, shaking him urgently.

I looked over at Loukia and James. They were standing now, eyes glowing red.

I dropped my forehead to Bree-yark's chest, which was compact and still. "What do you want?" I asked through gritted teeth.

"The whip," Edgar replied. "For starters."

"Bring him back first," I said. "And then let them all go."

Edgar laughed sharply. "Do you really think you're in a position to negotiate? You're trapped here. Your doddering Order is lost. None of your friends can help you. You can't even help *yourself*, Everson. You know what will happen if you try."

I sensed Thelonious standing by, ready to jump in again.

"The whip," Edgar repeated. I lifted my head to find him extending a hand.

I reached into my pocket and squeezed the duct-taped grip. It was the weapon I'd been banking on, the weapon that should have destroyed him. Instead, it had only destroyed a copy of him—one of several, most likely.

He hadn't needed to know our plan. He'd only had to watch us run the play and then adapt.

Still, I'd *felt* his pain when the whip had seized his duplicated form and torn it apart. The whip's angelic power could destroy him. The thought heated my blood again, and a sizzle ran the whip's length.

But when I drew it from my pocket, it was just an inert cable.

"If you insist on delaying," Edgar said, "I'll be happy to have your friends dispose of themselves."

I looked over to find James aiming his wand at his own face, while Loukia held one glowing blade out from her chest and the other from her stomach, tensing to deliver the lethal blows.

"All right, all right," I said quickly, drawing the whip back to toss.

"No," he said sharply. "You'll hand it to me like a proper gentleman."

He shoved himself from the piano and landed lightly on his oiled boots. He opened and closed the slender, pale fingers of his extended hand in an exaggerated show of patience. I stood and walked toward him.

Though he was hiding it well, the whip made him nervous. Did I channel all my power into it and hope for the best? Because as I drew closer, I began to wonder if there were no more duplications of himself. If this was all he had left.

His eyes stopped me. Though I couldn't see them, something in the shades told me that if I bet wrong, he would have Loukia and James join Bree-yark without giving it a second thought.

Desperate for guidance I tuned into my magic. *What next?*

But it was back to its seemingly aimless motion. Whether it was trying to arrange something, I had no idea. But it was too late. I was standing in front of Edgar now, offering him the whip, handle out.

As he took it, his thin lips pinched into a grin that looked like relief. "Excellent."

He regarded the threaded length of steel before dropping it in front of him. Infernal flames burst up, engulfing the whip. The fire burned small but brightly. Soundless detonations of white light went off inside. Then the fire disappeared, and the handle of the angel-powered weapon landed on the floor, melted and disfigured.

Edgar dusted off his hands.

"Now," he said. "I'm actually glad you're here. We were going to have to hold this conversation sooner or later, and it was easier for you to come to me than vice versa. You have questions, I know. Chief among them why you're still alive. I'll explain everything, but only if you promise to stay on your very best behavior." He said it like a teacher stooped over a grade school student, and it chaffed like hell.

"I promise," I muttered.

He clapped his hands twice and addressed the room. "A couple of chairs, please?"

The druid staggered into motion, seized a chair, and carried it to him. He thanked her and spun it around, straddling it backward.

"Please," he said to me. "Have a seat."

Something butted against the backs of my thighs. I turned to see that Loukia and James had carried another chair over by the armrests, the horrible glow of possession seated deep in their unblinking eyes. Beyond them, Bree-yark remained down among the pieces of his shotgun, smoke drifting from his still body.

Furious, grieving, and out of options, I drew a sleeve across my mouth and sat.

"Talk," I said.

40

Edgar drummed his hands on the chair back before resting his elbow across it. Though his shades made it appear that he was staring me down, the angle of his head suggested he was trying to puzzle something out.

"You had me in your hands twice, a helpless babe," he said at last. "And you didn't destroy me. Why?"

"Just tell me what you want."

"Relax, there's time." He checked his watch, a slick Rolex, before shaking his coat sleeve back over its gold face. "No, I honestly want to know. Why didn't you drive that beautiful blade of yours through me and scatter me to the four corners? It would have worked. I was in no position to stop you."

I didn't know his game, but I refused to play along.

He leaned back and opened his arms. "I mean, your magic couldn't have put it to you any more plainly: 'Kill the child.'"

My mind snapped to attention. *Find the child.*

Edgar straightened. "Is that what you thought it said?"

Demons at his level possessed powers of telepathy, and I'd replayed the memory so clearly, I might as well have broadcast it in Dolby surround. Even with the obfuscation enchantment, I needed to be more careful.

But I couldn't *not* wonder now whether I'd heard wrong.

Edgar's perfect teeth flashed like a picket fence as he laughed in surprise, slapping the chair back twice for emphasis. "Are you kidding me? Well, that would explain it. Talk about dropping the game winner."

Find the child. That's what my magic had told me—I was sure of it. *Find the child.*

But I paused to test the variation: *Kill the child.*

I went back and forth until the key verbs blurred in my mind and I couldn't be sure what I'd heard.

"Wow, think of it," Edgar said, pausing to draw a finger under his right shade as he chuckled some more. "You could have closed the curtain on this whole show. I'd be history, along with this horrible air quality you're suffering. And today was supposed to be pleasant—dry and cool with highs in the upper sixties. Not to mention the thousands upon thousands of *souls* you might have spared."

I fought to block out his goading words, to empty my mind. Demons were master manipulators. He was trying to get inside my head, psych me out.

Find the child... Kill the child...

I peered back at James and Loukia, who were planted behind me like wax statues, then over at Bree-yark, who remained down. Then I thought of all the innocent souls ripped from their bodies, fuel for Sathanas and his son.

A fresh wave of grief and anger rose up.

Clear your mind, I urged myself. *Stay with your faith, your magic.*

"You know what I think?" Edgar said. "You heard what you wanted to hear, because the thought of harming that *poor child* was too much for your precious morality. You needn't have worried. I strangled him early on—in the womb, in fact. He was just a flesh suit by the time I came out. I was one hundred percent *démon*," he said in exaggerated French. "But that's the line of Saint Michael for you. A bunch of do-gooding sheep."

I ignored my own counsel as anger gripped my neck and burned in the hollows of my face. "Those 'do-gooding sheep' banished your father from the world twice now," I growled. "What does that say about him?"

Edgar stiffened as if I'd caught him with a left jab but then relaxed around another teeth-baring smile. "We learn from our mistakes, Everson. Unlike your Order." He shook his head. "So pathetically predictable."

Were my fears founded? Had the Order been led astray again?

I hardened the muscles around my eyes to hide my anxiety, but I was too late. Edgar had caught it.

As his smile grew, the room darkened. Deep infernal light glowed from the baseboards. Edgar stood, shadows springing around him. They gathered into a massive set of wings, horns that jutted from his cheeks and punched through his hair in a ring, and a barbed tail that raked the floor at his back.

"*Alone,*" he rumbled, in Sathanas's voice. "*The poor wizard is all alone.*"

For a terrifying moment, I was back in the subbasement in St. Martin's, facing the demon lord. I'd forgotten his size, the wrath and power of his presence. I shrank back as his laughter shook the room. And now a timid voice inside me was whispering that I'd had no right to banish a demon lord, not as a novice practitioner.

No right at all.

The darkness withdrew, the shadows dispersed, and Edgar became a slender red-head in a trench coat once more. He waved a flippant hand as he turned his chair around and sat in it properly. I collected myself, hating that I'd cowered, hating even more that I could see Father Vick in his features. It seemed as much a taunt as the trench coat.

"Look, what's done is done," Edgar said with a sigh. "Here I am, and there you are. Now, why didn't *I* kill *you*?" He leaned forward, his knees supporting his narrow elbows. "I wanted you to see the city for yourself. The state of it. The hopelessness. I wanted you to understand that I was in control and there was nothing you could do. But I mostly kept you alive because I have three tasks for you."

A finger of hope flickered inside me. He needed me. And if he needed me, he lacked something to complete his second return.

I kept a poker face. "What are they?"

"First, I want you to kill the Nephilim."

Was that what the demons called those with Faziel's blood? "The pale woman?" I asked to be sure.

"I called off your incubus, but you failed to finish her," he said sternly.

He was referring to our melee at the IFC Center. That explained why my power had returned. Not because Thelonious had shrunk from the holy threshold, but because Sathanas had ordered him down.

"Why her?" I asked.

"That's not for you to know."

"Then why should I kill her?"

"Your friends." He nodded past me. "I'll restore them."

"Sure you will."

"Or I can destroy them right now. You're in no position to stop me. Neither are they—especially your stubby chum on the floor over there. He's going on five minutes without a pulse." He shrugged as though to say *your choice.*

I reset my jaw. "The second task."

"I need access to St. Martin's Cathedral."

I stiffened. "Why?"

"For a powerless wizard, you really ask a lot of questions. That's not for you to know," he repeated, agitation growing in his voice. "In exchange for access, I'll give the city a twelve-hour respite, a chance to clear out. But I warn you not to use it to bring in supernatural backup. I understand you have a little girl now? It would be a shame to have to deprive her of that sweet, sweet soul."

Adrenaline ripped through me and my breathing quickened. "Third task," I growled.

"Before midnight tonight, you're going to deliver the Nephilim's sword to the basement of St. Martin's. I think you know the place."

He meant the grotto in the ossuary, the same spot where I'd denied Sathanas his sacrifice of Bishop Sheridan four years earlier. Midnight was the alignment of the Child and Father stars, the event that would propel Sathanas into the world. Only there would be no Contest. Sathanas was making sure of that by having me kill the pale woman and deliver her sword, which he would no doubt destroy, just as he'd done the whip. But the sword was no shadow weapon—he needed that fount of ley energy, the most powerful in the city, to fuel the sword's incineration and nullify its threat.

"And if I don't?" I asked.

Edgar flashed a cruel smile. "Do you really want to know?"

In my peripheral vision, infernal smoke gathered, morphing into faces I knew: Ricki's, Abigail's, Tony's, our friends'. Their eyes were wide, horror ringing them white. Then came the tortured screams.

The worst were Abigail's infant squalls.

"Okay, okay!" I shouted, squeezing my eyes closed. "Enough, *goddammit!*"

The images dispersed. "I didn't think so," Edgar said. "And that would go for *any* of the three tasks you fail to complete. So if you think you're going to outwit me, some-how, I would seriously think again."

I kept my head bowed and eyes closed, my breaths coming hard. "What do I get for this one?"

"How about not undoing the last two? That's rather generous: restoring your friends and releasing my grip on the city for a full twelve. You can't win, but you can mitigate your losses. That's the best you're going to get." His visage turned dark with humor. "You already know the worst."

The images of my family and friends took brief form in the smoke between us.

"And you never know," Edgar said, waving them away. "Please Sathanas in your work, and he might find a use for you that doesn't involve eternal torture. My father may not give selflessly, but he gives."

"You mean the two-time loser?"

My head rocked to one side. The explosive pain in my jaw

and the hot taste of blood arrived a moment later. Edgar stood before me, nostrils flaring, fist poised for a follow-up blow. But he restrained himself.

"You have your tasks," he said hotly. "Thelonious, get him out of here."

41

The creamy white light receded, and I found myself washed up on the steps of my apartment building. I checked my watch. Less than an hour of missing time, meaning Thelonious had skipped the carousing. I did the post-Thelonious pat down anyway.

Faziel's whip was gone, of course, but I found all my other implements where I'd put them. They were no threat to Edgar. He may even have wanted to ensure I had everything I would need for my tasks. Even so, I was surprised to find my coin pendant still tucked under the front of my shirt. The obfuscation enchantment must have been powerful enough to have worked on Edgar, too.

That's something, I thought dimly. *Even if everything else has gone to absolute shit.*

Hacking infernal smoke, I pushed myself to my feet and staggered up the steps. Somehow, I made it to the top floor. Ricki opened the warded door of our apartment and I stumbled into her arms.

"Everson!" she said, helping me to my chair, where I sat heavily. "Are you all right?"

She touched the knot on my jaw where Edgar had struck me, then brushed my hair from my brow.

"Did Jordan or Petra come back?" I asked.

She shook her head. Before I could ask her to contact the Sup Squad driver or send another vehicle to check on them, Mae came rushing in from the kitchen, drying her hands on a towel. She looked from me to the closed door. The questioning concern in her eyes said it all: she'd been expecting Bree-yark. As I recalled his dim, vacant stare, I covered my face with my hands and shook my head.

"What is it, hon?" Mae asked. "What's happened?"

I could hear Tony playing with Buster in his room. I imagined little Abigail down for her afternoon nap. I took a deep, steadying breath and scrubbed my face. This was no time to break down. My loved ones were counting on me. Still, it took all my strength to meet Mae's anxious gaze.

"Bree-yark..." I swallowed. "He's still at the hotel. Things didn't go as planned."

And then I told them what happened.

When I finished, Mae remained standing, one hand to her mouth, another to her heart. Ricki was beside her, hugging her shoulders. She finally coaxed Mae to sit on the couch with her, where the woman who'd become like a grandmother to me broke down in great, heaving sobs. It went on for several minutes and was as gutting as it sounds.

I leaned forward and held her hand. It was feeble consolation, but she squeezed back. In her drowning grip, I felt the death of her first husband and the long, cluttered solitude that followed. I felt the spark of Bree-yark's arrival and the steady, swelling love that filled her life again. And then I felt the pain of collapse as she anticipated losing that, too. I brought my other hand to the back of hers.

Tabitha regarded the whole thing with a flat stare. That, plus her silence, was the closest to sympathy we were going to get.

"What are the tasks again?" Ricki asked quietly.

"Kill the pale woman," I said. "That will restore Bree-yark and the others. Then I have to give him access to St. Martin's. In exchange, he'll release his infernal hold over the city for twelve hours. Finally, deliver the sword to him at St. Martin's before midnight. That will ensure he upholds his first two promises."

"It will also ensure his release," Ricki pointed out.

I nodded, trying not to show the utter defeat I felt. I didn't tell her what would happen if I refused the tasks—I didn't want to relive those images again.

Thankfully, she didn't ask.

Mae sniffled and patted my hand. "Well, we're not going to let you do any such thing, Everson. You let that evil into this world, and it's only a matter of time before it comes for all of us—restored or not, in or out of this city. I just know there's another way." She smacked her knee for emphasis. "There's *got* to be."

I nodded again, even though I could see nothing right now but smoke and death.

Understanding the dilemma, Ricki's eyes remained dark. "What are you going to do?"

If there was one fingerhold Edgar had given me, however small, it was time.

I pressed my hands to my thighs and stood. "I'm going to start by checking in on the kids. Then I'm going to sit down and have a heart-to-heart with my magic."

I settled into my casting circle in the basement lab and exhaled, trying to center myself. But I was too pissed off.

I'd listened to my magic. It had shown me the angel-powered whip. It had nodded at every goddamned step of the planning. And then I'd lost the fight to Edgar, I'd lost James and Loukia to possession, and I'd lost Bree-yark, my closest friend, to death.

I wiped my eyes fiercely.

And now my magic was back to its aimless, *what, me worry?* bullshit. No urgency, no direction. But beneath my anger, there was the question Edgar had planted, a question that burned like a splinter caught in the pulp of my conscience. Had I ignored my magic's most crucial directive?

Find the child... Kill the child...

Because if my magic had told me the second, maybe it had been playing catch up this whole time, trying to reroute me after two missed opportunities. Doing the best it could with a flubbed hand.

Could I have followed through, though?

I'd considered the question while looking down at Abigail asleep in her crib, haloed in the soft light of my mother's emo ball, innocent to the horrors outside. What if the scantest sliver of Edgar the child had remained? Could I have done it? Could I have killed him?

No, I decided. Not even knowing what I knew now, and if that made me a do-gooding sheep, so be it.

From the circle, I released my breath, my thoughts. I descended, down, down, into the depths of my magic. Having been so thoroughly defeated, the surrendering came easy. I had nothing left. The currents of magic grew stronger and heavier. They pushed, pulled, and upended me, like a seashell in a vast ocean.

And then everything went still.

My space had become small and enclosed. A fuzzy weight that smelled of moth balls pressed in on me from both sides, and my legs ached from crouching. Suddenly, I knew this place. I was in the closet of my grandfather's attic study, reliving a memory from when I was thirteen.

Aprire, I recalled myself saying in an awed, prepubescent voice.

Yes, that had been my first time speaking one of Grandpa's words. And, like magic, it had released the door to his empty study, the one room in our old house I was forbidden from entering.

I remembered the battered trunk beside his desk. It had looked like a pirate's chest and felt alive under my hands. Then I'd heard him coming up the steps, and I'd plunged into his closet of hanging coats and pulled the folding door closed behind me.

Now, true to the memory, the door to the study creaked open. The floorboards clicked with someone's weight, and a dangling bulb filled the seam above the closet door's middle hinge with light.

But what am I doing back here?

From my hiding place among the coats, I leaned toward the seam.

A tall figure entered my view, his back to me. Apprehension drew my stomach tight, partly because I knew what was going to follow. At any moment, Grandpa was going to open the closet, seize my wrist, and use the blade of his cane sword to cut my first finger. Deeply. I could already feel the bright burn. He would use my blood to prepare his sword, the Banebrand, for my eventual use, but I hadn't known that at the time.

Even knowing it now did little to lessen my anxiety.

I almost shouted when the closet door folded opened and light rushed in. But the hand that gripped my wrist wasn't harsh and it wasn't my grandfather's. I blinked out at a man whose shoulder-length hair was mostly silver now. His scar-etched face was handsome and familiar. Intelligent gray eyes smiled into mine.

"Everson," he said.

In a voice weak with love and wonder, I murmured, "Dad?"

He drew me from the closet and held me solidly against him, rocking me from side to side. "Hello, son."

42

My father clapped my back several times, and held me out by the shoulders. He looked over my face before his rich gray eyes settled on mine. The moment was like our last face-to-face, right before he plunged into Dhuul's pit.

I have to go, he'd said. *But I go with the joy that I finally got to see you, to know you.*

Then as now, his image blurred as I blinked back tears. As though to spare me any embarrassment, he released me and lifted his gaze to my hair.

"I see your salt's starting to compete with your pepper," he said. "It's been trying out there, yes?"

I nodded, still unable to speak. He and my mother had placed me in my grandparents' care for protection right after I turned one. Days later, my mother was killed by the corrupt magic-user Lich.

Years later, I found my father in the Refuge when I'd become a magic-user myself. We joined forces to defeat Lich, but our time together was brief. Before his demise, Lich released a world destroyer named Dhuul, the Whisperer. My father sacrificed his life to repel the ancient being and prevent the world from falling into chaos. He'd been my role model ever since, the man and magic-user I aspired to become.

He would know what to do.

"God, it's incredible to see you again," I said, finding my voice. "But are you...?"

"Actually your father?" His eyes crinkled when he smiled. "For centuries, the same magic that now moves through you moved through me. And just as I learned to become that magic, it came to know me, both within and without—as intimately as the water knows its stream bed or the wind a slot canyon. So, yes. You're seeing your father."

It was my father, but it was also my magic.

He smiled. "You said you wanted a heart-to-heart."

"So you know the situation with Sathanas and my friends?"

"Of course."

"Sathanas is forcing me into tasks that will ensure his successful emergence, and I can't see a way out. Not without losing my loved ones—who I'll probably lose anyway if I free him," I added helplessly.

The old boards in the attic clicked as he began to pace, hands clasped behind his low back. "Yes, we're working on that," he said.

I pictured the Order arriving en masse, spells blazing. "And you'll have something by midnight?"

"There is another reason I appeared to you as your father," he said, as though he hadn't heard the question. "He left you a message. Well, *I* left you a message. Here, in your magic." Though he was smiling when he peered over at me, it was a sad smile.

My breathing thinned. "What is it?"

"You know of the angel Faziel. It's okay, we can speak his name here."

I nodded, already sensing the weight of what he was about to share.

"Well, it was my line that passed his blood to you. Not pure blood, no, but pure enough. Of course none of us knew this at the time. We'd thought the age of the Avenging Angels had passed, that nothing more of them existed in this world or any other, save perhaps in the diffuse particulates of the universe."

As when I'd last seen my father, I marveled at how much we talked alike, even paced alike.

"Long ago, when your grandfather and I and the rest of the Order were battling the forces of the Inquisition, I took an urgent trip to Venice for supplies. This would have been in the sixteenth century. My business took me to the bustling Rialto market, where I found what I needed. But instead of leaving, I made a side trip to St. Mark's Square. It was just to see the palace and church—that was what I told myself—but it wasn't true. I was pulled there, Everson, to the basilica specifically."

"As if by Fate itself," I said, recalling my dream.

"Yes, very much. I made arrangements through one of the servants to enter alone that night. Then, as now, the basilica was an awesome sight with its many domes and rich mosaics, even more so by lantern light. But I only cared to find the source of what was pulling me, *willing* me, into its vast depths. Though the threshold had left me vulnerable, I went ever deeper. At last, I arrived in the back of the church, in an old brick grotto, where I knelt before the tomb of a forgotten bishop."

I nodded fervently, seeing the grotto from my dream.

"I removed the tomb's lid, and there it was: a sword in the bishop's skeletal grip. The pristine metal was nearly white. Not a spot of age along its gleaming length. I almost snatched it up. The idea felt as natural as taking one's own child into his arms, Everson. But as my hand went near it, I sensed a great and terrible power, and I withdrew. Before I could reconsider, I took what magic I had and wrapped the power in a Gordian Knot. I then sealed the tomb and rushed from the basilica, feeling as if I'd just looked upon Death."

That was how I had felt upon awakening from my dream. I didn't remember seeing a tomb, though, just the angel and my shadow's decapitated body.

"The sword was Faziel's," I said.

"Yes, though I didn't know it then. I'd *wanted* to make inquiries into the bishop's identity, into the sword, but I was needed at the front. And then events took over from there." He meant joining the secret resistance with my grandfather and moving to the Refuge, where he eventually met my mother. "We can only surmise that Faziel created the sword as a focusing relic before his demise. Meaning only those of his blood can free him. *That* was why it was calling to me. Thank the stars I resisted."

"But I didn't," I said hollowly. "Not in the shadow realm."

I pictured that version of me, a young academic saying goodbye to his wife and three-year-old child for his doctoral research. He'd been drawn to St. Mark's Basilica, like his father centuries before, to the bishop's tomb. Then, in violation of all research ethics, he'd pried open the lid and seized the powerful sword.

The images felt true, possibly from having been bonded

to his cremated remains for a time. I could all but feel the sword's cold, thrumming metal in my grip.

"Most likely, yes," my father agreed. "But by no fault of his own."

"But how did I undo the knot? I wasn't a practitioner in that reality—I didn't even know I was a magic-user."

"My magic would have degraded with time. By then, all it may have taken was for the knot to recognize your aura—one very much like mine, after all. From there, your angel blood would have awakened the relic's power. I imagine the angel Faziel emerged and slew you so as not to be beholden to you as master. He then went in search of demons, since that was his original purpose. Finding none, he turned his wrath on the ones who replaced him."

"St. Michael's line," I said. "All the magic-users."

I remembered the desolation of the shadow present. A reality without magic.

"Before returning to the sword, a plane unto itself, he would have instilled those of his blood with his power," he said.

Those must have been the founders of the Street Keepers and the other extreme law-and-order cults. Empowered to eradicate demonkind and the line of Michael, the Street Keepers had hunted me and Alec.

"Faziel's version of keeping the grounds salted, I suppose," my father continued. "That never happened here, of course. Faziel's power is still locked in the sword. But the sword is no longer entombed."

"Emma has it," I said, "the pale woman."

As he spoke, I'd been connecting her attack on me to what Caroline had said about Emma's recent travel to Venice.

And then, of course, there had been the sword she'd wielded at the IFC Center.

"Yes, another angel-blooded, like us," he said. "But not a magic-user of the Order. The impending return of Sathanas has awakened this young woman to her nature. She was called to the tomb of the forgotten bishop, where she found and recovered the sword. But she cannot open the knot. Some of the sword's latent power comes through—you've felt it, yes?—but not the full power of Faziel. Not even close."

That explained why I'd been able to overcome her when we fought at the IFC Center. Still, the limited power of the blade had made sliced kebab of the pitch demon. I could only imagine the world-shaking kickassery the knot was holding back. More than enough to destroy Sathanas's son, certainly.

But once again the thought of releasing the Avenging Angel filled me with a graveyard dread. I'd seen what would happen—and the annihilation of the Order was only the beginning.

"What if I attempted another truce with Faziel?" I asked. "Like in the shadow realm?"

My father shook his head. "He won't be amenable. Too much pent up vengeance and a wrath to rival Sathanas's. Upon his release, he'll do here exactly what he did in the other reality. He only granted you a truce because he'd already destroyed the line of saints, and he recognized your blood as his."

"What does that leave?" I asked.

"There's the Refuge," he offered. "Elder built, no demons can penetrate that thought realm. You and your loved ones and the rest of the Order would be safe. From there, you can plan your response."

"And abandon the ones we're meant to protect?"

The notion felt like an ice-bath in my chest. Centuries trapped in the Refuge, like my father and Arianna and the rest of the senior members, while the world burned and suffered unimaginable tortures? I couldn't do it.

"Did the Order know about Sathanas's son?" I asked.

He shook his head. "Certain conditions hid him from them. Until his emergence, that was."

"So why aren't they here?"

I braced myself for the assertion that they'd become trapped again. Instead, he said, "Don't fear for them, Everson. They're doing important work at the moment, but they're also heeding their magic."

Sensing that line of discussion would lead nowhere, I lowered myself onto Grandpa's old trunk with a ponderous sigh, no closer to a solution. I couldn't abandon the city to the demon lord.

"There is another way," my father announced quietly.

I looked up "There is?"

He'd turned toward the attic window, his profile staring at the dust-coated glass. "We're called magic-users, but what we really do is alchemy. Taking raw energy and channeling it through our essence to create manifestations. The most practiced of us heed that essence, for it is the will of the First Saints. What manifests is the best expression of that will." He blinked slowly. "Faziel is a form of energy."

"Are you suggesting I can, what, channel his essence?"

"And alchemize it into something less violent and vengeful, yes."

In the shadow realm, Faziel had annihilated the entire Order, then deputized the angel-blooded the world over, probably before breakfast. That was the kind of essence we were talking about.

"Is that even possible?"

My father remained staring out the window, not answering. The light through the dust paled his face, making him appear older.

"This should have been my burden, Everson. As I stared down at the sword that night, my magic was also talking. It suggested that, yes, what you behold is terrible, but you can resolve an old enmity that will rid the world of a threat and bring even greater power to the Order." He gripped the window sill and bowed his head. "My magic had compelled me to the tomb as much as the sword had. But I didn't stay long enough to listen, to understand what was being asked of me. Though I was powerful at the time—perhaps powerful enough—I was afraid of what would happen should I fail."

"Afraid?" I echoed.

I saw my father diving into the nightmare pit, his flapping robes consumed by the vast darkness and horrid whispers rushing toward him. I remembered the Word he shouted, more potent and resonant than anything I'd ever heard. I remembered the light of an exploding star and Dhuul's dying scream.

As unfair as it may have been, I hadn't imagined the man capable of fear.

"Yes, afraid," he said. "And so I locked up the sword's power and left it." He lowered himself beside me on the trunk, hands clasped between his knees. "I'm sorry, Everson. A son should never have to bear his father's burden."

How could this great man be apologizing to *me*? But in his apology, I also heard my odds of success. Practically nil.

I gripped his shoulder and pulled him against my side. His arm wrapped my back. We remained like that for a long while. Downstairs, the old townhouse creaked and I heard the occasional voice—ghosts of my grandparents in this reimagining of my childhood home.

I examined the faint scar on my finger left by Grandpa's blade: my early initiation into magic.

"I don't expect you to undertake this," my father said. "But we'll do everything in our power to help you. If your choice is the Refuge, just say it, and we'll make it happen. There would be no shame."

I sensed that the collective magic could put its efforts toward one or the other, but not both. In other words, I couldn't pack my loved ones off to the Refuge and then attempt to channel Faziel.

I would have to commit to one.

As I considered that, I recalled something I'd told Alec, the son of my shadow.

Magic isn't all spells and invocations. It's trusting that the work you've done—that effort and intention—that it's swimming in the collective magic and will emerge as the right solution at the right time. That's real magic.

I cleared my throat. "Are there times when magic *doesn't* have the answer?"

My father straightened from my side and smiled tenderly "Yes and no. Sometimes it can only take you so far, to the very edge, even. Then it's up to what's inside *you*. For even as users of the collective magic, we're all uniquely composed."

Once more, I saw him diving into the pit to repel Chaos itself, headlong and without hesitation. That had been his choice.

There was something else I needed to know.

"Did you tell me to 'find the child,'" I asked, "or 'kill the child'?"

"I told you what you heard," he answered mysteriously, suggesting that I could have heard either one.

"I should go, then."

When we stood and hugged, he felt smaller than he had earlier. "Again, I'm sorry—"

"I love you, Dad," I whispered fiercely, cutting him off. "And everything you've passed on. You're always with me. *Always.*"

43

"How do I look?" I asked Ricki when I returned upstairs.

She allowed a wan smile as I performed a slow twirl. "Like you've come to a decision."

I'd showered in the basement unit, then shaved and combed my hair. I changed, swapping my old trench coat for a fresh one that still smelled like its packaging. Then I cleaned and prepped my most powerful magical items until they hummed with fresh energy.

The work was absorbing, reminiscent of my time in Romania when I'd been awaiting Lazlo's decree—whether he would train me into the old Order or destroy me. I'd spent the day confined to a small room, organizing my belongings, reflecting on my life, and considering what future, if any, I might have. Fifteen years later, I was doing the same. The difference was those fifteen years. I wasn't a rube anymore. I was a magic-user of the true Order, and everything my father had said during our heart-to-heart had landed in a way they couldn't have even fifteen *days* ago, much less years.

My magic would deliver me to the edge, and I would take it from there.

I'd prepared his sword last, instilling it with an important spell, before slotting it home into my grandfather's cane.

"Yeah, I know what I need to do," I replied, glancing down at the cane.

"Spill it, then," Ricki said. "You've been married to me long enough to know I have a kink for specifics."

"First, any word from Jordan or Petra?"

"I finally got ahold of the driver. While Jordan was working on Petra, demons attacked the vehicle. A fight followed. The driver's escort was wounded, and he rushed him off in the carrier. Says he didn't realize Jordan and Petra weren't on board. He returned to the scene, but couldn't find them."

Damn, and that was with Petra's condition uncertain. Even so, I could think of few people better equipped to handle that kind of a scenario than Jordan. And his staff had been loaded with powerful magic for the mission.

"The Sup Squad is keeping an eye out for them," she said.

"Good. You still remember the location of our safehouse?"

She stopped as if she'd been tazed. "You're going to do them? His tasks?"

"The first two, anyway. Taking down the pale woman and getting him access to St. Martin's. It will restore Bree-yark and the others and give Manhattan a twelve-hour respite. Give everyone a chance to clear out."

Ricky went quiet. She knew both would also give Sathanas a major boost.

"What about number three?" she asked.

Delivering the Sword of Faziel to St. Martin's. The task that would place me in direct reach of the demon lord. Was that the edge? The call I would have to make? Or would my magic show me the way?

"I'm not sure yet," I replied honestly. "But I'll know the right course."

She slid her arms around my waist and pressed herself against me. "To answer your earlier question, you look about as handsome as I've ever seen you, so the 'right course' better involve a future date night."

We were both trying to keep things light, but neither of us were very good at it. Not with Armageddon knocking. After another minute of holding her, I kissed her head firmly.

"Pack only the essentials," I said.

"Don't worry. Bree-yark had us organize bug-out kits earlier."

"Good, because I want you to be ready to move when the smoke lifts."

She separated and looked up at me. "I'm not going to be able to do that."

"What do you mean?" Irritation burned the edges of my puzzlement. "Why not?"

"When the smoke lifts, we're talking about an evacuation on a scale Manhattan's never seen before. Two million people, and only twelve hours to get it done? The OEM will need every available body from every major service—police, fire, transit. I may be a wife and mother, but I'm also NYPD."

Exhaling through my nose, I nodded. "Of course."

I wasn't the only one with a duty to protect the city. She gripped my hands.

"Mae will be with them," she said of the kids. "I'll make sure they get the safest transport out of here."

"Bree-yark will be with them, too," I said. "Also James and Loukia."

Understanding that I was referring to the deal for completing task one, she asked, "Do you even know where the pale woman is?"

"Not exactly, but I have a good idea who does." I'd missed some earlier clues, but I was all but certain now of the identity of the IFC official who had sponsored her. "That's where I'm headed first."

She squeezed my hands more forcefully. "So, this is goodbye for now?"

"For now," I echoed, even though it wasn't a promise I could make any more than she could.

The rest of the apartment overheard the announcement. Mae came over carrying Abigail, whom she'd just fed, while Tony appeared quietly from his room and hugged me around the waist. Taking his cue from the others, Buster stroked my shoe with a claw. I took my time telling each of them goodbye.

I finished by assuring Mae she would see her fiancé again soon.

"Hold on a second, baby," she said, hustling to the kitchen and returning with a brown paper bag. "I thought you might have to be off in a hurry, so I packed you a dinner. I'll just put it in your satchel over here."

"Thank you," I said, already plenty misty. "For everything."

She hugged me again, one of her Mae Johnson specials, but then regarded me sternly. "You shouldn't be doing this business all by yourself, Everson."

"I'm not," I said, thinking of their love, the gifts and heirlooms I carried, and, of course, my magic.

"Oh, you know what I mean," she said, shaking my cheek in a firm pinch-grip.

Ricki arched an eyebrow. "Wait, wasn't someone just saying she doesn't get enough credit for helping you?"

"Hmm, that's right," Mae said.

We all turned to the ginger mound on the divan. As though sensing the collective attention, Tabitha stirred and squinted back at us.

"What?" she asked suspiciously.

44

"Could he be driving like any more of a roided-up brute?" Tabitha complained from the seat beside me.

We were in a Sup Squad carrier, speeding north, the driver veering to avoid crashed and stalled vehicles. We'd already heaved on and off the sidewalk twice. At a sudden turn, my harness held me fast, while Tabitha, who'd refused any form of restraint, was left to swear and dig her claws into the hard plastic. Her body sloshed forward, like warm dough overspilling a bowl, before settling back again.

"We *are* in the early stages of an apocalypse," I pointed out.

She made a sour face, as if it made no difference. "I can't believe I let myself get talked into this." Mae's power as a nether whisperer had had something to do with the getting-talked-into part, but I gained nothing by sharing that info.

"Well, Ricki's right," I said. "You've helped me in the past."

"Nice of you to finally notice, but what did I get for my troubles?"

"Besides a lifetime supply of goat's milk and prime cuts?"

She scoffed. "More like a lifetime of domination and derision."

She'd done more pitching than catching in those departments, but once more I held my tongue.

Though I'd debated the wisdom of bringing Tabitha along, she was sensitive to demonic as well as angelic energies, making her a good early-warning system. And then there were the intangibles. If this *was* to be my last hurrah, it was nice having someone alongside who'd shared in my struggles and victories since the beginning. Even if some of those struggles had been Tabitha's own doing.

"Hey, remember our early cases?" I said, trying to fan a little comradery. "There was the smallpox hospital on Roosevelt Island—or how about when we went undercover at that punk club in the Bowery?"

I brought up a couple more of our Greatest Hits. But with each mention, Tabitha let out a derisive grunt, altering the pitch slightly to indicate where they ranked on her could-give-a-shit-o-meter.

"Admit it, you enjoyed some of those."

"Maybe," she allowed. "But I'm retired now."

"Well, I'm glad you're here."

She turned to me, the bunches of her face letting out slightly. She appeared ready to make some concession to the quality of my own company, however small, but then swore as the carrier heaved to a stop.

The driver's voice crackled over the speaker: "*Manhattan General.*"

Armed guards allowed us through the front doors of the hospital, Tabitha waddling behind me. The Sup Squad had been delivering the injured to the hospitals all day, including the patrons of the Kitten Club. Others must have found their own way, because the lobby was a bloody, screaming chaos.

I dodged and edged my way to the front desk, while Tabitha shouldered people and plinths aside.

I managed to wave down an elderly receptionist with a frazzled display of red hair, who'd no doubt been on duty since the night before. The blood on her gloved hands suggested she was being recruited to help with patient transport. She adjusted her glasses with the same gloves, having forgotten to strip them off, apparently.

"What?" she rasped.

"I'm here to see Swami Rama." I had to shout to be heard above the noise. "I'm a friend."

Without asking for ID, she consulted a notebook and shouted back a room number. "Fifth floor. Take the stairs." She waved absently down the corridor before heeding a call to help with another patient.

"Did she really just say, 'take the stairs'?" Tabitha asked.

A buzz droned through the tumult—the sound of giant batteries powering the lights, equipment, and probably a single emergency elevator. "Don't worry, I wasn't expecting you to walk. Here." I lifted her with a grunt and placed her across my shoulders.

After a laborious climb, I set Tabitha back down on the fifth floor. We weaved through a bustle of scrub-clad workers. It was less chaotic here, but still too hectic for anyone to address the forty-pound cat on the unit. I started to scan door numbers before spotting a pair of Sup Squad members on guard duty.

They recognized me as I hustled over, and stepped aside to let us pass.

I entered the private room and noted the occupants. "Where is she?" I demanded. "Where's the pale woman?"

"Everson!" Bishop Sheridan said in surprise. She straightened from the swami's bedside and glanced around. "Who are you asking?"

I looked from her to Swami Rama in bed, his blood infusion appearing to have restored him. From beneath the thick bandaging on his head, he regarded me with keen, questioning eyes. I raised a finger and aimed it at the man sitting forward in the reclining chair at the foot of the bed.

"Him," I said. "He's the one who let her in."

"What this?" Rector Rumbaugh asked, straightening.

"You received the letter from Emma," I said. "I believe that much."

"Yes?" Though his eyes were alert, the rest of him appeared drained.

"I also believe you answered it," I continued, "granting her permission to use the old cathedral house on your campus. The stalled construction gave her cover, but you also had your security team guard the site, putting them under secrecy orders." He was the most well positioned, plain and simple.

He shook his head. "I've already said that didn't happen."

"When the boy disappeared from the cathedral house, you sensed a familiar energy in his room—you let slip earlier that you're sensitive to holy energies, said you saw them as colors. You didn't know who'd taken him, but you picked up the St. Martin's color left by my coin pendant. That was my fault." When the building's threshold stripped my stealth potion, I hadn't considered the residue I was leaving behind.

"Regardless, as a member of the Council, you had the power to grant Emma access to St. Martin's, too."

"This isn't only absurd," he said. "It's insulting."

"*That's* where she found Mary," I continued over him. "Probably in the courtyard, having a smoke." Emma would have recognized her right away. They had spoken a few days earlier at Mary's apartment. "When Mary wouldn't say who she solicited help from, Emma applied pressure, causing a massive brain bleed. But not before she got a name." I pointed to myself. "Mine."

Bishop Sheridan and Swami Rama looked over at the rector. He'd gone from shaking his head to staring back at me defiantly. Still, he maintained a certain self-possession.

"I already told you what happened," he said. "Why would I show you a letter I answered?"

"As an excuse for why you left the IFC Center," I replied. "Which, talk about absurd, didn't make a damned bit of sense, not under the circumstances. Whose first thought is to run home for a letter when gunfire breaks out?" Something my mind had glossed over in my post-Thelonious, pre-apocalyptic fugue. "You left to alert Emma. I was on her hit list, and I was asking some uncomfortable questions."

"I don't even *know* her," he said, coming to his feet.

"Father, please," Swami Rama warned in a voice that said *I want to hear the rest.*

"By the time you came back, everyone had cleared out," I continued. "That part was true. Then the infernal smoke blew in. Also true. I'll even spot you the dropped glasses. But Emma's arrival was no accident. You had her lure me outside —I'm guessing you didn't want blood spilled in the holy space—but the fight didn't go as planned."

"Wasn't I just telling you he's divisive?" he said to his colleagues.

I'd been struggling for the last piece, but he'd just clicked it into place for me.

"When I heard you were here instead of with your family, I thought you'd come to help bolster the faith of the Interfaith Council. I even admired you for it. But you came here to shoulder me out, deny me the IFC's support and protection."

"Is that what you were building up to?" Bishop Sheridan asked him sternly.

Bingo. I also suspected he'd helped Emma compose the threat note found in Mary's apartment. It had used "we" and "our," whereas Emma's letter to him was strictly "I." Rumbaugh may even have been the photographer caught in the bedrail's reflection during the kidnapping, but I had him cornered now.

He remained silent, his lips a taut line as he looked back and forth between us.

"Well, was it wrong?" he asked at last, recovering his poise. "Have you looked outside lately? Have you seen the demons, or, or the victims in this very lobby? Have you seen his head?" He gestured to the swami's bandages. "If the wounds had been a quarter inch deeper, he'd be in the morgue and the faith of the city would be on its knees. Everything is happening just as Emma said it would."

"She killed an innocent woman," Bishop Sheridan said severely.

"And he harbors a lower demon," Rumbaugh countered. "He freed a demon prince. What does that make him? Not our ally, that's for certain."

He was as steady in his confession as he had been in his

denials. Fanaticism didn't always show up spitting and screaming.

"Where is she?" I asked. "Where's Emma?"

He leveled his condemning eyes at me. "Cleaning up your mess."

Though I held his gaze right back, the accusation rattled me. I could have prevented this: *Find the child. Kill the child.* But I remembered what my father had said when I asked which one he'd told me.

I told you what you heard.

That had to mean something.

"Um, darling." Tabitha nudged my leg. "Angel at six o'clock."

I wheeled toward the door, already separating my cane into sword and staff. Pale light grew around the frame as the door opened. The Sup Squad members stood back, evidently awed, as Emma strode between them.

45

"There she is," Rector Rumbaugh announced. "Our gift from the Lord. She'll strike down Sathanas and rid us of his evil. We don't need a corrupt wizard."

Tabitha hissed and shrank from Emma's aura until she was backing her vast bulk under the bed.

Bishop Sheridan and Swami Rama stared at her in a kind of transfixion. I couldn't blame them. She was a sight—even more so when she drew Faziel's sword. Its fiery white light illuminated her pale face and hair and resonated with her angel blood, altering the pitch in the room, sending it higher.

As I readied my weapons, I glanced around. The private room was on the larger side, but it still made for a terrible battle venue. That went for the entire hospital.

"I'm not going to fight you here," I said.

Pinning me with her bottle green eyes, she spoke in her clear, declarative voice. "Then remove yourself so I don't have to."

"If I remember, you had a little trouble with me the last time," I growled.

"That was then. I'm in the presence of holy ones now."

The frequency leapt another ear-piercing octave. I winced and shuffled back as the window behind the shades began to rattle. She wasn't just capable of drawing power from holy spaces; she could draw it from holy *people*, and she was drawing from two of the city's most powerful: the bishop and the swami.

"Stop," I ordered her.

"It's just until she has the strength to destroy Sathanas," Rumbaugh explained, seeming to appeal to me as much as the others now.

He must have been preparing to lobby the bishop and swami for Emma's emergency inclusion on the Council. That would have given her a connection to *all* the members. But she wasn't sharing in their energy—she was draining it off them like a sponge, explaining Rector Rumbaugh's depleted state.

I watched the bishop and swami's auras thin like a receding tide, laying bare the psychic scars Bishop Sheridan had suffered from Sathanas's attack.

With a sword thrust, I shouted, "*Vigore!*"

The force threw the pale woman into the wall, felling a framed portrait of a forest meant to induce calmness and healing. It shattered against the floor. The pale woman came down on a plastic couch, her sword arm ending up behind it. I planted a foot against the front of the couch and shoved, pinning her arm.

Nice going, young blood, Thelonious rumbled. *Now do the deed for the big fellow.*

Like the last time, Sathanas was holding the incubus back, allowing me my full power to complete task one: kill the Nephilim.

Activating the spell I'd baked into my blade, I drew back the sword. But Emma released her gathered energy. It hit me like a fist, knocking me down beside the recliner. Bishop Sheridan covered the swami with her upper body, while Rumbaugh stood back with a smug smile, confident in his chosen horse.

Tabitha's eyes flashed from under the bed. When they met mine, they shook back and forth: *I don't do angels.* She'd been jerked to Faziel's realm once already and had barely made it back alive.

Emma recovered her arm—by bringing Faziel's sword *through* the couch. The couch's far end toppled outward, exposing a smoking foam core. Hair whipping across her face, Emma lunged and brought the sword down.

I caught it with my own, the collision sending out a dull ring. She ground down against the contact, pulsing power from her blade, the effect like repeated blows to my head. I was gathering a repel invocation when I saw something that scared the crap out of me.

The lines of the Gordian Knot, the strands that bound up Faziel's power and presence, were coming undone. It was the contact with my magic—magic very much like my father's, which had originally bound the blade. A few more blows, or even prolonged contact, would take the knot apart completely.

Through my blurring vision, I saw Emma's thumb coming for my forehead.

Grunting in desperation, I planted a foot against her hip and shoved. She reeled backward, allowing me space to scramble to my feet.

"Stop," I panted. "There's a binding on that sword. If it comes undone, it'll release an Avenging Angel that will slay everyone in this room... possibly the entire hospital... before wreaking mass destruction out there."

"Lies," Rector Rumbaugh said.

"They're not fucking lies!" I shouted.

Not normally how I liked to speak around holy figures, but I was already picturing my decapitated body on the floor. I was seeing the annihilation of the Order and the collateral damage from the battle between Faziel and Sathanas. A battle where the angel's victory would bring about a soulless shadow realm.

"Don't listen to him," Rumbaugh told Emma.

She looked from me to her sword before raising it again. Like a modern day Joan of Arc, she was heeding the call of the divine. She'd even found her Charles VII-like patron in Rector Rumbaugh. But she was new to this. She didn't understand the Gordian Knot or the power of Faziel. Her infallible belief in her virtue blinded her to the fact that an angel could be just as nasty as a demon.

"Call her off!" Bishop Sheridan ordered the rector.

"But it's all lies," he said. "His lower demon is whispering in his ear."

"Do what the bishop says," Swami Rama told him.

Emma's descending blow grazed my shield as I lunged out of the way. More of the Gordian Knot frayed. I backed from her next swing, this time placing a foot behind the reclining chair and shoving it between us.

What's with this scaredy-cat running away? Thelonious asked. *Just do the deed.*

"If you're not gonna help," I grunted, "you need to shut your incubus mouth."

"See?" Rumbaugh cried.

Emma lopped off the top of the reclining chair, the tip of

Faziel's sword narrowly missing my retracted chest. But the proximity to my shielding popped another strand of the knot and loosened two more. Swearing, I took mental inventory of my spell items. Did I have anything that wasn't imbued with my own magic?

Petra, I thought suddenly. The druid had planted a powerful cantrip inside my staff before the first hotel mission.

Tapping into it, I swung the staff around: "*Liberare!*"

The opal end coughed out a dispersion of red dust, not so powerful anymore. Emma sliced at the hovering magic that looked like a swarm of tiny gnats. They flared up before dimming, then disappearing.

Damn, it must have hit its shelf life.

But then Emma released a chattering cry and stumbled forward, the tip of her sword dropping to the floor. Her eyes went spacey, and her lips deepened to a bruised blue that matched the darkening hollows of her cheeks.

Rumbaugh's smile fractured. "What are you doing to her?"

Designed to draw the fire from the possessed druids, the cantrip had stolen Emma's body heat. She was in an advanced stage of hypothermia. She skipped shivering and went straight to giant shudders, the end of her sword bouncing against the floor.

"Stop it," Rector Rumbaugh said to me. "Stop it now!"

When Emma lurched toward me, I dropped my staff and caught her.

"Release the sword," I said, gripping the back of her frigid neck.

The Gordian Knot was down to its last several strands, and those were in bad shape. Even as I drew my magic in, another one popped. Emma struggled to bring the sword up, to wield it against me, but she was shaking too badly.

"*Drop it,*" I repeated.

Her fingers spasmed open, and the sword clanged to the floor.

She clung to me with both hands, either to wrestle me down or draw off my warmth. Gripping her icy neck more tightly, I spoke a Word that sent a lavender sheen of magic down the length of my blade.

"I'm truly sorry about this," I whispered, and grimaced.

The blade crunched through her core.

46

Emma's body held onto its final spasm. Then it released it along with an expiring breath that brushed my ear with chill air. I withdrew my sword and lifted her limp body onto what remained of the couch, tucking her legs in. The silence in the room stretched out until Rector Rumbaugh released a clogged gasp.

"Did you just...?" He swallowed and started again. "Did you *kill* her?"

"I had no choice."

He looked from me to her, his expression stark with disbelief as if I'd just slain a prophecy. "But she was... she was..."

I began a complex incantation, restoring what I could of the Gordian Knot. I then drew a salt-impregnated cloth bag from my satchel and shook it out. I stooped for the sword, anxious to get it into safe storage. But Rumbaugh rushed forward and seized my arm. Teeth bared, he twisted his hand back and forth like an older brother trying to give his sibling a skin burn. This was probably his first attempt at violence.

"Let me finish my work," I said firmly.

"I knew you were trouble," he seethed. "I knew—"

He hollered and shot up straight. Tabitha had scaled his back and perched atop his shoulders. Not used to bearing forty-plus pounds that high above his center of gravity, he flailed backward and toppled to the floor. Moving with surprising deftness, Tabitha squatted atop his chest, her succubus eyes glowing into his.

"*Incapacitate*," I stressed. "Don't eat."

With an irritated scowl, Tabitha mesmerized Rector Rumbaugh until he stopped struggling.

Gripping the sword, I pulled the salt sack around it. I then bound it with duct tape, smothering its power.

"Did you catch all of that?" I asked Thelonious.

That was cold, young blood, he replied appreciatively. *Dead cold.*

"'Dead' being the operative term," I said, staring down at Emma's body. "Tell him task one is complete."

As I felt Thelonious withdraw to inform Sathanas, Bishop Sheridan arrived beside me. She brushed Emma's white hair from her neck and pressed her fingers into the pulse groove. When she straightened, I didn't have to ask if she'd felt anything. It was written on the bishop's very somber face.

"Did you intend for this?" she asked.

"Yes."

I tapped into the fae enchantment that whispered through my coin pendant. The whispers reversed direction, restoring the obfuscation that hid my words and deeds from Thelonious.

"But she's not dead," I said.

The bishop looked at me dubiously. "I just saw you run

her through… she has no heartbeat. Are you saying this is all illusion?"

"My magic healed her when I retracted the blade." I lifted the hem of the pale woman's shirt to her navel. There was no blood, just the faintest line where the blade had entered and exited. "I also left a spell in her system, a *paralytic vice*. She'll remain in a state of suspended animation for the next several hours."

The bishop shook her head. "I don't understand."

"I was *supposed* to kill her," I explained. "It was the deal I made with Sathanas for him to restore my friends. He thinks I've done it. But he wants something else, and for that I'm going to need your help."

"I'll do what I can," she said cautiously.

"I need you to allow the demon prince into St. Martin's."

When she squinted, I saw her old scars cresting again. "Whatever for?"

"It's another deal. Once he's inside, he'll lift the infernal smoke and call off his demons for twelve hours to allow the city to evacuate."

"But why St. Martin's?"

I held up the wrapped sword. "He needs the fount of ley energy to destroy this."

I glanced over at Swami Rama, who'd been observing the events around him with a look of concern and profound confusion. Both understandable. He squinted from the sword to where Tabitha was squatting on the rector's chest, her lamp-like eyes staring into his face with a succubus's hunger.

"Can Sathanas be contained again?" Bishop Sheridan asked me.

She meant letting him into the cathedral, then restoring the threshold until he could only bat around like a trapped moth, like the last time. It was a good thought, but one I'd already discarded.

"He's too powerful this time, unfortunately. A prophetic celestial event and ten thousand souls will do that for a major demon."

"Then why would we ever surrender St. Martin's?" she asked. "Even with what he's offering, it sounds like a stay of execution at best." Though the bishop remained in front of me, I could feel her pulling away.

"Look, I know it's a huge ask, but it goes back to the rhyming I talked about the other day. This came together in much the same way as his first coming in the modern era. And I don't think it's an accident that events are converging on the same site. Sathanas wants me there, maybe for no other reason than to gloat, but I have to believe he's caught in a bigger pattern. Quite possibly to his detriment."

She looked to Swami Rama, who was already shaking his head.

"Allowing a demon into one of the faith houses?" His tone made it clear he thought her insane for even entertaining the idea. "It will undermine everything the IFC stands for, everything we've worked to uphold."

When Bishop Sheridan turned back to me, I placed my hands on her shoulders and focused into her eyes until it felt as if we were the only two in the room.

"All I can do is listen to the force that guides me," I whispered. "Granted, I don't always understand it—and it often challenges my sense of... well, everything. But it's the same force that placed me in front of Sathanas the last time, that helped me overcome him. You have a guiding force, too. What's yours telling you?"

Her gaze shifted slightly, as though taking in the stormy

horizon again. After several moments, she wiped her eyes and nodded.

"I'll grant it," she said quietly.

As her invitation to Sathanas went out, the usually composed swami sat up in alarm, agitating his IV lines. "What? No, you can't do this! Not without a unanimous vote of the Council, and I can already tell you that you won't get it!"

"I can't speak for the IFC," she said, "but I can speak for St. Martin's."

"You would do this to our faith?" Swami Rama asked.

"I do it *because* of faith. How can we claim to be its stewards if we can't heed it ourselves?"

Thank you, I mouthed.

As she went to his bedside, I reversed the obfuscation enchantment. "Two tasks done," I told Thelonious. "He has access to St. Martin's now. I expect him to uphold his end, or there's not going to be a task three."

Hold tight, young blood, he rumbled.

I circled the bed, past Tabitha, who had tired of Rumbaugh and left him sprawled out on the floor. At the window, I parted the blinds. The air remained smoky, but I could just make out the top level of the parking garage. Was the smoke starting to thin? I was checking my phone for a signal when it lit up with a call.

"Hello?" I answered.

"Hey, baby, it's Mae," she said, speaking through tears.

My heart rate skyrocketed. "What's wrong? Is everything okay?"

"I just heard from the Sup Squad. They found Bree-yark and your two magic-user friends outside that hotel."

"Are they...?"

"They're good," she said with a wet laugh. "They've been checked out and everything. They're on their way to the apartment."

"That's fantastic," I said, releasing my breath alongside a very relieved laugh.

He's lifting the siege, Thelonious rumbled in my head. *Says you know what to do next.*

I peered outside, where I could make out the opposite wing of the hospital now, a gibbous moon glowing above the rooftop.

"Okay, be ready to move," I told Mae. "The smoke is clearing off."

"We're all packed," she assured me. "Ricki headed out about twenty, thirty minutes ago with a team. She informed those emergency management people about the twelve-hour window, so they're getting everyone in place for the evacuation."

"How are the kids doing?"

"They're fine. Little Abigail's right here, kicking those powerful legs of hers. Excited to be taking her first trip, I think."

When I heard my daughter gurgle, I smiled sadly. "Get to the safe place, and we'll go from there."

"Aren't you coming with us?" she asked.

I turned from my phone, eyes closed. Because as I'd been talking to Bishop Sheridan about the rhyming, my magic had been nodding. I was to go to St. Martin's. I was to face Sathanas. The alternative, fleeing to the Refuge to fight another day didn't carry the same resonance. It wasn't even close.

I returned to the phone.

"No," I told her. "You guys go ahead."

47

By the time Tabitha and I left the hospital, traffic had begun moving along the hazy streets. From a port window in the back of the carrier, I watched NYPD squad cars flashing at intersections, officers directing cars along cleared routes. A loaded city bus trundled toward the Queens Midtown Tunnel. Belowground, the subways would be running soon, carrying carloads of evacuees to Brooklyn and the Bronx. And on the water, ferries and barges would be converging on the city's docks.

"You sure know how to kick a hornet's nest."

I turned to find Tabitha's front paws parked on the seat-back beside me, her bland stare taking in the evacuation efforts.

"At least it's orderly," I said, thinking of Ricki as I took a seat.

"So far, but I've seen how you humans behave when there's any sense of urgency. Remember that riot at Macy's last Christmas, all over a stupid doll? Anyway, I'm not talking about here. I mean down there."

"There's activity in the Below?" I asked, surprised.

She turned from the window and took her time settling into her seat. With smoke blowing off and the emergency routes cleared of wreckage, our ride out was much less of a rodeo. "Activity?" she repeated with a snort. "Try a stampede. Every demon and their second cousin is making for the Outer Reaches."

"Why? Sathanas has always ruled the roost."

"Yes, but the other demon lords were always within striking distance. If you want to know what it normally looks like down there, it's a constant reshuffling of alliances. Sathanas to hold his place, the other lords to hold theirs. A lot of movement, but nothing really happening. A bore, if you ask me. Yes, once in a long while, an ambitious lower demon makes ripples, but that rarely lasts." She dropped her voice conspiratorially. "But there are rumors that Sathanas has gotten his hands on something that will put him horns and shoulders above the others. He'll use it to destroy those who've opposed him. He'll use it to destroy those who've *helped* him, just to prove he doesn't need them."

This was new and alarming info. "How long have you known this?"

She squinted in thought. "Oh, I can't remember, darling. Sometime before my nap?"

I set my jaw at the notion that she hadn't bothered to tell me, but there was no time for one of our back-and-forths.

"Any idea what this 'something' is?" I asked.

Tabitha yawned as if the outpouring of information had exhausted her. "There's really no telling, darling."

Horns and shoulders above the others? Maybe it was the all-you-can-eat soul buffet he'd prepped for himself. If I failed, it would number in the millions. My hands were trembling when I looked down. I balled them into fists.

"Then why aren't *you* reacting?" I asked.

She shrugged. "I think I've stopped caring. I'm a succubus trapped in an overweight cat. There never really was any future for me."

I could see her point, but it saddened me anyway. "Hey, thanks for your assist with Rumbaugh back there."

"You could have allowed me just one small bite."

"Yeah, well, I've seen what you consider 'small.'"

Outside, an official voice boomed from a speaker, citing pickup points for evacuees and encouraging the able-bodied to walk or bike over the closest bridges. I snuck another look out the window. We were approaching downtown and St. Martin's Cathedral.

I removed my coin pendant from my neck and held it in my palm to study the family symbol: a circle with two squares inside, one offset at forty-five degrees to look like a diamond. Having done its job, the enchantment Caroline had installed was on its final whispers. I concentrated, infusing the metal with a portion of my own essence, then extended the necklace toward Tabitha.

She shrank away. "What are you doing?"

"Leaving it in your care. Can you make sure it gets to Ricki?"

"But why?" She stopped pulling back enough for me to place it around her neck, looping it twice to fit her.

"If I don't..." I swallowed. "If I don't make it out, I want my daughter to have this someday."

Tabitha regarded me for a long moment, her brows going up and down and then twisting, as if she were in the early stages of a seizure. But then coming to some decision, she relaxed her face with an aggrieved sigh.

"If you do manage to survive this, I'll deny what I'm about to tell you." Her brows convulsed into another fit. Finally, she looked at me flat-faced. "You've been very decent to me these past years, darling."

I blinked, then laughed in surprise.

She squinted away, muttering, "I knew I shouldn't have said anything."

"No, no, it's just that I never, ever thought I'd hear those words coming from that mouth. Look, we've had our spats, and yes, there are some things I regret having said—and I'd like to think you feel the same—but the truth is you got me through some pretty dark times. I can't imagine home without you."

When she nodded in a way that expressed satisfaction, or maybe just acceptance, I gripped her front paw.

She drew it back. "Cats hate that."

"Oh, right. Sorry," I chuckled.

When I noticed smoke out the window, my smile shrank. It was back and thicker than ever. Was Sathanas reneging on our deal?

I pressed the commo button for the driver. "Where's the smoke coming from?"

"*Looks like the church,*" he answered over the speaker. "*But it's contained per the aerial views. Covers a three-block radius around St. Martin's, which is on fire. And we've got some company.*"

I picked up a passing shadow, then another. Demons. What was going on?

Just an escort, Thelonious's voice rumbled in my head. *The big man wants to make sure you get inside safe.*

I communicated that to the driver before returning to my incubus. "Anything else you can tell me?"

Afraid not. For the first time since his revival, Thelonious sounded somber, if not scared. *It's been a gas running with you, young blood. But things are gonna be changing here real soon. This is probably our last blow session.*

Was Tabitha right? Was Sathanas becoming so powerful he'd be routing enemies and allies alike?

"What's changing?" I asked Thelonious in a lowered voice.

But he didn't answer. I couldn't even feel his presence anymore.

"*This is as close as I can get,*" the driver announced, rolling to a stop.

I heard a steady roar of flames down the block, the heat already warming our vehicle's armor. I looked over at Tabitha and flicked the coin hanging from her neck. She nodded to say she'd deliver it to Ricki. I gave her a final scratching around the ears, a final kiss on the forehead, and then I exited out the back of the carrier.

48

I wanted to recoil as I rounded the vehicle and faced St. Martin's Cathedral.

Once an awe-inspiring sight, an architectural wonder and divine sanctuary as old as the city, the cathedral now looked like a gateway to Hell. Rabid flames fused with the fount of ley energy, gushing into the sky in an unholy spire. Its soul-scalding heat thrashed my hair and snapped my coat sharply.

Am I really doing this?

The wrapped Sword of Faziel gripped to my chest, I lowered my head and forged toward the cathedral. The demons remained back, their wings scraping embers from the foul smoke as they cut to either side of me. They were creating a nightmare promenade, ensuring my only path was forward.

As I arrived at the front steps, the flames thinned across the cathedral's entrance. I paused and squinted up the raging spire again. The Refuge option remained. I sensed it shimmering in my magic like a lucky penny.

Was that such a bad idea, given the new info about

Sathanas's power boost? Getting us all to safety to plot our next move?

I peered back. Through the smoke, the personnel carrier that held Tabitha looked like a lunar explorer on an alien moon. I watched myself from a hazy distance as I waved for the driver to move out. He obliged, leaving my solitary, coat-clad figure before the steps.

In a dizzying rush, I was back in my body, but more firmly rooted in my magic. I'd made a promise to heed it—above head, heart, and gut—and it was telling me one thing:

Let's fucking go.

As if in response, the bronze doors yawned open. My invitation to enter.

I ascended the steps and crossed the threshold. A wave of infernal heat rushed through me, flash-broiling my blood and sending a sharp hiss through my teeth. A different pain than before, but by Bishop Sheridan's decree, the cathedral's old protections were no more.

This was the House of Sathanas now.

Shattered glass from the interior doors crunched under-foot as I stepped into the vaulted nave. The enveloping fire illuminated trashed pews and puddles of black ichor that smoked here and there.

Above the chancel, where the altar had been split in two, the fire lit up the vast stained glass window. But it wasn't the magical, majestic display from my childhood. The cast was too dark and red. The depicted saints and angels were still there in the glass, but a host of cackling demons were savaging them, the bloody carnage of a slain humanity littering the ground at their feet. And presiding over the nightmare display was a demon lord, his wings extending from one end of the stained glass to the other. In his taloned hands he held the Archangel Michael, torn in half, his storied sword shattered.

As I met the demon lord's eyes, they glowed harshly.

From somewhere below ground, laughter echoed, shaking the cathedral's mooring. The fire went out, casting the nave in total darkness. I adjusted my grip on the sword, my other hand digging at the tape, ready to pull the salt-impregnated cloth away.

It had crossed my mind that Sathanas was only using me as a courier. That once I arrived, the demons would grab the sword, rip me apart, and present my soul to the demon lord and his eternal torments.

I spun toward the flap of a wing, real or imagined, prompting more laughter.

But then flames licked up in a line, revealing an empty nave. They beckoned me to follow. I heeded them, the flames leading me along a familiar path through the cathedral. As I descended a flight of stone steps, my old phobia of going underground crept in, cinching my chest around my galloping heart.

I arrived in a low-ceilinged basement, stored items, bound and covered, looming to either side. Though I hadn't seen any demons since entering, I could sense them back in the shadows, watching me.

They fear the sword, I understood.

Ahead, two flames illuminated an arched doorway. Beyond, a stone staircase spiraled down. More laughter echoed up, but my magic urged me onward, straight into the mouth of madness. Holding tight to the sword, I descended, around and around, until the staircase deposited me into a cave-like corridor.

I stopped.

In the aftermath of the Demon Moon case, the old ossuary had been cleaned out, the remains properly buried. But by some trick of infernal magic, they were back—great drifts of dusty-brown bones and staring skulls.

As I picked my way between the morbid slopes, the air grew damper and heavier. Things skittered here and there. I glimpsed the tail end of a red centipede before it disappeared into a skull's earhole. It felt as if I were walking back in time, traversing the four intervening years in reverse.

That's what this whole show is about, I understood. *Sathanas wants to diminish me, make me feel small and afraid again.*

But I was moving forward, not backward, in step with my magic.

Up ahead, where the corridor bent around a corner, a demonic incantation rumbled out, rattling the bone piles.

I arrived to find a large brazier of dark flames. A tall figure in a black robe stood beyond it, head bowed, arms outstretched. Each of his words seemed to gather and warp the energy coming up through the foundation. The same energy twisted darkly into his being, while the rest fed the brazier's hellish flames.

He was standing in the center of an elaborate pattern of blood and bone ash. Once again, the grotto had been transformed into a demonic casting circle. This time, though, there was no Bishop Sheridan. It was just me, the demon prince, and the angel's sword.

"I'm here," I said.

He wound down his chant, brought his arms in slowly, and drew his hood back from his red hair. He'd ditched the sunglasses, and my breath caught as I found myself staring at the gentle, blue-eyed visage of Father Vick. But then his features thinned and hardened, and an inky blackness filled his eyes, drowning all color and warmth. Edgar grinned maliciously and clasped his hands in front of him.

"So you are," he said. "If I'm being honest, I didn't think the little wizard had it in him."

There he went again, trying to diminish me. But why?

"You kept your word, and I kept mine," I said simply.

He gave two slow claps. "Oh, such bravado. A touch more and you might actually convince me."

I shrugged. "Okay."

His grin spread, the fire of the brazier glistening along his teeth. "Your breath betrays you, Everson. It reeks of fear. And why not? Returning to this place, having to descend into darkness and death once more? That would wilt even the staunchest soul. Especially knowing how lucky you were the last time. I was nothing then. A flicker—nay, a *shadow*—of the being before you. And yet it took the full power of this place, a power I now command, to dispel me. And you didn't emerge unscathed, did you?"

His black eyes glinted with mischief as he twisted the fingers of one hand. A pain unlocked in my left shoulder, a horrible freshet of agony that deepened into a violent, rotting ache. I grunted—I couldn't help it—and seized the place where Sathanas's tail had impaled me those years ago.

"Come now, let's hear it," he said. "Belt it out."

Despite my best effort, the agony spasmed up my throat and emerged as a ragged cry. He closed his hand suddenly, taking back the pain.

"There."

He sniggered as I recovered my breath, the sound less Edgar's now than his father's, the wrath that constituted him seething just below the surface. The alignment of the Child and Father was at hand.

"I knew you still had it in you."

"Pain?" I gasped. "Who doesn't? I had the pleasure of feeling yours back at the hotel."

His smile stiffened for a moment before recovering its gleeful spite. "You've held on to your malice too, I see. That comes from me. My gift to humanity."

He was really trying to crank me through the wringer of emotions: fear, pain, and now anger. But I used each as a reminder to stay present, to remain rooted in my magic. It raised questions, though. If he held such a huge advantage, why try to break me down? A demon's cruelty or something more?

When I didn't react to his last taunt, he waved a hand. "The important thing is you've returned. This time bearing my *gift*." His face canted down to the wrapped weapon I'd been holding against my chest. "Now, then." His pale hand reached through the flames, the long fingers opening slowly. "The sword."

I saw the same nervous anticipation as when he'd asked me for the whip, only the stakes were heightened now. By incinerating the sword, he would avoid the Contest with Faziel and emerge unopposed.

"The sword," he repeated.

I would also forfeit any chance to alchemize the Avenging Angel.

I started to draw away, but a detonation of nerves in my head, heart, *and* gut gave me pause. This was a demon lord, a master of deception, and he was throwing all kinds of conflicting signals my way.

What did he *actually* want of me?

Focus, Everson, I thought. *What's your magic telling you?*

I checked, but it was absent. It wasn't even giving me the

aimless motion. It was as though it had taken a giant step back. Because it had. I was standing alone at the edge, and it was up to me now to leap—or not.

The sword began to shake in my grip.

If I failed to contain the released angel, he would destroy me. Then, he would face Sathanas. If he won, he would go on to annihilate the entire lineage of Saint Michael, including my precious daughter, before abandoning the world to fear and darkness. If Faziel lost, though, Sathanas would bring about a Hell on Earth, reserving special tortures for those who opposed him. Neither option felt great.

Edgar sighed. "I thought you might make this difficult."

He swept his arm out behind him as he stepped to the side. The shadow he'd been casting over the back of the grotto leapt away to reveal a trussed-up figure on her side, midnight hair across her face.

It was Ricki.

49

I knew my wife's energy signature inside and out. This was really her.

My shock and terror collapsed into a low note that shuddered through me and seemed to rattle the entire grotto. It was the kind of power I'd felt when handling the whip. My angel blood coming to life. When I spoke, the note merged with my voice, promising a level of violence I'd never heard before.

"*Release her*," I said.

Edgar's mocking smile grew until it was disproportionate to his narrow face. "That would defeat the purpose, no?"

"*You promised*," I seethed.

"As did you. But let's be honest with one another. You didn't *really* kill the Nephilim like I asked."

Dammit, he knew. "*Ricki*!" I called past him.

"Oh, rest assured, she's alive. I want her to feel *everything*."

He snapped his fingers, and flames hissed up into a ring around her. Then, as if heeding a command, they began to creep inward, converging toward her. Their demonic light glistened from her hair.

"Just relinquish the sword," he said, "and I'll spare her."

I seized a tube of ice crystals from a coat pocket. "*Ghioccio!*"

But no frost blast shot forth to extinguish the flames. Just an icy sludge that dribbled to the floor like a spilled Slushie. I ran toward her—or tried to. The twisting energies of the demon circle kept me perpetually in front of the brazier.

"*You're running out of time,*" Edgar taunted, his voice undergoing its own transformation.

He was growing now, his robe jutting out. Dark blood spilled from a spreading fissure in the center of his brow. It opened in a crackling burst, obliterating his nose. The right side of his grinning mouth dangled and fell away while a constellation of dark, jutting horns punched through the rest of his face.

I'd seen this movie before. The transformation may have been happening at 4x speed, but it didn't make it any less horrifying.

By the time the final scraps of his robe fell away, Sathanas's monstrous form filled the grotto. I stared at the incomprehensible fusion of muscles and exoskeleton, at the horned wings that touched the walls, at the barbed tail that curled around him, the dark flash of its tip reawakening the ache in my shoulder.

Child and Father had aligned.

Beyond him, the ring of flames continued to close in around Ricki. I shouted a series of invocations, but each one was absorbed by the twisting infernal energy and suffocated from existence. Wrathful laughter thundered from the demon lord's giant fangs.

"*See where obstinance gets you, stupid wizard?*"

He rose above me, the firelight glistening wetly over his grotesque form. There was no self-duplication in play. This was all Sathanas.

"*Want to see her hair go up in cinders?*" he roared. "*Or watch her skin bubble and blacken like a tar roof? Want to hear her scream herself raw as she fights from being grabbed and pulled into the lowest pits?*"

Indeed, the ring of fire would become a portal.

The brazier's flames parted around his thrust hand—not the pale, slender appendage of just moments ago, but a taloned monstrosity.

"*Give me the sword, and I'll make it stop. But you must fall to your knees and call me 'Master' now, for I am claiming you as my servant. My stupid wizard servant. The sword and your eternal bondage for her life.*"

Ricki moaned, like someone desperate to escape a paralyzing nightmare. I peered past the demon lord in time to see the tips of her splayed-out hair popping into flames. The low, rumbling note of my angel blood shot up an octave.

Without thinking, I tore the bag from the angel's sword, focused into the Gordian Knot, and shouted, "*Disfare!*"

The knot didn't just release—it blew apart.

I barely had time to set my feet before Faziel's power slammed into me on a shrieking gale. I reeled before getting low. Then, choking up on the sword's grip, I placed everything into holding my mental prism together, to funneling the angel's arrival through my being and... altering him, somehow.

Crack!

The sound landed like a pistol shot in my head. One of my prism's faces had already fractured. Two more snaps followed, their fissures joining up. My prism was going to shatter, my mind along with it.

When my vision began to fragment, I released the sword with a frantic grunt and threw myself backward.

I staggered for several steps before landing seat-down against the wall of the grotto. Head reeling, I stared my vision into a semblance of cohesion and blinked up. I expected to see Sathanas bending for the fallen sword and plunging it into the brazier. Instead, the sword was suspended where I'd released it.

No, not suspended. *Wielded.*

A shadowy figure, gray and growing, was taking form around the weapon. I'd seen him before—a misty impression with a spreading pair of angelic wings whose size now rivaled Sathanas's. But Faziel's arrival didn't stop there. He was coming into being in a way I *hadn't* seen before.

Feathers sharpened throughout the span of his wings, somehow light and dark at the same time. Thick, striated muscles filled out his body. Bronze plates etched with powerful symbols glistened over his forearms, while a pristine white pallium wrapped his waist and fell, fluttering, to his chiseled calves.

Sathanas stared at him, hesitant to advance or retreat, it seemed.

A glance down showed me that I'd landed outside the circle, its demonic energies no longer confining me. Free, I scrambled around to Ricki's side of the grotto. The ring of flames hadn't reached her yet, thank God.

I pulled a flask of holy water from a pocket and doused the entire thing.

"*Ricki,*" I whispered, crawling over the smoke and diminishing portal.

The damage appeared to be limited to the ends of her hair and the smoldering soles of her tactical boots. I removed the twisted metal that bound her. Then I worked my lap under her head and pushed the hair from her face.

She was clad in NYPD tactical gear, all except for the helmet. A demon must have grabbed her off the street and flown her here ahead of me. Her breathing came in shallow hitches, while her aura spoke to a demonic fugue. With an intact mental prism, I could have dispersed it, but mine remained in a state of healing.

That's what you get for trying to channel a frigging Avenging Angel.

Out in the grotto, Faziel raised the dome of his head, his face all cheekbones and granite jaw. His eyes manifested, glowing crescents of callous blue light. When they met mine, I felt the depth of his judgment and violence, and the incomprehensible weight of their power.

My earlier misgivings had been right. I'd had no chance of channeling him, not even with the help of the collective. He was an elemental force of Creation. From the moment I'd opened the Gordian Knot until I'd let go of the sword, only three, maybe four, adrenaline-fueled breaths had elapsed.

Some leap, I thought dismally. *But why else did my magic lead me to the edge?*

I looked between the combatants. Was I supposed to battle the freaking winner?

The angel's eyes glinted at me with soul-shattering hatred before shifting over to his original enemy, the demon lord. The two of them had faced off before, in the Earliest Days, before the Creator deemed the Avenging Angels too cruel and heedless and replaced them with the First Saints.

"*Greetings, Faziel,*" Sathanas said. "*Long time.*"

I couldn't see his face from my position, but his voice was thick with malice.

"*Greetings, Sathanas,*" the angel replied, the word as stentorian as a thousand voices woven into one, but no less malevolent than the demon's.

Though the reunion was thousands of years in the making, that was the extent of their salutations. Faziel brought the sword around in a blinding, bluish arc. Sathanas produced a sword of pure fire. The two weapons clashed above the brazier, producing a soundless force that shook the cathedral's foundation.

I scooted back with Ricki until we were flush against the wall. I tried again to awaken her, but the demonic fugue had put her too deeply under. I unfastened my cane from the satchel and checked the staff. Scant, but some of the magic I'd used to dispel the fugue around little Edgar remained inside.

"*Liberare,*" I whispered carefully, as though working with fragile glass.

In a way, I was. My repairing prism rattled, but allowed enough ley energy through to send magic from the staff and into the fugue. It failed to scatter the demonic mist, but it kicked off a thinning process.

The angel and demon traded two more prodigious blows.

"*It really is like old times,*" Sathanas said. "*I'd all but forgotten your power.*"

"*I have not forgotten your vileness, nor your deception,*" Faziel replied in a resounding voice that made you want to break into choral verse and vomit out your guts at the same time. It wasn't meant for mortal ears.

Still, the battle, the sheer fact of an original Angel and Demon facing off, was disturbingly hypnotic. For a moment, I became lost in the interplay of feathers and horns, muscles and scales, light and fire.

"*Deception*?" Sathanas said, swinging his sword down in a great roar of flames.

Another collision of blades was followed by another seismic rumble throughout the cathedral. Faziel backed off a step.

"*Yes, Sathanas. I am not foolish. I know where I stand.*"

The demon lord's mouth spread into a diabolical grin. "*Do you mean the Sigilum Angeli?*"

I looked down in horror. Indeed, the demonic circle had changed, reconfiguring itself into a powerful angel trap.

As Sathanas broke into booming laughter, my blood froze. Because I understood now, understood with arctic clarity, why he'd kept me alive and assigned me the tasks. He never planned to destroy the Sword of Faziel. Just the being it could summon. And he'd needed me to release the Gordian Knot.

There were other ways he might have compelled me, but like a true demon, he'd manipulated me into doing the deed willingly.

"*You can thank Everson Croft,*" Sathanas said, confirming my theory. "*He made all of this possible.*"

The Avenging Angel peered over at me, the glow of his eyes narrowing again into a penetrating hatred. When he turned his sword on me, I crouched over Ricki and gripped the back of my neck, visions of my shadow's headless body returning in a rush. His sword came down—and crashed into the side of the angel trap.

I looked over as Faziel staggered from the dispersion of dark energy, his wings erupting into dark flames. But there was no raging or screaming on Faziel's part. As his feathers lifted off in blazing embers, he stood tall, set his granite jaw, and stared straight into the laughing face of the demon lord.

"*Poor, judgmental Faziel,*" Sathanas taunted. "*I'm sorry our reunion had to be so brief.*"

Inky energies climbed from the trap, penetrating the angel's legs like wormy black veins.

By gaining access to St. Martin's, Sathanas had claimed a site with enough raw energy to power an angel trap. And in so doing, he—correction, *I*—had tilted the Contest steeply in his favor. Unless I acted, Sathanas was going to win.

I set Ricki's head down and gained my feet.

"Hey!" I shouted up at Faziel. "I pledge to free you in exchange for clemency for the line of Saint Michael!"

I brought the tip of my sword to the edge of the trap in preparation to breach it.

I was taking a giant gamble, but if Faziel agreed to preserve our line, we might mitigate the fallout of his return.

The angel didn't respond, however. His wings were mostly gone, reduced to charred stumps, and the veins had reached his neck. When the inky tendrils spread into the glistening dome of his head, his only feature still unblemished was the blue glow of his eyes. But there was still no pleading or panic in them. They continued to stare at Sathanas as though marking him for their next encounter.

"*Liberare,*" I hissed, creating the breach anyway.

Energy narrowed through my repaired prism, shot the length of my sword, and fissured the edge of the trap.

The outrush was so violent that I was on the ground before realizing I'd been blasted from my feet. The angel Faziel swayed inside the wild disorganization of released energy. The black veins narrowed to pencil-thin lines.

Then they erupted all at once, smashing the angel apart

from the inside.

Sathanas's laughter filled the grotto as Faziel's sword clanged to the floor.

"*Well done, stupid servant,*" he said to me. "*You have completed my work.*"

He seized the fallen sword. The energy that had been feeding the angel trap now gathered around the brazier, heating it to bubbling. But instead of plunging the sword into its molten depths, Sathanas passed the blade through its dark flames as he incanted in a garbled tongue. He did this several times, holding the blade up between passes to assess its darkening length. I stared in dawning comprehension.

A corrupted angel's sword, I realized, staggering to my feet.

That was the "something" Tabitha had picked up on, the weapon that would put Sathanas horns and shoulders above the other demons and enable him to reign unopposed.

I looked from the sword to the dusty suspension of Faziel's remains, soon to join the other angels as impotent universal static.

But not yet, I thought. *Not yet.*

Because I was venturing a very dangerous thought. What if Sathanas had just helped me in my task as much as I had helped him? The dangerous thought propelled me to the next one. What if the way forward, what everything had been building toward, wasn't for me to battle the winner, but to more easily harness the loser?

I tuned into my magic, but it remained back. This was my call.

Summoning power to my sword, I stumbled forward and jumped into the breached circle—my second leap from the edge.

Only there would be no take-backs this time.

50

I landed in the center of the circle, stirring up the charged dust that had once been the angel Faziel. The demon lord was so engrossed in corrupting the angel's sword in his roaring brazier that he didn't seem to notice me.

"*Ritirare*," I murmured, calling Faziel's energy.

The scattered particles arrived one by one, two by two. They passed through my mental prism, through my essence, and then fused into my blade's banishment rune in tiny flashes. Driven by the urgency to finish my work before Sathanas finished his, I increased the flow to a trickle and then to a small stream.

"*Ritirare*," I repeated.

When my prism hit capacity, I tried to ease off, but the flow had assumed its own momentum. It arrived faster and thicker, the friction of the angel matter sending out charges in vicious snaps and sizzles. I lowered myself to my knees and pressed my forehead to the flat of the blade, fighting to retain control.

C'mon, man, I thought, urging myself through the pain. *This has to be it.*

But if my first attempt to channel Faziel had felt like my mind shattering, this felt like being cooked from the inside. I was struggling with the raw, elemental energy. More particles stormed in, and with them came more collisions. They culminated in a crackling bolt that branched my entire length.

It rendered me blank for an instant, out of space and time. And then my nerve endings lit up in a constellation of agony so bright that I nearly dropped the sword. How much longer could I do this?

Behind me, Sathanas was exulting over his beautiful blade.

Another bolt. The blank-out lasted longer this time; the return to pain felt more hellish. Then something burst inside me like a lanced water balloon, and a lurid red mist washed past my vision.

My blood?

I don't expect you to undertake this, my father had said. *But we'll do everything in our power to help you.*

"Help me," I rasped.

The roar and agony of the grotto disappeared. I was standing in my grandfather's attic study, the light from the dangling bulb dancing as if the chain had just been pulled. I turned, expecting to find my father beside me, but I was alone.

"Hello?" I called.

Remembering the voices I'd heard downstairs the last time, I hurried toward the study door and opened it.

"Hello?" I called. "Anyone here?"

The old townhouse creaked as I descended the steps.

At the living room, I pulled up suddenly, like I might have when I was a child and my grandparents were hosting unexpected company.

The guests filled the upholstered armchairs and couches where Nana spread her quilts. Others sat on the floor around the potted plants and beside the doily-covered end tables with the porcelain lamps and family photos. The voices I'd heard the last time belonged to them: Arianna and the senior members of the Order.

They hadn't become trapped in an outer dimension—a part of them was here!

But though my heart swelled, this was no joyful reunion. They didn't even acknowledge my presence. Their heads were bowed to the last, hands joined, as though they were holding a funerary wake.

It's for me, I realized.

The thought landed with the gray weight of certainty. *I'm dead.*

The angel's power, even ground and scattered, had overcome me. Doomed me.

As I peered around, faint with the idea, I saw the ones who had gone before. They stood ghostlike on the edges of the living room. My father and mother. My grandparents. Lazlo, my very first mentor, wearing his country coat. Pierce Dalton, the magic-user who'd covered the outer boroughs...

There were others, so many others, slain by the Knights of the Inquisition or Lich or simply victims of time and circumstance. Their lines extended beyond the walls, beyond the townhouse itself. A large rotating galaxy of them.

The vision was devastatingly beautiful and just as tragic.

I'd asked everyone to trust me. I'd positioned myself as

the savior, even after my own father—standing there beyond the bookcase, holding my mother's hand—had intimated my chances were slim. I'd claimed that mantle anyway, and I'd let everyone down.

My family most of all.

I turned a slow circle, taking in the galaxy. I knew without being told that I would join that collective, supporting the remaining line of St. Michael.

In fact, it was already starting. I was fading into the totality of our magic. And for a moment it was all there, laid out in its incomprehensible perfection, like the view from a great height. I could see everything that had led up to the moment I'd confronted Sathanas. So many pathways, only some of them true. And I'd followed one of the true paths right up to the edge my father had described.

Only from up here, I could see the gap it abutted and it appeared narrow enough to leap.

There *had* to be a way over. I searched and searched before sensing that the answer wasn't up here. It was down there, still inside me. That was what my father had meant: *For even as users of the collective magic, we're all uniquely composed.*

"Wait," I said.

The single, resonant word delivered me back to the living room. The deceased members of the Order faded back into the walls, while the living members raised their heads. I met Arianna's maternal eyes.

"Send me back," I said.

"Is that truly what you want?"

In the solemnity of her question, I understood. Split between planes, the Order had been working this whole time to hold me together. They had done all they could. They would help again, but if I failed to find the way across the gap,

I would become scattered like the angels, no longer able to join our line or access the collective. I would drift throughout the cold reaches of the universe, truly alone.

I nodded anyway. "Yes."

I would find the answer.

I drew a wet, ragged gasp and squinted my eyes open.

I'd fallen onto my side, the faint dust of angelic matter scattering from my outstretched sword. Torn skin and shredded muscles screamed as I grunted myself back upright. My coat was in tatters, shirt soaked through with blood. Wavering on my knees, I raised my sword to my brow again.

"*Ritirare,*" I rasped.

Angelic particles returned in a rush. The collective was there, holding my prism together, but they could do nothing about the raw energy. It was the violent essence of the Avenging Angel. I needed to alchemize it, somehow—that was the gap I had to leap—but the damned particles were ripping me apart.

I bit down against another bolt and another sensation of rupturing.

More red mist circled around me, joining the angelic matter in the growing storm.

Fresh laughter shook the grotto. I squinted over a shoulder to find Sathanas drawing the blade from the brazier. It was several times larger now and black as pitch. He ran his tongue along its edge, leaving a trail of infernal fire.

"*It is done,*" he rumbled jubilantly. "*The Holy Sword of Faziel is now the Dread Blade of Sathanas.*"

His eyes canted toward me.

I opened my mouth to invoke a protection, but blood spilled out.

His laughter resumed, louder. "*What is my stupid wizard servant trying to do now?*"

I turned from him and concentrated back into the angel energy. What the hell was I missing?

"*Alone,*" Sathanas boomed, his voice elevating as he rose to his full height behind me. "*The poor wizard is all alone again.*"

The angelic particles smashed and crashed inside me, at war with one another. Something else broke open, and a long streamer of blood washed past my vision, sending me to the grayest edges of awareness.

You're not alone...

The voice hooked me, drew me back.

"Can you hear me, Everson? I'm right here. You're not alone."

I squinted through the storm of blood and angelic matter until Ricki's face grew into focus. Not an apparition. She was awake now and kneeling at the edge of the circle, leaning toward me.

I could hear her. In fact, hers was the only voice I heard.

"Whatever happens, I'm staying right here," she said. "I'm not leaving you."

Tears were tracking down her sooty cheeks, probably from the sight of my very messy dissolution. But her eyes were large and resolute. In them I saw the vastness of her love and commitment. I also saw little Abigail, who shared her eyes. I tried to smile, but my mouth had no lift. That couldn't be good.

"Keep going," Ricki urged. "I'll be right beside you. You are *not* alone."

I turned back to my sword, a gift from my father, the man I aspired to become.

Did you tell me to find the child, I'd asked him, *or kill the child?*

I told you what you heard.

That was the answer.

How could I take the power of an Avenging Angel and transform it into an Angel of Mercy? Through compassion, even for a demon's child. *Especially* for a demon's child. A capacity I already possessed.

To channel Faziel, I needed to shape that compassion into a focusing object.

I closed my eyes and immediately saw my mother's emo ball. I'd left it on my dresser, ever protective of its glass craftsmanship. But the ball took solid shape behind my closed eyes. I imagined it pulsing in time with my heart. As it warmed me, I took that warmth and grew it around my prism and the inflowing particles.

Little by little, the reactivity that was tearing me up softened into a mutual counterbalancing. Another way, but no less powerful. The new energy streamed into the first rune of my father's sword.

I rose from my knees to my feet, Ricki mirroring me from the circle's edge.

As my sword absorbed the last of the alchemized energy, it took on a solar glow. The glow expanded, growing into a rotation of four nested rings—the new form of the angel's essence. They hummed with protective power as each ring rotated in a different direction, encompassing Ricki and me at their common axis.

I turned to face Sathanas, who was no longer laughing.

"Raise your sword, demon," I ordered. "The Contest isn't over."

He squinted from the powerful light and seethed, *"What magic is this?"*

"Stupid wizard magic."

With a roar, he swung his blade around. It slammed into the side of a moving ring, releasing a burst of infernal fire. No damage. He withdrew and smashed his sword against the protection's other side. This time, the blade wedged between two rings as they rotated closed. Sathanas fought to retract it, but the blade was stuck.

The rings compressed it further, squeezing out a thick slick of black ichor.

"No," he grunted, muscles swelling from his glistening arms, wings slamming furiously as he struggled to free the blade. But he only succeeded in knocking over his brazier and extinguishing their flames.

Angelic light grew in their stead, and the two rings ground onward. The sword's metal groaned. Sathanas had invested the lion's share of his power to convert Faziel's sword into his own, and now it was bleeding, on the verge of—

In a series of deep snaps, the blade ruptured.

Sathanas released a wet roar and dropped to his knees before the fallen pieces. He worked desperately to scrape them back together, to reconstitute the weapon that would have given him dominion over Hell and Earth. But corrupted or not, the blade couldn't be turned against its maker. I felt that in my atoms.

"You've lost," I told him. "Again."

When he peered up, I drove my sword into the mantle between his eyes.

The nested rings collapsed around his weakened form,

their rotations crushing wings and horns. Angelic fire licked over the destruction.

Sathanas's eyes locked onto mine, their outrage demanding to know how I'd managed the impossible a second time. I wiggled my fingers at him in farewell—right before his eyes burst open like oil drums.

Though he would have tortured me for an eternity, I chose a quicker, more merciful end.

"*Disfare!*" I bellowed.

The banishment invocation shone bright from my first rune, lighting up the demon lord's form with white fire before blowing him into a storm of ashes. No longer under Sathanas's control, the fount of ley energy whipped his ashes around and ignited them. I felt his vanquished energy blast up the spire and out into the night.

I remained in my thrusting stance until I was certain he was truly gone. Then, very slowly, I lowered my dimming blade.

Ricki came up beside me, and we both listened a minute more. As the natural darkness settled into the stones, we found the other's hand. I was in rough shape, but I could smile again. Something that pleased me beyond all proportion.

"C'mon," I whispered. "Let's go home."

51

We spent the rest of October recovering along with the city. Ricki took a medical leave to recuperate from the lingering effects of the demon fugue—weakness and fatigue, mostly. With the college closed, I was able to shift from class work to full-time daddy duty, giving her a true break. And it gave me a needed respite from casting.

The city's recovery was more involved. Though not catastrophic, the damage was widespread, which meant a lot of labor crews and closures. And then there was the body removal. Sathanas didn't get his ten thousand souls, but he'd come close enough. It left me with the ill feeling that I could have done more to prevent them.

Budge was surprisingly honest with the public about the cause and consequences of what was being called the "Great Smoke Out." The public's reaction was predictably mixed, from shoulder-shrugging acceptance of a demon attack to outright denial to all kinds of wild cover-up theories—including that a nearby military lab had ripped a hole into another dimension, releasing a creeping, creature-filled mist.

Sounded like the makings of a fine horror story.

I talked to the mayor a couple of times during this period. He'd spent the siege in an emergency bunker, communicating with key officials. I also learned that he convinced Bashi to put his personnel and fleet of boats to use in helping evacuate Chinatown and the Lower East Side. In exchange, Bashi received some of the cleanup contracts at a generous markup. He got his hotel, too.

Naturally, I asked about my immunity agreement. Budge said it was all set as long as I kept my nose out of Chinatown. I thanked him while wondering how long I'd be able to honor that pledge.

The mayor and I agreed to close the task force on the conjurings, leaving the paperwork to Ricki's partner. Hoffman put up some token grumbling, but I think he was just happy to have missed the siege altogether. He'd been home in Long Island, and his wife later told us that he'd slept through most of it.

James and Loukia returned to their corners of the world to continue their own work. It was a difficult goodbye—every magic-user of the Order was family, but those two especially now. They invited us to come out to Grimstone and Athens anytime. Ricki showed considerably more interest in the second.

As for the druids, Jordan and Petra had undergone their own adventure the night we separated. After subduing her Black Earth sisters through the pact, Petra suffered a punitive attack from her goddess, Brigit. Jordan returned to the carrier to find her engulfed in smoke and badly burned. When he set about healing her, two of Sathanas's demons swooped in, and he had to spirit her to a nearby bakery.

Jordan worked on Petra throughout the day, but all he

could accomplish was a stalemate with Brigit. To save her, he needed to break their connection, and that meant breaking her wand. He carried her to where the wand was originally vested with the goddess's power—North Woods. The journey was a trial in itself, beset with demon attacks and friendly fire from a Sup Squad unit. At last he arrived and destroyed the wand. He then buried her in a healing barrow and applied powerful magics into the night.

By the time the smoke lifted, Petra was conscious. She insisted they return to the hotel to help her Black Earth sisters. But when she and Jordan arrived, they found that Edgar had slaughtered them to the last.

Grieving and powerless, Petra left the city. After consulting with his circle, Jordan and his wife, Delphine, went out in search of her. They found her at a shelter in Jersey City a week later. Over lunch, they invited her to Harriman State Park to become the Raven Circle's newest initiate. I imagined the offer to have been as important for Jordan as Petra. Seeing into her truer nature had no doubt brought out his.

Last I heard, Petra was kicking butt in training.

Because I survived the night, Tabitha returned my coin pendant. As promised, she denied confessing anything to me in the carrier, speculating aloud that I'd been suffering auditory hallucinations from the smoke. But I was perfectly content knowing what I had long suspected—she and I were alright. Plus, a more appreciative Tabitha would have been weird for everyone, I think.

And my incubus? Thelonious was still with me, but as insignificant as I'd ever felt him. It was safe to say he wouldn't be visiting again. As to whether I'd be visiting him, the chances were roughly zilch.

I finally made it down for some man-caving with Bree-yark, watching more TV and eating more double-loaded meat pizzas than was probably healthy. But it was a blessing all the same. Befitting his goblin stubbornness, Bree-yark had recovered faster than any of us. And a good thing, because he had a November wedding to attend.

His own.

The two had originally planned their ceremony for spring, but Mae reasoned they should go ahead while there was a lull in the action. "Plus, I'm not getting any younger, and poor Bree-yark's died twice since we started dating."

Both solid points.

The wedding was held at a rec center in West Harlem. It was a refreshingly low-key affair, with Mae wearing her nicest dress, and Bree-yark a secondhand suit he'd had tailored down to his size. The guests were mostly family, some Mae hadn't seen in years and, in Bree-yark's case, quarter-centuries.

The best man and bridesmaid honors went to me and Ricki, with Abigail playing baby bridesmaid at Mae's insistence. Abi seemed to enjoy the attention (she did look extra adorable in her hair bow). Bree-yark made Tony the ring bearer, a job he took with the utmost seriousness. And he got to do it twice, as there was a Baptist ceremony and another for The Cult of the Hidden Hoard, which Bree-yark held for the sake of his more orthodox kin.

The reception kicked off in the adjoining basketball court. In lieu of gifts, Mae and Bree-yark asked that everyone bring a dish, which made for an interesting buffet line. Everything from traditional chicken marsala to an ochre-colored stew that stirred with living things and went down a storm with the goblins. The choice of music was even more eclectic, but it didn't stop either side from scuffing up the dance floor.

It was the most fun I'd had at a wedding since I could remember, not least because Mae and Bree-yark looked like they were radiating pure sunshine. They'd each come a long way from how I'd met them.

But as much as I wanted to stay, I had to excuse myself to catch a cab downtown for a more solemn affair.

———

St. Martin's Cathedral was ringed in scaffolding as I pulled up —Sathanas's infernal doings had shifted and cracked some of the stonework—but my business was in the graveyard. I hustled through the iron gate, arriving as Bishop Sheridan concluded a small burial ceremony for Mary Swal's cremated remains.

As the scant crowd thinned, she and I walked the grave-yard's beaten path under a leaden sky.

"I'm sorry I got here so late," I said. "Two of my closest friends were getting married up in Harlem."

"You have nothing to apologize for. I just regret the burial was so long in arranging. Sites here are scarce so there's a petitioning process that goes up to the presiding bishop. Mary deserved a place here as much as anyone."

I reflected on all the young woman had gone through, from her seduction by Sathanas, to raising his spawn, to her demise at the hands of an angel-blooded. And yet she'd remained devoted to her child and her church throughout.

I nodded. "There's still no news on Emma."

"Yes, I've been following the case as well."

When my paralytic vice on the pale woman had expired, she'd simply gotten up from the couch and left the hospital. She presumably returned to Los Angeles, but without a full name to chase, detectives could only share what info they had on the suspected murderer with LAPD and hope for a break. Nothing yet.

"What's the latest on Rumbaugh?" I asked.

"He remains the rector at Grace—we have no authority with the Catholic diocese. But he's on indefinite suspension from the IFC, pending further inquiries. He claims to have no memory of his contacts with Emma."

"Do you believe him?"

"Strangely enough, yes."

"Well, maybe not so strangely," I said. "Emma isn't a Nephilim in the true sense of the word—those are the offspring of angels and mortals. But I've been researching the topic these past weeks, reconciling it with what I observed of Emma. Like the Nephilim, her angel blood is pure enough to enthrall mortals. You and I both felt it at the hospital, but Rector Rumbaugh felt it more. He's what's known as an *enthusiast*, one who really resonates with a Nephilim. And he wasn't just exposed to Emma, but the Sword of Faziel, upping that resonance several-fold. The effect can warp brain waves, even cause brain damage."

"Would you mind writing that up for the IFC's consideration?" she asked.

"Not at all." I watched her from the corner of my eye as we veered onto a faint path. "Is there anything I can do for *you* in that regard?" I understood there had been some fallout from her granting the demon lord access to the cathedral.

"Thank you, Everson, but no." We arrived under a knotted

willow in the corner of the old graveyard. We turned and looked back at Mary's burial site, beside the cathedral's north wing. "The hearings I'm currently involved in go deeper than my conduct. They get to questions of faith itself."

"Oh, yeah?" I asked, interested.

"That moment in the hospital when you urged me to consider mine... it gave me a clear answer and so I heeded it. But had I deferred to the IFC, or even to my own superiors, I would have denied its guidance—despite it showing me the alternative, a city burned to the ground. Still, it seems some institutional structure is necessary. Otherwise, anyone could claim to speak and act on behalf of 'true' faith. Rector Rumbaugh believed he had it. Emma too, for that matter. It's a tough question, a vital one, that we're still trying to come to terms with. I'm afraid there aren't any easy answers."

"No," I agreed.

"But one thing is clear to me, and it involves you."

When I looked over, I found her regarding me intensely.

"What's that?" I asked.

"I know your guilt, Everson. I see it in the shadows of your conscience. You feel your lineage conflicts with this place that was so special to you and your grandmother. You feel you've abdicated your home here. But you haven't, even if you never attend another mass—or set foot inside again, for that matter. Our stories may differ, but your magic and the faith that supports these walls come from the same place. You don't have to reconcile them. Honor one and you serve both."

When I looked away, she pressed a warm hand to my back.

"Thank you, Bishop," I said, because the guilt was real.

It had been there in my final conversations with Father Vick those years ago. It was why I'd dodged the bishop's masses. I just hadn't understood its hold over me until her words loosened its grip.

We resumed walking, back toward Mary's gravesite.

"I know you banished Sathanas," she said at length. "But you haven't told me how."

I reviewed those final moments in my mind. Attempting, and failing, to channel Faziel's energy... hearing Ricki's voice through the storm... seeing our child in her eyes. And with that vision of our union had come the final insight: My father's blood gave me the power to summon Faziel, but my mother's compassion was the key to alchemizing his essence, and she was already inherent in my makeup.

For even as users of the collective magic, we're all uniquely composed.

She was why I'd heard *Find the child.*

I opened my mouth to explain this to the bishop, or try to, because the words already felt pale and insubstantial. That seemed true of words in general for me these days, even the ones I'd honed for casting.

"I changed," I replied after a moment. "In ways I'm still trying to understand."

52

Mae and Bree-yark returned from their honeymoon in Vermont shortly before the holidays, Mae bearing two large suitcases of gifts, and Bree-yark a giant keg of cider ale. Ricki and I hosted Christmas in the apartment, an event made more memorable by a snowy nor'easter that blew in the night before, socking us in for two days.

On the morning of the third day, I took everyone's drink order, pulled on a pair of galoshes, and ventured down to Two Story Coffee. As the barista rang me up, I added one of their swag stickers to put on Abigail's bottle, so she wouldn't feel left out.

While I waited for the drinks, I moseyed over to the plush window-facing chairs. In my solitary days I would come here whenever I had problems to mull over, which was often.

I lowered myself into one of the chairs now and gazed past the frame of holiday lights to the snow-plowed street. Going back to the Demon Moon case, it still struck me how normal everything could look so soon after our reality had been tilted on its edge. Before my professor's mind could start theorizing away, a bevy of bundled kids raced past the window, shouting exuberantly and throwing snowballs.

"Wonderful, isn't it?" someone said.

I looked over to find an older woman sitting in another of the plush chairs, a steaming drink cupped over her crossed knees.

"Arianna!" I exclaimed, loudly enough to turn some heads.

I ran over and hugged her from the side. The senior member of the Order laughed and squeezed my hand. "I would have come sooner, but there's been so much work. Also, I wanted you to enjoy this time with your family."

"So the rupture...?" I asked, angling the neighboring chair toward hers.

"The primary and secondary sites are in good shape. We're still working on some tertiary fissures. Had we not acted, the damage would have spread beyond our control. Sathanas studied hard for this one. He found a remote site to strike that would compel a response while challenging our limited resources."

So Sathanas *had* been responsible for the rupture, probably through a contracted saboteur. It also explained why Claudius had been so frustratingly vague when we spoke—to sell the head fake that the Order was overcommitted and couldn't help me. Then again, that could have just been Claudius, who'd only recently located his lost magic-user.

"We've also been engaged in some recovery work," she continued. "After you banished Sathanas, chaos reigned in the Below. We took advantage of this time to deliver the souls he claimed, freeing them from their suffering."

"That's great," I breathed. "I've been thinking about them a lot."

She smiled tenderly and rested a hand over mine. "They were Sathanas's victims, not yours."

"I know, but still..."

"Take heart in knowing that you'll be able to help more now. Last we spoke, I said you would soon be ready for work of another nature. Important work. We were waiting for your angelic potential to manifest into something more... *definitive*, I guess you could say. It's happened, and with it has come new opportunities."

"Oh, yeah?"

"You've met one of them already," she said. "Emma Bellinger is her full name."

I straightened. "You found her? That's great! Ricki's taken up the case again and—"

She raised a hand. "I'm not going to defend Emma's actions, but I want you to hear me out. You saw into her, just as we did. She was under the influence of a force beyond her capacity to control or direct. It was far too powerful. But you brought that force to heel," she said, peering into my eyes. "The justice part is done. Your role now will be that of the surrogate."

"The surrogate?" I repeated.

"Faziel's power remains in Emma's blood. She will need guidance."

"I'm supposed to *work* with her?" I said, the distaste clear in my voice. I couldn't unsee the charred thumbprint between Mary's staring eyes or her granite headstone.

"Yes, and it should be soon," Arianna continued calmly. "Before others can influence her. I'm not saying it will be easy.

But we must allow her the opportunity to learn another way, much as you allowed Petra the same."

I nodded reluctantly, seeing her point.

"And this is bigger than Emma. Though she may be the purest expression of Faziel's line, we know there are others. They will eventually need guidance too, though not from you. Your main work will remain here in the city."

So I wouldn't just be guiding Emma, but training her to lead? Oh boy.

"We are still short magic-users, Everson. The next generation of practitioners remains years away. The demons will not rest in the meantime. If the *angel kin*, as we're calling them, can be organized under a banner of mercy rather than vengeance, they will become crucial allies. And Sathanas may have other seeds."

I'd been thinking about the possibility of "other seeds," too. I pictured them gestating, waiting for the right conditions to break into the world, just as the last one had broken from little Edgar.

"I was writing up a report to send you," I said, "but I might as well tell you now. A friend connected me with a computer expert who goes by Rusty. He cross-referenced women who may have attended St. Martin's at the time of Father Vick's possession with birthing data at area hospitals for the appropriate period. Four women matched the criteria. Three are here in the area, all with healthy toddlers. The other one moved, but hers seems fine, too. Rusty will let me know if he finds any other matches."

Arianna nodded. "We'll remain vigilant as well."

As she paused to sip her tea, I eyed my seated reflection in the glass. Since alchemizing the angel Faziel, I felt different. And it wasn't just the power I'd channeled into my sword. My cells were busier, as if my own reality had tilted and everything was trying to reorient itself to a new normal.

"What *have* I become, exactly?" I asked.

I could see Arianna's eyes in the glass, studying my reflection, too. "What you always were, but I don't think that's what you're asking. This will be a discovery period, Everson. All I can tell you is that your work will grow along with your changing nature. And you will not be alone. There is the Order, of course, and your family and friends. But others are coming. I see a new and very capable team around you."

I looked over in surprise. "Who are they?"

"You will know them by their integrity, if you do not already. When they've completed their own work, they will come."

Behind us, a barista called out loudly, "Order for Emerson?"

"That must be me," I said to Arianna with a sigh. "It usually is."

"I should let you go, then. Your loved ones are expecting warm drinks."

"Wait, you mentioned something about a new mentor the last time?"

"We'll begin soon."

I stared at her. "*You?* No, no, I didn't mean for it to come out that way. I'd love to train under you, it's just that you're the most powerful member of the Order and isn't the disparity in our abilities a little... immense?"

"Don't underestimate yourself, Everson. In channeling Faziel, you not only reconciled the final enmity between Avenging Angels and First Saints, but accomplished something no magic-user of the Order had ever done before. Not even your father," she added slyly. "We'll be learning from one another."

That was almost too shocking to respond to, so I kept it simple and honest.

"I'm looking forward to it."

THE END

BLUE CURSE

BLUE WOLF BOOK 1

ELITE SOLDIER TURNED WOLFMAN

Cursed on assignment, a special ops soldier finds himself transforming into a creature of local legend.

Seven feet tall, 400 pounds, and packed with lupine assets, Jason is now the dreaded Blue Wolf — a role he never asked for in a land far from home. The price for a cure? Eliminating the region's most notorious warlord, the White Dragon.

From the icy peaks of Central Asia to the urban canyons of Manhattan, and with the help of a bookish wizard named Prof Croft, Jason pushes his newfound powers to their limits. Because with the curse now eating away his mind, he's running out of time...

Succeed and he returns home to his fiancée and a future.

Fail and he dies a bloodthirsty beast..

Blue Curse
(Blue Wolf, Book 1)

AUTHOR'S NOTES

From *Demon Moon* to *Angel Doom*...

Twelve books that saw Everson go from a lost and lonely wizard to a husband and father with an extended family that *I* wouldn't mind having. He also wowed his magic-using community enough to earn a training spot with the Order's top brass. As an added bonus, he and Tabitha succeeded in not poisoning each other.

So, yes, this concludes the Book 9-12 quadrilogy that had Everson stumbling into the shadow realm, learning about its dearth of magic users, discovering the reason for said dearth, and then managing to harness the vengeful being who'd made it so. But it also completes the larger circle that goes all the way back to *Demon Moon*, where a novice Everson Croft confronted Sathanas with little more than his luck and pluck.

So where does our hero go from here?

Arianna gave us some hints. He has a side quest of sorts to track down the pale woman, Emma Bellinger, and show her the right way to angel. That will be explored obliquely in an upcoming series that introduces our third and final feature character in the Croftverse. Don't worry, it's not Emma. In fact, it's not anyone we've met, but this character's story will tie into events that relate to Croft's doings in Los Angeles.

Arianna also mentioned a new team. I've made no secret about my plans to place Prof Croft, the Blue Wolf, and this as yet unnamed third character into a kickass team series. It's time for Everson to have some permanent, powerful colleagues who share his do-gooding tenacity and will complement his abilities. It will also be a more interesting venue, I think, to explore his angelic potential.

A quick note on Everson and Arianna's meeting place. Two Story Coffee is where I wrote *Demon Moon* back in 2016, though it was located in Athens, Georgia. I remember those months fondly. I had zero idea if Prof Croft would find an audience, but I understood his character, and I couldn't wait to return to my favorite table in that old American Foursquare-turned-café each day to delve into his next crisis.

I can still see the view out the back window: a depressed gravel lot, hopelessly potholed, with vine-covered trees and a crumbling brick wall. I stared out at that view often during the writing, superimposing it with whatever scene I was sussing out. Indeed, except for me and that back lot, no one else knew about Everson Croft, Vega, Tabitha, or post-crash New York. Thankfully, the audience grew to include actual people—something that continues to humble and inspire me.

Sadly, Two Story Coffee is no more. But with Faziel as my witness, it will live on in Everson's world and continue to serve the best darned Colombian dark roast around!

Angel Doom also alluded to a couple of Everson's side series that you may or may not be aware of. *Croft & Tabby* is an ongoing series of mini-adventures that chronicles his and Tabitha's very early years together, when getting along was half the battle.

Croft & Wesson is a trilogy of short novels, where Everson teams up with fellow spell-slinger James Wesson out West. When Everson said that *ridiculous* barely began to describe their adventures, he wasn't kidding. While *Croft & Tabby* brings the snark, *Croft & Wesson* delivers the outrageous.

I designed the Croftverse to be read one series at a time, with readers free to start anywhere. Not every series has to be read, either. (Though the characters can appear in each other's stories, the main plots don't intertwine.) But I get it, many of us like to know what's happening where. Check out the **Croftverse Catalogue** at the end of this book—it includes a link to the series chronology, which we've designed as a colorful visual guide.

I have many people to thank for their help in bringing *Angel Doom* into the world...

Thank you to the team at Damonza.com. They have designed every cover in the *Prof Croft* series, and the palette of all twelve books (plus the two prequels) is a thing of beauty. Thanks to my beta and advanced readers, including Beverly Collie, Mark Denman, Fiona Harford, Bob Singer, Erin Halb-maier, Susie Johnson, and Larissa, who all provided valuable feedback during the writing process, as they've done for so many books in the series. And thanks to Sharlene Magnarella and Donna Rich for, once again, taking on the painstaking task of final proofing. Naturally, any errors that remain are this author's alone.

I also want to thank James Patrick Cronin, who brings all the books to life through his splendid narration on the audio editions. Those can be found at Audible.com. We also feature a catalogue of our shorter works on YouTube.

Writing on *Prof Croft 12* mostly happened in Mexico City. This time, I have Blend Café and Cleotilde Barra to thank for keeping me stimulated while I banged out Everson and company's latest adventure.

The expanding Croftverse wouldn't be possible without the Strange Brigade, my dedicated fan group whose enthusiasm serves as motivation rocket fuel, book after book.

And last but not least, thank you, fearless reader, for taking this crazy journey with the Prof.

Best wishes,
Brad Magnarella

P.S. Be sure to check out my website to learn more about the Croftverse, download a pair of free prequels, and find out what's coming! That's all at **bradmagnarella.com**

CROFTVERSE CATALOGUE

PROF CROFT PREQUELS

Book of Souls

Siren Call

MAIN SERIES

Demon Moon

Blood Deal

Purge City

Death Mage

Black Luck

Power Game

Druid Bond

Night Rune

Shadow Duel

Shadow Deep

Godly Wars

Angel Doom

SPIN-OFFS

Croft & Tabby

Croft & Wesson

BLUE WOLF

Blue Curse

Blue Shadow

Blue Howl

Blue Venom

Blue Blood

Blue Storm

SPIN-OFF

Legion Files

———

For the entire chronology go to

bradmagnarella.com/chronology

ABOUT THE AUTHOR

Brad Magnarella writes urban fantasy for the same reason most read it...

To explore worlds where magic crackles from fingertips, vampires and shifters walk city streets, cats talk (some excessively), and good prevails against all odds. It's shamelessly fun.

His two main series, Prof Croft and Blue Wolf, make up the growing Croftverse, with over a quarter-million books sold to date and an Independent Audiobook Award nomination.

Hopelessly nomadic, Brad can be found in a rented room overseas or hiking America's backcountry.

Or just go to www.bradmagnarella.com